"This is not a smart thing to do,"

Amy gasped, tearing herself away from Paul.

"Smart?" He glared at her, bewildered, his breathing as ragged as hers.

"Getting carried away like this—with the night, the gazebo," she spluttered, backing away from him. "Discussing a personal experience or two doesn't mean we have to—to—"

"Hold each other? Kiss? Make love?" he said dryly, not sure if he was extremely annoyed, strangely amused or very, very angry.

"I meant we shouldn't take on more than we can handle," she insisted. "You don't really know me. And I don't know you."

"Wasn't that what we were doing—getting to know each other better?"

Dismay flashed in her eyes. "Not that way, Paul. You understand, don't you?"

Paul told himself to cool down. Disappointment shouldn't overshadow whatever was left of his common sense. "I understand," he said finally.

But he didn't like it.

Dear Reader,

We've another great selection of books for you this month, including some of your favourite authors.

Firstly, we've got a new mini-series to highlight. Trisha Alexander's *A Bride for Luke* is the first title in her THREE BRIDES AND A BABY series, which will continue early next year. Bestselling author Nora Roberts continues THE MACKADE BROTHERS series with *The Fall of Shane MacKade*—you'll love this story about the fourth brother, who certainly meets his match in Rebecca Knight!

Barbara Bretton's *Renegade Lover* is September's THAT SPECIAL WOMAN! title, whilst Jennifer Mikels' *Expecting Baby* is a tale to tug at the heartstrings! And rounding off this month is Ellen Tanner Marsh's touching *A Family of Her Own*, and Judith Yates' warm family story, *A Will and a Wedding*.

We're sure you'll be delighted with each and every one!

Sincerely,

The Editors

A Will and a Wedding

JUDITH YATES

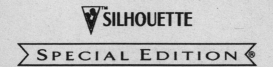

SILHOUETTE

SPECIAL EDITION ®

*Silhouette, Silhouette Special Edition and Colophon are
registered trademarks of Harlequin Books S.A., used under licence.*

*First published in Great Britain 1996
Silhouette Books, Eton House, 18-24 Paradise Road,
Richmond, Surrey TW9 1SR*

© Judith Yoder 1996

ISBN 0 373 24026 0

23-9609

*Printed and bound in Great Britain
by Mackays of Chatham PLC, Chatham*

For Stephanie and Willie Yoder,

You make each day come alive,
reminding me why love is the
most important thing in life.

JUDITH YATES

grew up in a tiny New England town where she secretly
wrote novels after school. After such an early start, she
finds it ironic that she didn't get around to "following her
bliss" of writing professionally until after working for
years in Boston and Washington, D.C., marrying and
starting a family.

When she's not busy writing and taking care of her two
small children, Judith volunteers at local schools and
enjoys speaking to young people about writing—especially
those who are secretly working on novels after school.

Another Silhouette Book by Judith Yates

Silhouette Special Edition

Family Connections

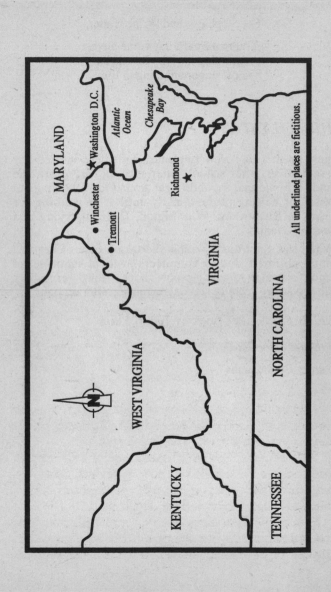

Chapter One

Amy Riordan's heart was at odds with her better judgment. The choice between facing the past and leaving well enough alone was tough. Very tough.

Explaining her final decision to her mother was no day at the beach, either.

"Mother, I have to go out there to take care of this. They've backed me into a corner."

Amy gazed across the polished mahogany table at her mother as the maid cleared the remains of another oh-so-elegant yet dull Windom Thanksgiving dinner.

"Oh, honestly. You don't have to deal with anyone you don't want to," Joan Holt Riordan Windom insisted, her manicured hand rapping the table in emphasis. "Certainly not that woman and her daughters."

Joan's objections came as no surprise. Still, Amy was relieved her mother had managed to hold her tongue until after the others had tottered off to the living room for dessert and coffee. Hearing the unsolicited opinions of her aging stepfamily was the last thing she needed.

"According to the lawyers, that woman and her daughters were like family to my father." More family to him than she'd ever been.

"Then Gregory should've left that entire godforsaken inn to them in his will, instead of tangling you up in this ridiculous legal snare. Why would you want part ownership?" Joan said, her voice edgy with indignation. "Even without your business, you'd have no financial worries—and Greg knew that!"

Why, indeed? It was the question Amy had been asking herself often in the months since she'd been notified of her father's death and the terms of his will. Why had he left her a half interest in the renovated old inn nestled deep in the Shenandoah Valley of Virginia?

She hadn't seen Gregory Riordan since her mother had divorced him when Amy was six years old. For a while, she'd heard from him twice a year—with a card and a ten-dollar bill on her birthday and at Christmas. But never a phone call or a visit. In time, her memory of her father had grown so vague she could recall only a gruff-sounding laugh gentled by sparkly blue eyes, and long, strong arms that would lift her onto the backyard tree swing. Then he had pushed her to exhilarating heights and they had played Touch the Blue Sky, a singsong game he'd made up especially for her.

"Someday you'll touch the blue sky, Amy sprite," he would call over her delighted giggles. "The elves will shower you with luck when you touch the blue sky."

By the time she was twelve, however, the cards had stopped coming. Save for that one enchanting memory, her father, for all intents and purposes, had disappeared from her life.

Her mother had had little to say about it except that she wasn't surprised. Her stepfather, Thomas Windom, had tried to explain—in his well-intentioned way—about men who drifted through life, incapable of family responsibilities. "Men like Greg Riordan can't be counted on," Thomas had cautioned. "You may never hear from him again."

Yet Amy did hear from Greg—years later, after she'd emerged from a stormy adolescence and was living away from home for the first time. She'd been in the throes of an important college romance when Greg had sent a letter, via Joan, announcing he'd just achieved a lifelong dream. He'd purchased an old fifteen-room inn in Tremont, Virginia, less than two hours from the Windom home in Washington. He had big plans for renovating it, and he had invited Amy to come see the inn—and him—whenever she wanted.

Whenever she wanted?

Her father hadn't been around all those years when she'd really needed him. And then he'd chosen to reappear when life was exciting and bursting with new possibilities. Was she supposed to be thrilled? Amy had waffled for weeks over how—or if—to respond. But when her mother had revealed that Greg had settled down at the inn with a woman who had two teenage daughters of her own, Amy's resentment intensified into anger and hurt. Clearly Greg Riordan didn't need her in his life, and with all the callow presumptuousness of a nineteen-year-old, she had concluded she didn't need him. Not ever.

These days, at age thirty-one, sadder but wiser after a frustrating string of relationships, Amy realized Greg could have been reaching out to her with that letter, trying to reconnect. Maybe he hadn't been looking for a handout, as her mother had suspected. But then, why had he tried only once? Why hadn't he tried harder? For now all she had left of him was the special memory of their private game, Touch the Blue Sky. And, of course, the inn....

"Can't your attorneys work out a deal with this Ryan woman?" Joan said, pouring herself more coffee from an exquisite china pot. "It would seem to me she'd either want to buy out your share or sell hers."

Amy shook her head. "She refuses to sell, and I don't think she has the means to buy me out. Apparently the inn's been teetering on a financial tightrope for the past three years."

"Somehow I'm not surprised. Your father was horrible with money. I'm amazed he managed to hold on to that inn as long as he did."

"Well, he did hold on to it, and Bernadette Ryan is not about to let it go. She refuses to take any action until I go down there in person. She's adamant about that."

"Greg Riordan's *mistress* has no right to make demands on you," Joan declared. "It's probably some ploy to get money out of you. Greg must have told her we're wealthy."

The same thought had occurred to Amy, if only because Bernadette Ryan's refusal to negotiate with Amy's attorneys seemed so unreasonable. Because of her stepfather's wealth and social position, some people sought her out for whatever advantages they hoped her connections might bestow. Except for one recent, glaring exception, she had become quite good at keeping such users at arm's length.

But in this situation, as Mrs. Ryan's insistence had held firm over the past few months, Amy's resistance had grown weak from curiosity and confusion. She'd begun to suspect something other than money was behind Bernadette's demand.

"Mother, the lawyers advised me to meet with her and stay at the inn as she's asked," Amy explained. "They believe it's the quickest way to resolve the matter."

Her mother sighed. "Are you sure that tawdry business with Jeffrey Martin isn't influencing you in all this? Because reaching out to those people is no way to compensate for—"

"Mother, this has nothing to do with what happened with Jeff."

"Well, either way, I think your plan is utterly misguided." Joan tossed down a white linen napkin and got to her feet. "*I* certainly wouldn't give in to that woman."

True enough. Her mother rarely gave in to anyone.

Yet Amy wasn't fazed by Joan's indirect criticism of her decision. She had realized long ago that her mother's approval would always be hard to win. Besides, Joan would never understand that Amy wasn't going to Tremont because of her lawyers' advice, Mrs. Ryan's conditions or even her father's bequest. No, her decision was clinched by the painful sense of regret she couldn't rationalize away and an innocuous bit of information that, strangely enough, she'd only recently learned.

How could Amy tell her mother, the ultimate realist, that she'd agreed to go to Tremont only after she'd forced herself, finally, to read Greg's entire will and discovered he'd long ago changed the inn's name? Her mother wouldn't, *couldn't,* understand how her heart had spun fast and her curiosity had run wild when she'd learned Greg Riordan had called his lifelong dream *Touch the Blue Sky.*

* * *

Amy sped along Interstate 66, anxious to beat the dark. She was concerned about navigating the unfamiliar, winding roads at the foothills of the Blue Ridge Mountains, which loomed ahead of her in the distance. Passing the first sign announcing her exit, she gripped the steering wheel tighter as her pulse quickened. Soon she'd be seeing her father's beloved inn for the first time. Soon she'd be meeting Bernadette Ryan and her two daughters.

She knew it was silly to be so nervous. As a businesswoman, she'd learned to handle herself in sticky situations. Running a child's casting and modeling agency required capabilities that went beyond overseeing a profit-and-loss bottom line. She had the patience to be pleasant yet firm with pushy "stage" mothers, the ability to be cordial but persuasive when marketing to picky prospective client companies and her instinct was that of a mother hawk when it came to protecting the interests and safety of *her kids*—the children represented by her agency.

Yet, despite these strengths, Amy felt on shaky ground as she drew closer to the village of Tremont.

This journey of hers was about the past, and she had never liked dwelling on that. Memories tended to be bittersweet at best, and there certainly was no changing what had already happened. But the Ryans...the inn...her father...were like one emotional package shoved at her feet, one she couldn't skip over or kick out of the way. She had to confront it, deal with it and then move on quickly—just as she had with every other unsettling experience in her life.

A half hour after exiting the highway, she spotted a road sign directing her toward Tremont. Only five miles to go, she noted with relief. Dusk was fast deepening into nightfall, the state road was narrow and curving and a red pickup truck seemed to be tailing her car awfully close. But she was driving at the speed limit—which was as fast as she dared on this rolling, unfamiliar terrain. And as annoying as the trailing pickup was, at least the other driver wasn't flashing his headlights or honking at her to speed up.

Turning the corner onto a long, straight stretch of road, Amy spied a big, old gas guzzler of a car pulled over to the side several yards ahead. Its taillights were blinking. Drawing nearer, she could see an elderly couple standing by their disabled vehicle. The woman, her coat pulled tightly around her, appeared to be shivering, and the man seemed bewildered. Although she was in a hurry and alone, one look at their fretful condition made it impossible for her to drive past without stopping.

She pulled over in front of their car, which looked frightfully rickety next to her shiny, almost new Lexus. "Can I help you?" Amy called to the couple as she climbed out. "I can make a call on my car phone."

Walking toward them, she saw that the tailgating red pickup had pulled in behind their car. From its cab emerged a tall, lean man, wearing a rust brown leather jacket and blue jeans. "What's the trouble, Jake?" the man asked in a voice that was as rich and deep as his stride was long.

They reached the couple simultaneously, with the woman smiling sweetly at Amy and the man, Jake, shaking his head at the pickup driver.

"Got a flat, Hanley." He pointed to the rear of the car. "Goddang tire is practically new. Ain't got more than a hundred miles on it. Can ya believe it?"

"But this nice young lady kindly offered to call for help, Jacob," the old woman piped in. "Maybe we could call Harry's station."

"It's the day after Thanksgiving, Janie Lee," Jake grumbled. "Harry always closes up shop early around the holidays."

Although a flat wasn't that big a deal, Jake looked too old and too fragile to be changing a tire on this tank of a car. And Amy knew she wouldn't be much help. As far as she was concerned, changing flat tires was what automobile clubs were for. "I can call some other service station for you," she volunteered, "or maybe give you a lift somewhere."

"Excuse me, miss." The tone of the younger man's voice was less than polite.

"Yes?" She turned to find him eyeing her from head to toe, and she couldn't help but do the same to him. He was blue eyed, with sandy blond hair that was just long enough to graze his jacket collar; his body looked hard and angular. His face was tanned with a trace of windburn, and his features were both sturdy and refined—a combination that made the man outright handsome.

Within seconds, however, Amy realized he was not regarding her with a similar appreciation. Actually, she detected a wry glint in his eyes, as if he were amused by her. Feeling defensive, she stiffened, but covered herself by peering straight into his deep baby blues. "Well, what is it?"

"I thought I'd point out that by the time you reach an open gas station on that car phone of yours and get someone to come out here, I'll have put the spare on and Jake will be back on the road." He glanced over at the elderly man. "You have a spare in the trunk, right, Jake?"

"Of course I do, Hanley. I'm not dotty, just old."

"See? We're all set," Hanley said, turning to her. "It was kind of you to stop, but now you can run right along."

Run right along? Amy glared at him. What was this guy's problem? She wasn't expecting laurels for attempting a good deed, but she didn't expect to be scoffed at, either.

Ignoring him, she moved to Janie Lee's side. "Ma'am, you're shivering. Would you like to sit in my car while they're changing the tire? I'll turn on the heater."

"Oh, I couldn't hold you back, honey. But you're sweet to offer." The old woman patted Amy's arm. "Maybe I can wait in Mr. Hanley's truck."

Hanley nodded. "I have a heater, too."

The half-teasing smugness of his comment went right over Janie Lee's head, but not Amy's. Still, she wasn't about to let his orneriness intimidate her. "I'm on my way to Tremont, but I wouldn't mind giving you a ride home while the men are fixing the car."

"Well, our farm is just this side of Tremont," Janie Lee said, "and I am gettin' tired. You sure it'd be no trouble?"

Amy shook her head. "I'd love the company of someone who knows the roads around here, especially now that it's getting dark. Perhaps you can give me exact directions to the inn when I drop you off."

"The Blue Sky? You mean a pretty young thing like you is taking a vacation there all by yourself?"

"Actually, I'm going there on business."

"Business?" Janie Lee looked over at Hanley. "Did you hear that? She's got business over at the Blue Sky."

Hanley shrugged as if he couldn't care less. Then he motioned to Jake. "Let's get going with that tire."

While Jake and Janie Lee exchanged some parting words, Hanley turned on his heel without so much as a nod in Amy's direction. Which was fine by her. She'd had quite enough of him—even if he was the best-looking man she'd seen in years.

Paul Hanley left Jake to say his goodbyes and went to fetch the spare and a jack from Jake's trunk. Then he positioned the jack beneath the car and began pumping up the rear, glancing up only when the luxury car pulled out onto the road. He'd behaved badly, he knew. But damn... His head still ached from combing through last month's disappointing profit-and-loss figures back at the paper... and he was worried about his aunt's anxious phone call, begging him to come to the Blue Sky tonight. Nevertheless, he shouldn't have been so terse with the would-be Good Samaritan, especially since he'd be seeing her again soon. Real soon.

Probably should have told her that, he thought, shaking his head.

As soon as she had mentioned the inn, he'd known the woman was Greg's spoiled, rich daughter, finally deigning to come out to the old man's inn. She even had Riordan's black-Irish coloring with her glossy dark hair and vivid, sapphire blue eyes. But Greg had been a burly son of a gun, rough around the edges, imposing. His daughter was smaller than Paul would have expected, her build delicate. And despite all the makeup, she was damn pretty.

He shouldn't have been rude to her at all—before or after he'd realized her identity. Trouble was, he'd long ago lost patience with the trendy D.C. Type A's who seemed to flood the area every decent weekend with their flashy cars and fat wallets. He especially resented the whiny ones who stayed at the inn, bombarding poor

Bernadette with their overparticular "you-must-cater-to-us" demands.

By all appearances, Ms. Riordan fit the bill, what with the car, the expensive business clothes, the expert makeup job. Still, he shouldn't have allowed his bias to get the better of him. He sure as hell knew what it was like to have scads of cash and more than one head-turning car of his own. Amy Riordan couldn't help what she was any more than he could help what he used to be.

"Jake, hand me the socket wrench." He pointed to his beat-up toolbox.

"Hope Janie Lee gets home all right," Jake said while rummaging through the box.

"She will." Paul held his hand out for the wrench. "Don't let the hot car fool you. That woman is a cautious driver. I should know. I was stuck behind her for eight miles."

"Good-lookin' little gal, though, wasn't she? Wonder what kind of business she has at the inn."

"Guess that's *her* business, Jake." Grimacing, he wrenched hard at the first lug nut on the wheel.

"Okay, okay. Keep it to yourself, Hanley. But you dang well know the word's gonna be around town by breakfast tomorrow."

"No doubt." But he wasn't about to be the reliable source of this news. He had a strong aversion to the town's rumor mill, which he considered to be nothing more than a localized, more efficient version of the gossip columns and TV tabloids that had pestered him during his spell in the public eye.

"I bet Janie Lee gets the whole story before they reach our driveway."

"Probably," Paul said, yanking off the tire with a grunt. He thought of his Aunt Bernadette. She was on pins and needles about meeting Riordan's daughter. One evening of privacy with the young woman was the least she deserved, and probably all she would get. Because once word was out that Greg's girl had come to town, Bernadette would have no peace.

In the meantime, he hoped Amy Riordan had enough sense to keep her private business private.

Janie Lee peered through the open car window. "Sure you won't change your mind about that cup of coffee?"

"No, thanks. I'm late as it is." It was nice of Janie Lee to offer, but Amy half suspected the older woman wanted another crack at finding out why she'd come to Tremont.

"I understand. But if you get any grief from Bernadette Ryan about checkin' in after dark, you tell her to call Janie Lee Pratt. I'll set her straight."

"Thanks, I will." Amy started the engine, but Janie Lee leaned against the car door.

"Now remember, take a left on 612 about a mile after the Winchester turnoff," she said. "That'll land you right in the middle of town."

"And the inn's at the top of the hill?"

"Right there. Can't miss it."

After thanking Amy again, Janie Lee finally stepped away from the car and waved goodbye.

Amy eased down the Pratt's long, unpaved driveway, glad to escape with her privacy intact. Although Janie Lee was a likable, harmless woman, she was on the nosy side. And persistent! Amy now knew that a third degree could be camouflaged in sweetness and light. She breathed a wary sigh. For all her efforts, poor Janie Lee had gotten no satisfaction from her. Amy was having a hard enough time dealing with the whys and wherefores of this visit. She wasn't about to tell all to a complete stranger.

As she navigated the unlit country road, the dashboard digital clock clicked off the passing minutes, each one bringing her closer to Tremont and Touch the Blue Sky Inn. When she passed by the Welcome To Tremont sign, barely readable in the dark, the knots in her stomach tightened. The late-autumn moon afforded a misty light and she took in what she could of the village. Brick and clapboard houses and low one- and two-story commercial buildings were clustered on either side of the road. The general store and gas station were closed tight, as was Tremont Elementary School, of course, and the Baptist church just beyond it. Then she spotted a large white sign with elaborate black script announcing the inn. Amy turned right as directed and drove carefully up the steep road.

It seemed to take forever.

Finally, at the crest of the hill, the inn came into view, and Amy blinked in surprise. Shimmering between beams of ground lighting, the building was graceful and grand, and far lovelier than she had expected. The two-story structure was expansive, with the aura of an English country house, but the wide veranda framing the front bespoke old Virginia, gracious ladies, mint juleps and fluttering fans.

Unsure where to park, Amy pulled up to the front entrance and got out of the car. Melodic refrains from what she thought might be a mandolin floated softly through the open screen door and into the night air. Yet the music couldn't soothe the emotions roiling inside her. She leaned against the car, drinking in the sight of her father's dream come true. As her gaze roamed from the roof peak, down the white brick facade, to the holly and azalea bushes embedded at its foundation, her mind and heart contemplated the man she barely knew. Right now, Greg Riordan felt so near, his presence enmeshed in each coal black shutter, in each gleaming white picket of the veranda's railing, in each light glowing through the windows and in each muffled laugh and murmuring voice emanating from inside the inn.

Amy squeezed her eyes shut and swallowed hard. She was unprepared for these feelings . . . this sadness. Nervousness about meeting Bernadette Ryan had preoccupied her for days. She hadn't considered—or allowed herself to consider—how it would feel to come face-to-face with her father's domain, with his life.

If she had, she might not have come at all. The loneliness in her heart made her realize that.

The sharp sound of a creaking floorboard startled her and her gaze flew to the darkened porch. At first it appeared empty. But then the floor creaked again, followed by movement, enabling her to focus on the figure in the shadows. It was a woman rising from a wicker rocking chair.

"Good evening," Amy called.

The only response was footsteps as the woman walked across the veranda. Even in the dim light, Amy could see she was a handsome woman, tall and solidly built. Her hair fell loose past her shoulder blades and Amy guessed it must have once been a vibrant red. In any case, it was unusual to see a woman well past middle age wearing her hair that way or dressed in an oversize tunic sweater over a flowing pleated skirt.

The woman came down the front steps. "Amy Riordan?"

Amy's throat felt tight and dry, and she shivered in the cool night air. "Yes," she managed to say.

"Welcome to the inn. I'm Bernadette Ryan."

"I know." Though her voice had all but deserted her, Amy couldn't take her eyes off the woman. Greg Riordan was part of her, too. Amy half expected him to fall in step behind her, to hold his hand out to her just as this woman was doing now.

She searched the older woman's pale face, hoping to find some sign of acceptance. But Bernadette's gaze was as distant as her handshake was brief.

"Glad that you got here safely," Bernadette remarked, her voice honeyed by a light Virginia lilt. "This day has been a long time coming." She turned and started back to the inn.

Amy followed her up the steps. By now, however, the inn had lost its comforting glow and the encompassing sense of her father had evaporated. Why on earth had she come?

Bernadette held open the door for her. Amy hesitated a moment as the indoor heat rushed over her and out into the crisp night. The heat, the sounds, the aromas and the voices clamoring inside the inn reminded her she was nothing but a stranger here, a stranger from Greg Riordan's past.

Amy had never felt so alone in her life.

She stepped into the spacious front hall, where an older couple stopped Bernadette to tell her how much they had enjoyed their dinner tonight. Amy looked over her shoulder into the dining room entrance. There she spotted the mandolin player, sitting by the fireplace as he serenaded the few remaining diners relaxing at candlelit tables. Suddenly a young woman, carrying an empty serving tray, hurried out the dining room door.

"Bridget!" Bernadette stopped the waitress. "Amy's here."

Although Bridget's strawberry-blond hair was pulled back into a fluffy, girlish ponytail, she looked to be around Amy's age. She clutched the tray against her chest and held out her free hand. "Hello, Amy, I'm Bridget Johnson. I've been wanting to know you for a long time."

"She's my oldest girl," Bernadette said as the two young women shook hands. "Bridget, has your sister come in yet?"

"'Fraid not. But you know her. Some customer in the shop probably got her going on the powers of aromatherapy. Or she offered to read their tarot cards."

Bernadette rolled her eyes. "Heaven forbid."

"Paul just got here, though," Bridget added. "He's washing up down the hall."

"Washing up?"

"I didn't have time to ask why, Mom. And I can't chat any more now. I've got to get table four's drink order." She smiled at Amy. "I'll catch up with you later."

Without suggesting who this Paul happened to be, Bridget rushed off through another door. Amy was puzzled. The only people she had expected to meet were Bernadette and her two daughters.

"We're shorthanded tonight," Bernadette said, shaking her head. "One of our young waitresses got engaged last night and quit this morning. Didn't care if we were fully booked the entire holiday weekend."

"That puts you in a tight spot."

Bernadette shrugged. "These things happen all the time in this business. Luckily my girls can help in a pinch if they're—"

The sound of a door closing, followed by sharp footsteps on the polished oak floor, echoed through the hall, distracting the older woman. "Paul," she called, "Amy Riordan has arrived."

"So I see."

The rich voice snagged Amy's attention immediately. Peering down the lengthy passageway, she recognized the tall, blond man approaching. She recognized him, all right, yet she couldn't believe her eyes. "You!" she gasped.

But clearly he wasn't surprised to see her.

"I see I beat you here." He was drying his hands with a fluffy white towel. "Janie Lee must have taken you by the scenic route."

He didn't appear surprised by that, either.

Annoyed anew, she tried to compose herself before opening her mouth. But the sly smile teasing in his eyes was more provoking than her own good sense. Besides, she hated being in the dark about anything.

Straightening her shoulders, she gave him her most direct stare. "This time, why don't you just tell me who the heck you are."

Bernadette stepped between them. "Amy, this is Paul Hanley," she said, obviously baffled by the sudden tension crackling in the air. "He's family."

Chapter Two

"Family? Him?"

Amy glared over Bernadette's head at Mr. Paul Hanley. "You could have at least said something out on that road. You knew I was coming here."

"Out on the road?" Startled, Bernadette looked from Amy to Paul and back. "My dear, you didn't have any trouble, did you?"

"None at all," Amy said quickly, putting a hand on Bernadette's arm to reassure her.

"Janie Lee and Jake had a flat, Aunt Bernadette. That's all," Paul explained to the bewildered woman. "Ms. Riordan and I both stopped to help."

"Oh, thank goodness. I'd hate to have anything bad happen on your first day here." Bernadette took a deep breath, her relief obvious. "So, you two have met already."

"In a manner of speaking. I didn't realize he was your nephew, though," Amy commented, trying to keep rein on her annoyance with Hanley. Upsetting the Ryans was not how she wanted to start this visit.

"Paul is more like a son." Bernadette gazed up at him with affection. "I helped raise him."

"Mom!" Bridget called from down the hall. "We need you here in the kitchen for a minute."

"Coming, darlin'." Bernadette looked to Paul. "You take Amy into the dining room while I take care of this. I'll send in Bridget with drinks and appetizers." She turned to Amy. "It's gotten so late. You must be starving."

"Maybe a little." She was more apprehensive than hungry, and very, very tired.

"Well, I thought we'd all sit down to dinner together and get better acquainted. Hopefully Maura will show up soon," Bernadette added. "I'll have your bags brought up to your room while we're eating, if you'd like."

"That'd be fine. Thanks," she said, digging in her handbag for her car keys.

She would have preferred going straight up to the room. But Bernadette seemed to have the evening planned, so Amy said nothing. Better to go with the flow tonight, she decided, get a feel for the place—and for these people. Amy handed the older woman the keys.

"I'll come join you as soon as I can," Bernadette said. "Paul will take good care of you."

"I'm sure he will," Amy replied, although she turned a skeptical glance his way after Bernadette left them.

"After you, Amy."

With a gracious sweep of his arm, Paul gestured at the wide doorway to the inn's dining room. The humorous glint in his rather attractive grayish blue eyes made her want to smack him. How nice that he found the situation amusing. But she'd never found rudeness funny and she hated being misled.

Swallowing her irritation, she entered the dining room. To her surprise, Paul's hand cupped her right elbow as he guided her through the large, dimly lit room. He moved past the array of tables with confidence, his bearing so even, so smooth, Amy felt as if she were gliding along beside him instead of merely walking. Although she wasn't thrilled with the guy right now, Paul Hanley's presence—tall, tight and sleek—was compelling.

At a corner table set for five, he held out a chair for her. Settling in, Amy glanced about the elegant room with its low-lit pewter chandeliers and imposing marble fireplace. But the fire was dying out, the mandolin player was packing up his instrument and only a handful of diners remained. A lonely hush seemed to have fallen over the room. Finally, she looked across the table and met Paul's gaze. The flickering flame from the miniature hurricane lamp between them danced across his thick, blond hair and cast intriguing shadows across his face.

Dragging her eyes away, Amy reached for her water glass. She took a long sip. Yet Paul's attention remained on her. She could feel it, steady and unwavering, drawing her gaze back to his.

"I apologize," he said.

Amy put down the water glass. This was the last thing she'd expected.

"I was rude to you out there with Jake and Janie Lee, and there's no excuse for it. Washington weekenders tend to take over the roads around here, and sometimes my tolerance gets a tad low." He shrugged and leaned back in his chair. "I shouldn't have taken it out on you."

Okay, so he'd covered the rudeness; she'd give him credit for that. As far as Amy was concerned, however, the greater offense hadn't yet been addressed. "But you learned soon enough that I wasn't your run-of-the-mill Washington weekender. At least not to you and the Ryans."

A grin lit up his face, fine laugh lines crinkled at the corner of his eyes. Amy's pulse quickened. She wished she didn't find him so attractive. It left her feeling somehow off kilter, even vulnerable. And considering why she was here, this seemed counterproductive.

"At least you say what's on your mind." Paul smiled again. "That's good. I like to know where I stand."

"So do I, Mr. Hanley, so do I," she said. "Which is why I have a bone to pick with you."

"Over why I didn't identify myself out there?"

"You could've said something."

Paul sighed, clasping his hands across his waist. "Could've and probably should've. Running across you with the Pratts caught me by surprise, I admit. Your visit is something of a momentous occasion around here. You're all my cousins have been talking about. And Bernadette has been so anxious about meeting you, she insisted I be here tonight."

She frowned. Why would Bernadette, with two daughters, need him to rally around? *She* was the outsider here. If anyone needed moral support, it was she.

"Then there was the matter of the Pratts," Paul continued.

"What have they got to do with it?"

He chuckled and shook his head. "You've never lived in a small town, have you?"

"No, I've lived in D.C. most of my life."

"Well, the Pratts, like most folks around here, are good people. But like most folks in the area, they consider their neighbors' business their own. And your being the daughter that most people never knew Greg Riordan had, and of course this business with the will..."

Amy remembered Janie Lee's inquisitiveness. "I get the picture."

"I guess I was thinking more of Bernadette's privacy than anything else. I'm sorry for taking you by surprise in the hall."

He seemed sincere. "Forget about it," she told him, figuring it was pointless to belabor the issue. After all, he was one of the Ryans, and she'd come here to resolve her differences with them, not create new ones.

Amy leaned back and relaxed. They'd just gotten off on the wrong foot, she concluded, taking another drink of her ice water. Paul, however, had straightened in his chair, his posture much more formal. Her uneasiness returned.

"Having said that, I want to make one thing clear." His apologetic tone had disappeared completely; he sounded serious—dead serious.

"And that is?"

"Bernadette has been apprehensive about finally meeting you, and she's extremely anxious about the inn. She's still mourning Greg, and she's vulnerable. So I'm not about to allow you or your lawyers to take advantage of her. Understand?"

She stiffened and resentment bubbled within her. Who the hell was he to talk to her like that? Or to suspect her motives?

"Listen, Mr. Hanley, *I've* been trying to get this will settled for months. Your aunt is the person dragging her feet. It's your aunt who demanded I come out here."

Paul leaned in closer. "Everybody knows Windom and Hart is one of the premier law firms in Washington, if not the country. Doing what's best for you—not Bernadette—butters their bread. I'm sure they wouldn't have allowed you to come if it wasn't to your advantage."

"My attorneys advise me on legal matters. They don't tell me where I can or cannot go."

"Your self-determination is to be admired," he said, clearly scoffing at her. "But my concern is Bernadette, and I'll do whatever I can to protect her. This place is her life. So I'm going to say this one more time—I don't want her hurt."

Amy wanted to get up and walk out, out of the dining room and out of the inn. She didn't need any of this. First she felt like an outsider in her father's home, and now this overprotective boor, who'd known her all of fifteen minutes, was hell-bent on making her out to be the bad guy. But maybe his aim *was* to chase her away—or, perhaps, to cow her into complying with whatever Bernadette wanted. Well, he would just have to rethink his strategy.

"I hear you, Mr. Hanley," she said, squeezing her fists tight under the table while trying her hardest to keep her voice sounding perfectly calm. "And I, too, have one thing to make clear."

A blond brow rose with surprised interest.

"I want to resolve the matter of the inn fairly, equitably and—with luck—quickly. That, and nothing more."

Before Paul could respond, a woman's voice trilled from across the dining room, "Hi-hi."

Amy turned, spotting a tall, radiant redhead coming their way. Her tumbling wavy hair and gold tunic and long crinkly gauze skirt floated around her with each crisp, leather-booted step. Looking for all the world like a soft, burnished cloud, she was absolutely stunning.

The young woman came right up to their table, dropped a colorful yarn-embroidered handbag at an empty place and then bent over Hanley. She took his face between her hands and planted a big, affectionate kiss on his forehead.

Amy watched, feeling peevish. If she wasn't so irked with the guy, she might even be a tad envious of his friend.

"I've been waiting for you to drop by the shop for weeks, you crumb," the golden vision announced, giving his head a gentle shake. "You said you would."

"It's been crazy at work," Paul explained as he disengaged himself from her hold.

Amy noticed a teasing twinkle in his eyes.

"Besides, some of your customers give me the willies."

"Oh, you're not afraid of anything." The woman plunked herself in the seat next to Amy's. "Anyway, my customers are as normal as Mom, apple pie and baseball."

Paul laughed. "That's some stretch, sweetheart."

Ignoring this, she turned to Amy. "You'd think I was running a den of the bizarre and the occult instead of a New Age gift shop." She extended her hand. "Hi, I'm Maura."

"The perpetually late Maura," Bridget offered, approaching from behind, carrying a tray laden with a pitcher of iced tea and a carafe of white wine. "Does Mom know you're here?"

"Saw her at the front desk. She'll be right along." Maura lifted the platter of cheese and crackers from her sister's tray and placed it between Amy and herself. "I'm just ravenous," she said to Amy, "aren't you?"

Amy nodded, although her stomach was too numb from nervousness to register any sensation. She did, however, appreciate the younger woman's breezy friendliness. And due to her perfect timing, Amy had managed the last word in the tangle with Mr. Paul Hanley.

"Where are George and my precious nephew and niece?" Maura asked Bridget, after slicing off a hunk of ripe cheddar. "Aren't they coming?"

"George was on duty at the fire station all last night, so he was just beat. Since I'm filling in tonight, the kids would have been underfoot." Bridget looked to Amy. "Willy is four going on ten, and Jenny's in the terrible-two stage now. And I do mean terrible."

"Don't malign my sweet angels," Maura protested. "They always behave with me."

"That's because you let them have their way all the time," Bridget replied as she turned back to Amy. "I'll bring them by tomorrow. They both really want to meet you."

Amy smiled and nodded. Yet she felt awkward. Bridget and Maura were acting as if they'd known her for a long time, as if she were just another member of the family.

Following their mother's reticent welcome, and after what had just transpired between her and Paul, the Ryan girls' easy warmth amazed her. Although it was nice, Amy didn't know what to make of it. She wasn't sure she even wanted it. Because, no matter what the nature of their relationship with her father, Amy did not consider the Ryans *family*.

* * *

Paul watched Amy say her good-nights before Maura took her upstairs to her room. He'd been watching her throughout dinner, trying to get some sort of fix on her. But she wasn't an easy read.

"Well, what do you think?" Bridget asked after Amy had left with Maura.

"She looks so much like Greg," Bernadette said, sounding wistful.

Bridget nodded in agreement. "She's really quite attractive. A little shy, though."

Paul sat back quietly. He agreed with the "attractive," very much so. All evening, he'd kept stealing glimpses at those wide, dreamy blue eyes of hers. Then he'd catch himself wondering if her rich, dark hair could possibly be as soft as it looked.

But shy? Not that woman.

Amy hadn't shrunk from their rather testy discussion. She met him head-on, spoke her mind, made her intentions known. Then again, he expected nothing less from a rich, well-educated, urban professional businesswoman. She *should* know how to handle herself.

Still, he was surprised to learn she worked with children.

"Except for telling us about her business, she didn't say much during dinner," Bridget continued. "Even after we managed to shut Maura up for a while."

"I wonder how she really feels about us," Bernadette said, gazing absently in the air, apparently not expecting them to answer. "She has no feeling for this place—I can tell. She could sell her share in a blink of an eye and not care to whom."

"Mom, she just got here."

"She didn't say a word about Greg. Not a thing." His aunt lifted her worried eyes to Paul. "You spent a few minutes alone with her. What do you think?"

"I think you need to stop fretting. Give her a day or two to take this place in." He gently squeezed her weathered hand.

Although his discussion with Amy showed she could give as good as she got, Paul suspected she didn't find this situation easy, either. At times she even looked a bit lost. That's something he wouldn't have expected from a woman like her, and that's what was throwing him off. Amy Riordan was what he'd thought she'd be, and yet she wasn't.

"And I think we should call it a night." Bridget stood up and began gathering their empty coffee cups. "Are we going to have the pleasure of your company anytime soon, Paul? Or are the papers going to gobble you up again?"

"I'll come when I can."

It was the best he could offer. He was swamped at work. After three years of publishing a string of small-town weekly newspapers and regional shopping advertisers, he was mired in the inherent hassles of a growing company.

"Don't bother yourself about it." Bernadette patted his shoulder. "You've been so patient these past few days. I'm sure I've driven you crazy with my ranting and raving."

"Not a chance." Curving an arm around her, he pulled her gently against his side. "I'll be here when you need me."

Amy followed Maura up the wide, elegant staircase to the second of the inn's three floors. She was bone-weary tired, yet glad to be in the company of the one Ryan with whom, so far, she felt at ease. After Paul Hanley's intensity, and then feeling as if she were on display during the "family" meal, she found Maura's openness and quirky charm oddly comforting.

"Mom saved the Ivy Room for you, I see." Maura unlocked the door at the very end of the second floor hall. "It's my favorite."

Amy stepped inside and understood why. It was a huge room, with a high ceiling, polished wood floor, rich mahogany furnishings, lace curtains and a queen-size canopy bed. The wallpaper—graceful, leafy-green ivy vines on a clean, white background—was clearly the source of the room's name. The same ivy pattern trimmed the edges of the white bedspread and canopy.

"It really is lovely," she said to Maura as she walked around the room. Peeking into the bathroom, she couldn't help smiling at the big claw-foot tub and pedestal sink.

"Mom and Greg spent a ton of time renovating each room," Maura said. "This was one of the last to be completed."

"How many guest rooms are there here?" Amy asked. "Fifteen?"

"Sixteen. All on the second and third floors. For years, the inn was a continual work in progress," Maura revealed. "Greg would come up with one fantastic idea after another, and Mom would always pull him down to earth, working with him to sort the practical from the impossible. Watching them thrash out the details was such a kick."

It felt strange hearing her father talked about in such a familiar way. He'd been a distant, almost abstract figure to her, even in her discussions about him with her mother.

"Did you all live here in the inn together?" she asked, trying to sound casual. She was curious about what her father's life here was like, but she didn't yet feel comfortable enough to come out and ask. Maybe in a day or two, she would.

Maura shook her head. "We all lived in the innkeeper's cottage behind the inn. That is, until Bridget got married and then later I moved to Winchester to be near my shop. Mom's still there, though."

Amy sat on the edge of the bed and slipped off her navy pumps. "And did Paul live in the innkeeper's house, too? Your mother mentioned that she had raised him."

"Oh, Paul was long gone by then." Plopping herself down on the other end of the bed, Maura plumped up the pillow behind her and sat back. "He joined the service right out of high school. Then he attended college out west and lived in San Francisco for years."

"But he lives in Tremont now?"

Amy didn't know why she was even asking about him. Other than having appointed himself Bernadette's guardian angel, Paul mattered little to her.

"Close enough. He has this really neat house in the hills just outside of town. Came back about three or four years ago—after his divorce," Maura explained. Suddenly she smiled, and a knowing look popped into her brown eyes, a look with all the subtlety of a wink and a poke in the ribs. "Paul *is* something of a dish, isn't he?"

Amy's first impulse was to deny Maura's assumption, because—dish or not—Paul Hanley did not put stars in her eyes. Still, mindful of the boomerang effect of protesting too much, she reconsidered.

"He didn't say much at dinner tonight," she said, instead, hoping to derail Maura's misguided train of thought. Besides, Amy had found his relative silence at the family meal confusing, especially following his earlier outburst with her.

"Oh, that's just Paul's way," Maura said with an unconcerned wave of her hand. "He's what you might call a private person. I mean, the guy's like a brother to me, yet there's a lot about him I don't know. For instance, take his divorce—"

Two sharp rings from the bedside telephone cut her off. Amy reached over to answer it.

"Hi, it's Bridget. Would you please tell my little sister that her Jeep is blocking my car? I can't get out."

She relayed the message at once.

"Nuts, that's the second time I've done that this week." With a sigh Maura got to her feet, smoothing out her long, red hair with her fingers. "I probably should be heading out, anyway. You look beat."

"I am. But I enjoyed talking with you."

"Me, too, you. It's good to finally put a face to your name, and you're not like what I expected at all."

Amy was way too weary to touch Maura's last remark. "Well, I hope we can talk again."

"Absolutely. Come have lunch with me in Winchester some afternoon." Her brown eyes lit up with enthusiasm. "As one businesswoman to another, I'd love to know what you think of my shop."

Amy promised to get in touch and Maura was off, the clicking of her boot heels on the hall's bare floor echoing after her.

Immediately upon closing the door, Amy began unbuttoning her suit jacket and tugging at her skirt zipper. She'd been wearing this outfit since seven o'clock this morning. When she'd finally managed to drag herself away from the office, she hadn't wanted to waste time changing into more comfortable clothes. But she had packed them: jeans, slacks, sweaters, flats. Amy was happy to take a vacation from suits, panty hose, heels and makeup.

"Oh, my gosh," she gasped just as she was pulling her white, satin slip over her head. Letting the slip slide back over her breast and hips, she dashed for the phone. Tapping into an outside line, she quickly dialed her partner's number.

"Julie, I'm sorry," she said when her friend had answered halfway through the first ring.

"Amy, finally!"

"I know—I'm sorry. I got here late and then I had to meet all the Ryans," she explained. "Believe it or not, this is the first moment I've had to myself since I arrived."

"Ooh, how's it going?"

Julie Bauman, who was not only her business partner but also her best friend, knew the whole story.

"Overwhelming—more so than I'd imagined."

She told Julie everything, from butting heads with Paul the first time, when she'd stopped to help the Pratts, to Maura curling up on her bed like a chummy college roommate.

"Hmm, this Paul fellow sounds intriguing. Is he married?"

Amy groaned. Ever since her marriage three years ago, Julie had become a dauntless matchmaker. She was always on the lookout for perfect mates for her friends.

"Jules, you're not listening. I'm Ryan enemy number one as far as he's concerned. He thinks I'm out to get his aunt."

Julie gave a dismissing grunt. "Yeah, but once he gets to know you..."

"Give it up, Julie!" Amy lay back on the bed, frustrated. She shouldn't have even mentioned Paul Hanley. "I'm not in the market for anyone new. Remember?"

"All right, all right." Then Julie hesitated a moment before continuing. "While we're sort of on the topic—there's another reason I've been sitting by the phone waiting for your call."

Amy didn't like the sound of this.

"Jeff phoned you at the office, not more than fifteen minutes after you left."

Jeff Martin. Her ex-fiancé. Amy's thoughts clouded with discomforting memories. She had spoken to him only once in the three months since he'd broken their engagement. "Did you take the call?"

"Of course I did," Julie replied. "And he sounded genuinely concerned about how you're doing. He wants to phone you back."

"What on earth for?"

Again her friend hesitated. "Probably to tell you he's getting married soon. New Year's Day is what I've heard via the grapevine."

"That soon?" Amy said, although she'd been expecting it. Still, she was grateful her friend hadn't spared her the truth. Julie knew Amy would rather hear the news from her than from anybody else—Jeff included.

"He really wants to talk to you," Julie added. "I think he wants to know if you're okay about it."

Amy closed her eyes. She *was* okay now. The initial feelings of shock, betrayal and disappointment had subsided enough to allow her some perspective. To right the wrong he had done, Jeff had had to be brutally honest about himself and about his feelings. And although she'd been deeply hurt, Amy sensed that Jeff was experiencing a greater pain for having lied to her and to everyone else.

"You'll talk to him, won't you?" Julie prompted.

"Sure, why not?" She'd already forgiven Jeff, had even defended him to her stepfather.

"Thought so. That's why I gave him the inn's phone number."

Amy couldn't help smiling. Jules always knew the right thing to do. They read each other so well—both in their personal lives and in their business. It meant the world to Amy that she had one person in her life she could rely on and trust.

They talked awhile about their agency, agreeing on the secretary's Christmas bonus, disagreeing on the brash photographer who was angling for client referrals. Amy was concerned about Shawna, an adorable seven-year-old she'd recently signed. After sailing winningly through several interviews with both Amy and Julie, the little girl had developed unexpected jitters about auditioning for an upcoming toothpaste commercial.

"Are you sure she really wants to do it?" Amy asked. "Because I'm perfectly willing to cancel her audition if she's not ready. I told her mother that."

"Mrs. Darner isn't giving up that appointment for anything. You know how she is," Julie added with a huff. "But I talked to Shawna today. She claims she's okay."

"Maybe I should drive up Tuesday and go to the audition with her."

"No, you won't, Amy. You stay there and take care of your personal business. I'll go with Shawna. I promise I'll have her mother kept waiting outside—even if I have to bribe someone."

"I feel like I'm dumping everything in your lap."

"What are partners for? Besides, we agreed this was the best time for you to take leave. With the holidays coming and all, this place will be dead in a week."

"I'll try to get things settled here as soon as I can anyway."

"Now who's not listening?" Julie said with a sigh. "Don't worry about this place. Tend to family matters for a change."

"I wouldn't exactly call it a family matter."

"Wait a minute. I thought you wanted to find out more about your father because of what he named the inn. You having a change of heart or something?"

"I don't know. Maybe I was being too sentimental for my own good." Taking a deep breath while she collected her thoughts, Amy leaned back against the pillows Maura had fluffed up earlier. "It feels so strange being here. One minute I feel like they're circling their wagons against me, and in the next I feel like they're courting me with family dinners and chummy chats—just to get what they want."

Julie's disparaging mutters came over the phone line loud and clear. "Could be they're just nice people who are as torn and confused about this as you are. I know it's tough for you to let your guard down, but give them a chance."

She knew her friend was right; she had to accept people at face value. "I guess seeing the inn for the first time hit me hard."

"Understandable," Julie said. "Just try to relax. And take as much time as you need. Considering the past few months, you deserve a vacation."

"Ha! Some vacation."

"Amy—"

"Okay, okay. I'll start over again tomorrow, I promise. Clean slates for everyone—me, Bernadette, the girls, the inn, the town. Even Paul Hanley."

Chapter Three

"How do I get through to these guys?" Paul grumbled in his office. "Threaten to throw them all out on their rears?"

Five minutes after adjourning the Valley News Group monthly company-wide meeting, he was still fuming. "You know I hate to yell." He paced back and forth in front of Dirk Campbell, the group's production manager. "But I've tried incentives, pep talks, praise. I didn't want to resort to yelling—I really didn't."

"I wouldn't call it yelling," Dirk said, sitting on the edge of Paul's desk. "You were tough, and rightfully so. I was watching them—they got your message."

"Let's hope you're right. The thought of laying off even one person . . ." He shook his head.

"Look, you saved their jobs three years ago when you bought Tully out. They know what they have to do to keep them."

Paul sank down in his chair and stared again at the current revenue statement. Advertising income was down; operating costs were up. Every one of his twenty employees, including himself, had to work smarter and harder to make up for last quarter's losses. The bulk of his personal cash was tied up right now; he didn't have enough to cover a shortage this time.

"It's not the first rough patch we've hit," Dirk reminded him. "And, business being business, it won't be the last."

"True enough." He chuckled in spite of himself. "I had to be crazy going into business for myself. Life was a hell of a lot easier when I only had to worry about *my* livelihood. All I had to do was show up, read the news and get paid an obscene amount of money."

"And you gave that up for this." Dirk waved his arm at the contents of the dingy, minuscule office, most of which was taken up by Paul's crowded metal desk. "Hell, you *are* crazy!"

Paul didn't blink an eye. He and Dirk had been razzing each other since their high school newspaper days. Yet Dirk was the one friend in Tremont who knew at least some of the reasons for Paul's decision to give up broadcasting and come home.

"Crazy, maybe," Paul continued. "But at least I don't have to worry about wearing suits anymore."

"Or getting expensive haircuts," added Dirk.

"Or getting laryngitis."

"Or sneezing on the air."

"Or the TelePrompTer failing."

"Or getting food stuck between your teeth during close-ups."

Paul stopped pacing and shot a stern look across the desk. "You trying to cheer me up?"

"Actually, I'm angling for a free lunch." Dirk grinned.

Paul smiled. Despite tight times and headaches, he knew Tremont and the Valley News Group were where he belonged. "Okay, I'll spring for lunch."

"How about dinner at the inn, instead?" Dirk suggested.

"Dinner? At the most expensive place in town yet? Why not?" Paul quipped, certain Dirk was joking. His colleague tended to steer clear of the Blue Sky. "Sure you want to risk it, though? My aunt's still itching to fix you up with Maura." Bernadette believed Dirk was just the man to bring her free-spirited daughter down to earth. As far as Dirk was concerned, however, Maura was out in left field and could stay there. Without him.

"I will this time—if it means a chance to meet Greg Riordan's daughter. I hear she's quite a looker."

"How do you know about Greg's daughter?" Paul asked, though he could easily guess. After all, Amy had now been in town for a whole three days.

"Let's see, Ed at the general store heard it from Harry at the gas station, who heard it from Mary Frame, who found out about it from her dentist, who was dining at the inn the night she arrived."

"That's it." Paul slapped his leg. "Now I know why we're losing money. Who needs local newspapers when they've got the local grapevine?"

"So? Is the gang right about her being a looker?"

"I guess you could say she's attractive," he replied with deliberate nonchalance. For some fool reason, Dirk's interest in Amy bothered him. "The offer was for *lunch,* which, as you well know, is not served at the inn. Besides, didn't you hear about our cash-flow problem at the meeting?"

Laughing, Dirk threw up his hands. "Okay, okay, I get it. You want to keep the new girl in town to yourself."

Paul didn't bother responding. He'd spent more than enough time wondering about Amy Riordan since he'd met her. And he'd been worrying about what might be happening at the inn. He hadn't heard a word from Bernadette, so he'd assumed things were going smoothly. Yet, with Dirk mentioning the inn, his curiosity, or rather his concern, was raised anew. As he headed out to his pickup with Dirk, Paul decided he'd best check in on the Blue Sky very soon.

Amy was frustrated.

Although she was well into her third day in Tremont, she had yet to have any discussion of substance with Bernadette, either about her father or his will. But the older woman had dragged her through every inch of the inn, which Amy found lovely and maintained with meticulous care. Bernadette made a point of introducing her to the staff and to any guest who happened to cross their path. On Sunday, Bridget had brought her family and Maura had brought her tarot cards. Bridget's husband was quiet, but sweet, her kids rambunctious, but cute, and they all had a chuckle over Maura's cursory reading of Amy's cards. The only person missing was Paul Hanley, although no one said a word about him. Which, in Amy's mind, was just as well.

Having promised Julie to give the Ryans the benefit of the doubt, she had tried to get into the spirit of the family afternoon. Yet, as an only child from a small, formal family, she found the lively rhythm and flow of the gathering took getting used to. She also couldn't shake the sense that Bernadette and her daughters were watching her, studying her, weighing her actions and answers.

Considering this scrutiny—sometimes subtle, sometimes not—how could she let down her guard?

Now it was Monday afternoon, and Amy felt she was getting nowhere. The majority of the Thanksgiving guests had checked out of the inn last night. The few remaining had gone on a sight-seeing tour to Skyline Caverns near Front Royal. Except for Bernadette and a member or two of the kitchen staff preparing the evening's dinner, the inn was empty. Grateful for some time to herself, Amy went up to her room and attempted to muster interest in the historical novel she'd borrowed from the downstairs library. But she was too distracted by the unearthly quiet to concentrate. Instead, she closed her eyes and let herself drift off to sleep.

Within what felt like minutes, her eyes flew open when the bed began vibrating gently. An ear-pounding boom followed by a thunderous crash rattled the windows, jolting Amy to her feet. Suddenly everything was still, except for the footsteps clamoring up the staircase.

"Must be one of the rooms!" she heard Bernadette cry.

Amy flung open her door just as Bernadette reached the second floor, with Martin, the chef, fast on her heels. "It was upstairs!" she called out, running after them.

On the third floor, Bernadette unlocked doors in a frenzy, sticking her head inside each room to check before moving onto the next. Finally, at room 16, she stopped and gasped in horror as milk white powder floated into the hall like a foggy mist. "My God, it's ruined."

Breathless from running up the stairs, Amy poked her head inside the room. She was shocked by the destruction. Thick chunks of heavy plaster lay splattered across the guest room, apparently having fallen from the ceiling with crushing force.

"Be careful, ladies," the chef warned. "There still may be some loose pieces up there."

Slowly leaning farther into the room, Amy peered up at the ceiling. No loose, dangling hunks were evident, because the entire ceiling had collapsed. She could even see the attic through a few holes where the ceiling joists had been torn off by the chunks. And white dust coated every inch of the room.

"I think it's okay to go in," she told Martin. He and Bernadette followed as she cautiously stepped inside.

"Thank heaven the room was vacant," Bernadette said, her voice shaky. "Someone could have been seriously hurt. Just yesterday it was occupied...."

"And a good thing most of the guests were out of the building," Martin commented. "The noise alone would have scared them witless. It did me."

And me, Amy thought, as she surveyed the wreckage. Lamps and bric-a-brac had been shattered, curtains torn, the wood floor scraped and dented. A few sizable blocks had smashed into the furniture, chipping, splintering and even breaking many of the fine wood pieces. The mahogany four-poster had received the worst damage. The bed's dark frame had literally been split in two, the headboard cracked and both footposts broken in half.

"Oh, no," Bernadette murmured, approaching the bed. "It can't be."

Amy noticed she was shaking.

Eyeing the bed, Martin shook his head. "Looks beyond saving. Was it very valuable?"

"Only to me. It was the first piece we bought when we began renovating."

Hearing the catch in Bernadette's voice, Amy moved to her side. She surmised the "we" meant Greg.

"Your father found it in a junk shop." She glanced at Amy. "He mended the frame and refinished it. It turned out to be a beautiful piece."

Touched by the strength of Bernadette's emotion, Amy put her arm around the older woman's shoulder. For the first time, she felt the awkward distance between them ease. She also felt Bernadette's body trembling. Concerned, she suggested Martin take Bernadette downstairs for a cup of tea.

"No time for that!" Bernadette pulled away. "I've got to start cleaning this mess up, find a plasterer—and call—"

"I'll help," Amy insisted, for Bernadette's trembling was visible now. "I'll see to the room while you go down to make the necessary calls."

"You? You can't do it by yourself." Bernadette looked around the room, her expression dazed. "How can I leave it like this?"

"I'll make a start. It might help to sweep some of this stuff up—to see how extensive the damage really is. Certainly I can manage that." She began to edge Bernadette toward the door. "Besides, the tour group will be returning from Skyline Caverns soon and you'll need to attend to them."

"And the first dinner sitting needs to be set up. You have to oversee it," Martin added, taking Bernadette by the arm. The concern on his face matched Amy's. "Perhaps I should give Bridget a call, as well. Don't you think so, Ms. Riordan?"

Amy nodded as the chef led Bernadette down the hall, their shoulders and hair speckled with plaster—as she supposed hers were, too. Before turning the corner for the stairs, Martin looked back and suggested she check the maid's closet for brooms and other supplies.

After a moment of calculating exactly what she had gotten herself into, Amy went to fetch the items she needed for cleaning. Once armed with brooms, rags, sponges and plastic trash bags, she heaved a sigh of disbelief and then got to work. It was a messy job. As she waded through the wreckage, she had no idea how long it would take. She did know that the debris swirling about made her throat burn and her eyes itch. And she was convinced that every hair, every pore, every stitch of her sweater and jeans were coated with powdery white dust.

She had just bent down to scoop gritty plaster particles into the dustpan, when a long, low whistle echoed through the room. Still sweeping, she snatched a look over her shoulder. Catching a glimpse of the tall, lean silhouette at the threshold, Amy froze, not knowing whether to laugh or curse. It shouldn't matter if Paul Hanley saw her stooped over the floor, looking like an earthquake survivor. But matter it did.

"Well, I'll be damned." He squinted up at the practically nonexistent ceiling, making a quick perusal of it from corner to corner. "Guess we're lucky no one was hurt."

The man had an incredible voice, deep, rich and sexy. Amy swore it made her spine tingle in a way she'd never experienced before. Except right now, it made her feel self-conscious. Yet, with no choice but to face him in the state she was in, Amy put aside the dustpan and straightened.

"No such luck for the furniture, I'm afraid," she said, her own voice raspy from the drying dust. "Just look at it."

His blue eyes surveyed the room's contents before widening when they focused in on her. "And look at you."

"For heaven's sake, please *don't*." She began brushing furiously at her jeans.

"Can this really be the woman of the designer suit and two-hundred-dollar hairstyle?"

Her mouth tightened, a defensive reflex that suddenly relaxed into a smile when she caught the wry gleam in his eyes. As guarded as she'd been the past few days, she could still recognize good-natured teasing. And that was a relief.

But his gaze remained on her, even after the teasing glint had faded. It was as if he'd never seen her before. Then again, she thought dryly, no one had ever seen her looking like a ghost before. "Were you called to come save the day?" she asked.

"Actually, I'd just dropped by to say hello and found Martin at the front desk, frantically trying to reach Bridget on the phone. You don't have to clean this up, you know," he added, gesturing at the floor.

"I know." She shrugged, sending puffs of plaster dust dancing above her shoulders. "But Bernadette was pretty shaken and we couldn't get her out of here. How is she now?"

"Calmer, I think. I sat her down in the Pub Room with a glass of brandy and the telephone. Someone's coming in the morning to repair this and to check the ceilings throughout the inn. They'll probably take care of the mess, too."

Feeling awkward under his unblinking gaze, Amy reached for the broom. "I think I'll finish the sweeping and dusting, at least. Could help the room look less daunting to Bernadette."

"Okay, if you insist." Paul slipped off his leather jacket and, to her amazement, tossed it out into the hall. Then he started rolling up the sleeves of his blue chamois shirt. As his long fingers pushed the fabric up his muscular, golden-haired arms, she couldn't resist wondering about their strength.

Grabbing some trash bags, Paul got to work. He swept up the jagged shards of smashed lamps and glass, then he started moving damaged furniture out of the way. Together they worked in a silence interrupted by the occasional dust-induced cough or sneeze. After a while, Paul went downstairs in search of shovels and trash cans to hold the heavier pieces of plaster. When he returned with them, Amy took notice.

"Look at you!" she cried, then laughed as he ran a hand through his covered hair. It resembled a powdered wig. "You and I could get night work haunting this place."

Glancing down at his shirt and jeans, he smiled. "Maura is always complaining that the inn hasn't got a single ghost to boast about. Maybe we should get her over here tonight and give her a thrill," he proposed with a mischievous wink.

Amy giggled and moved on to another corner of the room. She had already noticed, and appreciated, the jesting relationship between Paul and Maura. Actually, she envied it—and Maura and Bridget's camaraderie as well.

"Bernadette just asked me if you were doing too much," Paul said as he heaved a hunk of plaster into a trash can. "I told her you had me doing all the work."

"That's not such a bad idea." Grinning, she dumped another dustpan load into a plastic bag. "Is she feeling any better?"

"A little. At least the initial shock has worn off."

"She was very upset about the bed."

"Yeah, she told me." Paul glanced over at the ravaged bed frame. "She's still shaky when it comes to anything connected with Greg. But that'll change in time."

"You're very supportive of her."

"Well, she's always been there for me."

Amy watched Paul hoist a second multilayered chunk into the trash can, followed by another. The task seemed effortless for him, yet she could see by the taut, extended muscles in his arms that it was not. She couldn't tear her eyes away as each corded tendon flexed beneath his skin when he grasped and lifted the heavy plaster. That is, she couldn't until the exquisite warmth stirring low within her began threatening her equilibrium.

She took the broom and swept hard for several seconds. But it was pointless. Her interest—among other things—was aroused. Amy cleared her throat, determined to keep this prickly new excitement from seeping into her voice. "When I arrived the other night, Bernadette mentioned she had raised you."

"That's right. From the time I was ten. My parents were killed in a car crash."

He was so matter of fact about it that Amy didn't know if she should express sympathy. "So you went to live with your aunt," she said, instead.

"*An* aunt. Not Bernadette—who is actually my father's cousin." He stopped working and pulled a red bandanna from a back pocket. Wisps of dust clung to it, so he gave it a good shake. "My mother's sister took me in," he explained, wiping the sweat from his brow. "She was single at the time, and she seemed to want me. I had just turned eight."

"So young," she whispered, more to herself than to him. She knew how hard it was to lose a parent when you were very young—but Paul had lost both of his in the ultimate, final way.

"Aunt Milly was very good to me, though I'm sure I wasn't the easiest kid. She pulled me through the blackness."

"What happened to her?"

"She met a man who wanted to marry her." Paul stuffed the bandanna back into his pocket and leaned against a relatively undamaged bureau. "But, when push came to shove, Milly's husband-to-be didn't want a preadolescent boy in the bargain."

"Don't tell me she—"

Paul cut her off with a nod. "Aunt Milly was heading for the altar, and I was heading straight for a foster home. None of the other relatives wanted me."

Amy thought this incredibly sad. How abandoned Paul must have felt. And betrayed. Yet now, telling her all about it, with his arms folded against his chest, he continued to sound and look so matter-of-fact. How could he do that? She couldn't speak of her father's desertion without getting emotional—even twenty-plus years after the fact.

"How did you end up with the Ryans?"

"When Bernadette heard about me through the family grapevine, she drove all the way down to Lynchburg to get me—even though she was widowed and had two little girls of her own to raise." For the first time in this discussion, his face softened. "Ten-year-old orphans usually don't get lucky. She saved my life."

He no longer sounded matter-of-fact.

Paul turned back to work, and Amy resumed her sweeping. She couldn't, however, get his story out of her mind. It must have been scary for the young Paul to come live with a virtual stranger after losing two homes in two years. Bernadette must have had her work cut out for her. Apparently she had done right by him. Paul's touching devotion to her was proof of that—as was his fierce protectiveness.

Finally, their work was done. With the dust and debris cleared away and the damaged furniture pushed into a corner, the guest room was ready to be repaired. Amy, her clothes caked with dust, her arms sore and neck stiff, gave the room a satisfied glance. After three days of passivity, she was happy to have accomplished something. "Not a half-bad job," she mused to Paul, who was pushing the last loaded trash can toward the door, "considering it took us over two hours."

"Seemed more like four," Paul countered, returning to her side. "And you've been great. This was above and beyond the call of duty."

She waved off his praise. "I didn't have anything else planned for this afternoon, anyway."

"I also appreciate what you did for Bernadette. Martin told me how you coaxed her back downstairs."

"She wanted to tackle it all herself. I couldn't let her do that."

"Sometimes I wonder how she's managed to run this place without Greg for the past six months. She's not getting any younger."

"The girls help her out, don't they?"

"When they can, sure. Still, Bridget has young kids, and Maura has the shop. It's damned difficult all the way around."

That he was expressing concern about Bernadette and the inn to her, the presumed threat, surprised Amy. Sweeping gunk this afternoon might have had its rewards, after all. For it seemed the door between them had opened a crack. After sharing such a personal, painful part of his past, Paul might be inclined to look beyond his preconceived notions about her. Perhaps she could trust him to believe the real reason she'd come to Tremont.

"I would like to make it easier for Bernadette," she began, somewhat tentative as she searched for the right words, "if only she'd let me. But she keeps me at arm's length, not only about the inn, but about my father. And he's why I—"

"He's why you came?" Paul interrupted, turning to her with skeptical eyes. "Isn't it a little late in the day for that?"

Stunned by his remark, Amy struggled with herself not to snap back. He was just extremely protective of Bernadette. By keeping calm and trying again, she still might get him to listen—despite his doubts. "Paul, my father *is* why I'm here," she assured him. "And since Bernadette lobbied for me to come, it's frustrating when she keeps putting me off."

"Why the rush, Amy? It's only been three days."

"What?"

"Maybe she needs time to get used to you. Have you thought of that?"

Not giving her a chance to answer, Paul started collecting the soiled rags scattered on the floor. "And you know what else?" he continued as he crisscrossed the room. "I think Bernadette's reticence is understandable—considering she stands to lose the one place she holds dear to a woman who couldn't be bothered about it or her own father until money became involved."

Amy winced, his words piercing her with the precision of an archer's arrow. Well, it was her own fault for making herself an easy target. She'd been a fool to believe that his oh-so-matter-of-fact recitation of his childhood misfortune actually meant something. He wasn't interested in her side of the story, and he certainly didn't care about her feelings. He probably thought she didn't have any.

Amy grabbed the broom she'd been using and marched it over to the overflowing trash cans. She had every intention of simply walking out the door, but she couldn't—not with Paul's unfair charge left hanging in the air. Steaming with resentment, she turned to him. "I'm really sick and tired of being suspect in everybody's eyes. Especially since none of you have considered what coming here has been like for me."

Paul looked startled by her vehemence. "Bernadette and the girls have gone out of their way to welcome you."

"Yes, and I don't fault their hospitality one bit. They *act* like I'm one of the family. But I'm not, and deep down they know it. So we all pretend, and the past three days have been nothing but a showy dance."

"That's not fair." Paul threw the soiled rags into a heap by the door. "They're not the kind to play games."

"And of course *I am*. Because you've decided I'm greedy and coldhearted, that I never even cared about my father." Her fingers curled tight around the broom handle as she swallowed back an errant sob. She would not cry in front of this man. "Bridget and Maura had him much longer than I did. He actually was a father to them. Do you know how that makes me feel?"

"Amy..." He reached for her with a dusty hand.

She moved away from him. "I lost my father when I was six years old. And for a moment there, I was crazy enough to think you were someone who could understand that."

"Amy, I'm sorry—I—"

She turned her back to him, heading for the door. Caught up in a spin of emotion, she had had enough of Paul Hanley—and everything else, for that matter.

She had barely made it out into the hall, however, when Paul grabbed her wrist. "Please, Amy, wait."

The look in his eyes was different now; suspicion had turned into sympathy. His gaze, clear blue and intense, held her for a moment—until her reflection came staring back at her. She felt raw and exposed, and embarrassed for having let her feelings fly. The last thing she wanted was pity.

She jerked her arm hard, but his hand held firm.

"Talk to me," he insisted.

Amy took a deep breath. This had gone far enough. She realized she had to get a grip on the situation and on herself. "I don't want to talk, Paul," she stated, struggling to feel the calm that, somehow, she was managing to project in her voice. "It's been a long afternoon. I'm tired, I'm filthy, I'm hungry. And frankly, I don't have to deal with you."

She yanked her arm again, and Paul released her. Although she could feel his eyes boring into her back as she hurried down the hall, he didn't say a word. Apparently he had the message.

When Amy reached her room, she headed straight for the shower. Never having gotten so dirty in her life, she lingered beneath the cleansing cascades of hot water for the longest time. It was hard not to replay what had just happened in room 16. Her annoyance with Paul remained high, but she was also upset with herself. She shouldn't have let her emotions get the better of her like that.

Finally dragging herself out of the shower, she wrapped her shampooed hair with a fluffy towel and was reaching for another towel, when a sharp rap on her room door made her jump.

"Amy!" It was Paul.

Her mouth tightened. The short, insistent knocks continued. She was sorely tempted to ignore him—to let him knock and call until he got good and tired. But she had a hunch he wasn't the type to give up easily. He had followed her down here, hadn't he?

Figuring she'd just have to make herself clearer this time, she pulled her china-blue silk robe from the cherry armoire and wrapped it around her wet body. She wasn't anxious to confront him again, and his persistent rapping tried her patience. Her slippery, moist hands fumbled with the heavy, old door locks, although she kept the chain secured. "What is it?" she snapped through the slight wedge of opening the chain permitted.

Paul, his hair and clothes still gritty with old plaster, leaned against the doorjamb as his fascinated eyes slowly roamed the length of her body. "You're looking much better."

She pulled the thin robe tighter around her in a self-conscious attempt to shake his scrutinizing gaze—and to dispel the steamy warm effect it was having on her damp skin.

Finally, *finally,* his eyes reached hers. Unfortunately his shift in perspective gave her no relief.

"Before you start chewing me out again, let me ask one thing," he said, his voice laid-back and low. "How'd you like to get away from this place with me for a few hours?"

Chapter Four

Amy's sapphire eyes flared—with astonishment or anger, Paul wasn't sure. He slid his foot inside the door, just in case it was the latter.

"A change of scene might do you some good."

She frowned. "No, thanks."

Despite her curt reply, Paul drank in the fragrance of fresh soap and shampoo while restraining his gaze from feasting on her surprising curves. Her robe clung to her wet skin, revealing the soft roundness that her business suit and today's loose sweater had hidden—unfortunately. When he'd first met Amy, he'd thought her pretty, but in a starched, too-polished way. Not anymore. Seeing her like this, stripped down to the almost bare essentials—scrubbed face, moist skin, curvy body—changed his perspective. Now she was real, warm, sexy.

Now he was in trouble.

Excitement seared through him like heat lightning, as his original intentions seemed to drown beneath the resulting cloudburst. Drowning with them, however, was out of the question. Paul coughed, clearing his throat and his thoughts. "I understand why you're upset. We—I— haven't been entirely fair to you. I can see that now."

Amy didn't answer. Her bright blue glare said it all. She was angry and hurt and in no mood to listen.

But she would have to.

"I'd like to take you out to dinner. You did say you were hungry, and I know a mighty fine rib place on the other side of Winchester."

"I'll eat here in the dining room, thank you."

"You've been cooped up in the inn for three days. Getting out of here might help your perspective."

Her eyes narrowed. "*My* perspective's not the one needing help."

"Okay." Paul tried not to grin. "But you clearly want to talk about this situation. That would be easier to do in a neutral place. Somewhere private. No interruptions."

Her shoulders sank and she leaned against the edge of the door. "I appreciate what you're trying to do. Except you're not the one I want to talk with. You don't have the answers I need."

"Maybe not. But I did know your father," he explained. "At least for the past four years."

"You did, didn't you?"

He nodded. "I'd be happy to tell you about the Greg Riordan I knew."

When she wasn't quick to accept, Paul figured she was still wary of him. "Look, I apologize for treating you like the enemy. I know you're not."

"As long as I do right by Bernadette." The sly gleam in her eye was unbelievably alluring.

"That goes without saying," he said, trying to shrug off the tantalizing pull of her gaze.

The opportunity to hear about her father apparently overcame Amy's reluctance, and she accepted his invitation. "Besides, barbecued ribs are my weakness," she added, "so this place better be good."

Paul was pleased, and surprised by just how much. "I keep a change of clothes in my truck, and I can run over to Bernadette's cottage to shower," he said, not wanting to give her time to reconsider. "Won't take me more than fifteen minutes."

"I'm going to need a little longer than that." She glanced down at her slithery wet robe.

"Shall we meet down in the Pub Room in, say, half an hour?"

It took Paul longer than he'd expected, however, to wash off all the plaster, dirt and dust. When he reached the pub, Amy was already there, chatting with Bud, the bartender. She was casually dressed in a sweater and long, floral-print skirt. Her dark hair was dry now and glossy clean. Paul was glad to find her wearing little makeup, allowing her face to still radiate the freshness he'd noticed upstairs.

She glanced up at his damp hair. "You shouldn't have rushed. You could catch your death that way."

"But I'd hate to keep a pretty woman waiting."

A slow, sleek smile crossed her lips, reminding Paul of flirting's small pleasures. It had been a long time since he'd dabbled in that particular art. Helping her with her coat, he inhaled her light fragrance and enjoyed the feel of feminine shoulders beneath his hands.

The main hallway was empty as they headed for the door. The inn's midweek occupancy tended to be light, especially between Thanksgiving and Christmas. Yet the clinking of china and glass signaled another full house in the dining room. Open to the public for dinner, the inn's restaurant was popular throughout the region; reservations were booked weeks in advance. Chef Martin's cuisine, traditional Southern dishes prepared with contemporary flair, was highly regarded by critics from Washington to Richmond and beyond. Paul was just glad the restaurant was busy because it allowed them to leave unnoticed. If they knew, Bernadette and his cousins would, undoubtedly, pepper him with questions after he returned with Amy.

Amy didn't flinch when he opened the door of his red pickup, climbing in without so much as a word. He'd half expected her to suggest they take her roomy luxury car. As he drove out of town, a self-conscious silence fell between them. Paul chided himself for letting his "dating" skills grow rusty—not that he'd characterize this as a real date. But he hadn't been out with a woman in months. For the first few years after his return to Tremont, he had pursued—and occasionally had been pursued by—several attractive, intelligent women. Nothing seemed to take. Perhaps his heart hadn't been in it. Or maybe, after his mess of a divorce, the trouble *was* his heart. Battered, tired, wary.

"I can't believe how dark it is out here," Amy commented in a clear attempt to break the lingering silence. "I'm glad you're the one driving."

Paul appreciated her effort. "Practically no moon tonight. And, of course, there aren't any bright city lights to mask the dark."

"Sounds like you're no fan of cities."

"I prefer the country."

"But I understand you lived in San Francisco for years."

"How do you know that?"

"Maura mentioned it. She said you've only been back here for three or four years."

"Four." He wasn't surprised Maura had talked about him. He just wished she hadn't.

"Because you got divorced?"

Paul turned to Amy. "She told you that, too?"

"Is it supposed to be a secret?"

He shook his head. "Like I said, I prefer the country. And after the divorce, there was no reason to stay in San Francisco, especially since I was fed up with my job as well. So I came home."

He gripped the steering wheel tighter. Paul hated talking about this, or even thinking about it for that matter. He hated being reminded of what he'd had to give up and how impossible it had been to remain in the same state with his ex and her new family. Besides, this outing wasn't supposed to be about him.

"Now you know why I'm here. Why are you?"

Amy cast him a wary glance. "You know why."

"Yes, yes, to settle your father's will. And I accept that," he said quickly, not wanting to irritate her again.

"And to learn something about him," she added.

"So why did you wait until now?"

"I would have come to his funeral—if there had been one. But I was told his body was cremated, and there was no service, no memorial, no burial."

"That's how Greg wanted it, Amy. He didn't believe in ceremony of any kind."

"I didn't know."

Although her response was barely a whisper, Paul caught the sadness in it. She even looked a little lost. He felt for her then. He really felt for her. "Greg was unconventional for a man his age," he offered gently.

"My grandparents thought him odd," she said with a rueful sniff. "My mother called him a nonconformist, and she didn't mean that as a compliment."

For pity's sake, no wonder the poor guy took off, Paul thought as he steered the pickup carefully through a winding patch of mountain road. What kind of picture had those people painted of Greg over the years? "Look, Amy, Greg Riordan was no saint—few men are. But he was a good man at heart. Bernadette wouldn't have stayed with him all those years if he hadn't been," he assured her. "And he was a heck of a lot of fun."

"Was he?"

Amy's voice cracked, and then he heard her deep sharp breath.

Turning to her window, she stared out into the dark. "You're wondering why I waited until after his death to come to the Blue Sky—aren't you?"

"Frankly, yes," he admitted. "I'd heard you'd been asked several times."

"Back when my father first bought the inn," she said, still gazing out the side window. "I hadn't heard from him for years before that."

"Why didn't you come, Amy?"

"Because it was too damn hard. Because I was nineteen years old and I couldn't cope with the situation." She turned to him, her jaw clamped tight as she struggled to keep her emotions in check. "I had grown up feeling like my father had abandoned me, and then he suddenly reappears not only with an inn, but with Bernadette and the girls, too. He had a new family. And I was an outsider. Even now that's hard to deal with."

New family resounded through his head, and Paul felt he had to pull his truck over. He wasn't sure why. Was it the silent tears streaming down Amy's face or the echo of his own disturbing memories? But when he stopped and Amy turned to him with glistening eyes, he reached for her because he understood. He understood better than she would ever know.

Murmuring her name, he held her trembling shoulders between his hands. Pressing his forehead against hers, he tried to soothe her with words.

"I can't believe I'm doing this," she gasped, her voice quivering. He felt her body fight back the sobs. "I never cry, Paul. Never."

"I know," he whispered against her cheek, his arms sliding around her back. She was still trembling slightly, but she felt warm and soft and good in his embrace.

Paul could no longer resist the temptation of her hair. He'd been wondering about it from the moment he first saw her approaching the Pratts' disabled car. The glossy, dark strands were now within reach. He had to touch.

Gently he combed his fingers through the length of her hair. He closed his eyes and relished the feel of it, smooth, luxurious and softer than fine, fine silk.

A breathless sigh seemed to shiver through her, yet she did not move away. "Crying is pointless," Amy insisted, as though she were arguing with herself. "It never changes anything."

"It might help you feel better." He stroked her hair again. "All this has to have been rough on you."

Finally, Amy lifted her head to look at him. "I haven't had it as rough as you. You lost both your parents and then your Aunt Milly."

His thumb smoothed away the last tear from her cheek. Although Paul appreciated her compassion, he had come to terms with his childhood losses long ago. He wished he could say the same for the more recent past.

Amy managed to compose herself, and Paul released her. He shifted back behind the steering wheel and switched on the ignition. She smiled at him from across the seat, and his heart revved up faster than the truck's engine. For a second, he thought about taking her to a place with more ambience than Fred's Bar-B-Que Bash. But he had promised the woman ribs and beer, not candlelight and wine. Besides, considering her frame of mind, she probably wasn't in the mood for such nonsense.

Which was probably for the best . . . he guessed.

They both said little during the rest of the ride to Fred's, but their silence was relaxed and companionable. The marked tension between them had dissolved with Amy's tears. When they pulled into Fred's parking lot, Paul wasn't surprised to see it less than half full. Mondays tended to be slow even at this popular restaurant. That meant less chance of running into anyone he knew from Tremont, less chance of fueling the already rampant gossip about Amy Riordan.

Pine-paneled walls, laminate-topped tables, nonstop country music and the smoky aroma of the barbecue pit were the perfect accoutrements for enjoying the best ribs for miles around. And any reserve left between him and Amy was long gone by the time they had finished their meal. Eating sticky, wet beef ribs with their hands freed them from polite formalities and created a lighthearted mood throughout the meal. In fact, it tickled him to see socialite Amy Riordan of Washington, D.C., chow down on a side of ribs with uninhibited relish.

"So you really were a TV news anchor in San Francisco?" Amy said as she pushed her plate away. "I can't believe it."

Paul watched her lick the last bit of tangy sauce from her delicate fingers. Somehow she managed to have it look dainty and sexy at the same time.

"I wouldn't make up something like that," he said, although his gaze was still fixed on her luscious mouth. "Besides, what's so hard to believe about it?"

"It's just that anchormen usually have perfect, slicked-back hair and smooth, booming voices."

"I supposed I've gotten a bit shaggy the past few years." He brushed a hand through his hair. "But I can still boom with the best of them."

"Oh, yeah?" She leaned back in her chair, provocative glints of challenge in her blue eyes. "Show me."

Without hesitation, he summoned up the tone and inflections that, in their heyday, could out-Cronkite Walter. "And so, Miss Riordan," he continued after describing the scene at Fred's Bar-B-que Bash, "that's the way it is on this Monday, November 30."

Amy applauded and laughed. Paul was just surprised that he'd done it. He rarely talked about his past profession, never mind conjuring up a display of skills. Yet with Amy he had opened up. The same thing had happened when explaining how he'd come to live with Bernadette as a boy. He had told her much more than he'd intended.

"Why did you give up the news, Paul?" Amy tore open one of the moistened towelette packets the waitress had left at the table. "San Francisco is a major market. You must have been a darned good newsman to be working there."

"Reading the news every night instead of finding it or writing about it felt hollow to me. But after five years at the anchor desk with great ratings, the station considered me too valuable for general reporting—other than the occasional high-profile puff piece." He took a sip from the thick-glass beer mug. "I came to hate it."

"So you went into business for yourself." Amy wiped her hands with the towelette.

"Maura told you that, too?"

Before Amy could reply, an older, heavyset man came barreling up to their table. "Why, Paul Hanley, I thought that was you I saw comin' in," the man declared loud enough for the entire place to hear. "But Edna told me to stay put. Since she went ahead to pay, I told myself I'd sneak a look just to see."

Effusive as the man was, his speech was somewhat slurred. Amy figured he must have taken advantage of the restaurant's Monday-night free refill offer. She glanced over at Paul. Although he was being polite to the man, he seemed perturbed by the intrusion.

"Amy, this is Harry Bradford," Paul said without smiling. "He runs the gas station in Tremont."

"Nice to meet you, Mr. Bradford."

"Call me 'Harry.' And I've already heard all about you, Miss Riordan." Harry pumped her hand in his thick grip. "Janie Lee told me about how you helped with Jake's flat."

"I only stopped," she said, trying to disengage her hand from his. "Paul's the one who did all the work."

"And ain't that just like him?" Harry continued without missing a beat. "I've known this boy since he began deliverin' newspapers for the Tullys. He was quite a hellion back then."

Amy grinned. "Was he?"

Paul rolled his eyes, but said nothing.

"Sure was. But now don't you go believin' everythin' you hear about him. He turned out all right, I guess.

Even ended up buyin' out the Tullys' business." He slapped Paul on the back.

"Harry. Get on over here," snapped a tall, skinny woman at the cashier's counter.

"Right away, honey bunch," Harry called before turning back to Amy. "You come by the station to say hello sometime. Okay?"

Amy promised at least to stop by for a fill-up.

"Old fool's had one beer too many," Paul muttered as Harry shuffled away. "Don't pay any attention to his rambling."

Harry seemed harmless enough to her; still, she could see Paul was annoyed. "What part should I ignore?" she asked lightly, hoping to get a smile out of him. "The part about you being a hellion? Or the part about you having turned out all right?"

She got her smile, the warmest one she'd seen from him yet.

"What's bothering you about Harry?" she prodded.

He shrugged. "It's not Harry per se. It's like I told you—people around here like to talk. The whole town will know about our having dinner together."

"So? Are you embarrassed to be seen with me?"

"Hardly." The look he gave her almost stopped her heart. Amy still considered Paul immensely attractive. After spending a few hours with him, however, she realized she was drawn to more than just his looks.

Paul drank the last of his beer before continuing. "I just wish people would leave well enough alone. Most gossip is innocent enough. But when the line gets crossed, it can be hurtful and, sometimes, downright destructive."

She sensed he was speaking from experience. Had he been the victim of small-town gossipmongers as a child?

Because Bernadette had taken him in? Because he had been a hellion? Or was there something else? And if Paul actually was the private sort Maura had spoken of, why had he revealed the painful details about his youth to Amy? Paul Hanley was a confusing and complex man, to be sure.

After the waitress served them coffee, Paul reminded her they hadn't come here to talk about him. "Would you still like to hear about your father?"

"Very much."

She listened intently as Paul told her what he knew about her father—facts, anecdotes, speculations. He even repeated a few of the jokes Greg had told him over the years. Paul was more than generous, digging back into his memory for every detail he could recall about Greg Riordan as a friend, townsperson and innkeeper. Still, Paul could reveal only the more obvious facts about Greg's relationship with Bernadette and the girls. He certainly couldn't tell Amy what her father had thought or felt about her.

Amy was grateful, though, and glad that she and Paul were no longer circling around each other with suspicion. Although he'd remain Bernadette's arch defender to the end, he had listened to her and understood. Irony of ironies, she had found an ally in Paul Hanley. Returning to the Blue Sky and the Ryans didn't feel like such a lonely prospect now.

Paul glanced at the dashboard clock when he pulled up to the inn. It was only a little past nine. Inside, the dining room was still busy with the second sitting, and outside, the evening was quiet, the temperature brisk. The earlier masking clouds had lifted. Now he could see the glow of a few low stars through the old willow oaks' leafless branches.

He realized he didn't want to go home. Not yet.

Amy was looking across the seat at him, her hand resting on the door handle. He supposed he could go inside with her, suggest a nightcap and then chat and mingle with other Pub Room patrons. But that would, effectively, end this time together.

"It's gotten kind of nice out tonight," he began, unsure what he intended to propose. Peering through the windshield, he searched around the low-lit grounds until he spotted the gazebo. "Would you like to sit outside for a while?" he asked. "It's not that cold."

Her eyes widened with surprise. "I don't know. It's kind of late, isn't it?"

Paul tapped the illuminated digits on the dash's clock. "We can sit up on the gazebo for a little while, anyway. I'll even run inside for some coffee to keep us warm."

"More coffee?" she said with a laugh. "I'll be awake all night at this rate."

"Bud always has a pot of regular and decaf going behind the bar."

"Well, if there's decaf. Why not?"

"Great." He liked the way her eyes seemed to smile.

Paul parked the truck and walked Amy to the gazebo. Then he hurried into the inn, hoping to get in and out without attracting his relatives' notice. He loved them dearly, but they would ask too many questions.

As expected, neither Bernadette nor his cousins were in the pub. He slipped behind the bar and asked Bud for a couple of paper cups with lids. Paul, anxious to get back to Amy, poured the coffee quickly. With a jaunty wave to Bud, he headed out, thinking he was home free.

As he marched through the Pub Room door, Bernadette came careening around the corner. They almost knocked each other over. He held on to the coffee for dear life. The bar tray she was carrying slipped from her hands, clanging when it fell on the wood floor.

"What are you doing here?" Bernadette stooped down for the tray. "I thought you went home hours ago."

"I just brought Amy back from dinner."

"*You* went out to eat with Amy?" His aunt's eyes were about to pop.

Deciding against further explanation, he simply nodded.

"Hmphf. Guess I can stop worrying about her gettin' home safe." Her gaze narrowed in on the two white cups. "Where are you going with those?"

"Outside. Amy is waiting for me."

"Waiting for you? You mean out on the veranda?"

The hopeful note in her voice did not escape him. "No, the gazebo."

"The gazebo?" She tried to hold back a smile.

"Bernadette, I'd love to stay and play echo with you," he said with a wink, "but this coffee is getting cold."

"Don't let me keep you then."

Paul turned to leave. He didn't have to be a mind reader to tell what she was thinking. That sly twinkle of hers said it all. At least she wasn't barraging him with questions.

"Oh, Paul, wait," Bernadette called after him. "I forgot something."

He noticed her smile had disappeared. Her sparkle had faded into concern. "Aunt Bernadette, what's the matter?"

"I forgot Amy had a phone call." Pulling a pink message slip from her apron pocket, she glanced at it before handing it to him. "A man named Jeff Martin from Washington. He wants her to call him as soon as she can."

"I'll see that she gets it."

"That's his home number, Paul."

Her voice sounded pained. It was as if she were warning him to be careful. He understood why. Bernadette was one of the very few people he had confided in when his life had gone to hell. She was the only person in Tremont who knew what actually had happened in San Francisco.

Heading across the side yard toward the gazebo, Paul told himself that Bernadette needn't worry. Whoever this Jeff Martin was, whatever this phone call meant, was of no concern to him. Sure, he enjoyed being with Amy tonight. But that was as far as it went. No way was he going to start wondering about her life in D.C. No way was he getting himself into a position where he had to worry about competition for her affections.

"Hi. I was afraid you'd forgotten about me."

He glanced up. Amy was leaning against the gazebo's latticework railing and smiling down at him. She looked lovely. "Bernadette nabbed me at the door. Sorry."

But somehow the mood had shifted. He felt the evening had lost its promise.

"Nothing wrong, I hope," she said, as if she'd picked up on the change right away.

"Not at all." He climbed up the steps to join her. "She asked me to give you this."

Her lips tightened as she scanned the message slip. Crumpling the paper in her palm, she shoved it into her coat pocket. "I could use that coffee now."

They sat side by side on a platform bench, sipping their coffees. For Paul, the silence was deafening. In spite of himself, he was curious about that phone message. Clearly it had disturbed Amy. And, whether it should have or not, whether he liked it or not, that damn piece of pink paper really bothered him.

He watched her out of the corner of his eye. Holding the cup between her hands, she looked deep in thought, closed off and far away. Oddly enough, this reminded him of how much they had shared this evening. Up to now.

Paul realized he wanted that back. After gulping down the rest of his coffee, he rolled the empty cup around and around with his fingers. Then, before he knew it, he had dredged up his newscaster voice for the second time that night and was using the overturned cup for a sound "mike."

"Ms. Riordan, a distinct pall has befallen this gazebo tonight. As an eyewitness, would you tell our viewers— in your own words—why this has happened."

Amy seemed taken aback at first. But when he pushed the paper microphone in front of her, she smiled and shook her head.

"Come, come, Ms. Riordan, your public needs to know."

"Do they?" Her dark blue eyes locked onto his.

"Yes," he admitted softly, dropping the anchorman facade. "Won't you tell me what the problem is?"

"There's no problem—not anymore. Jeff Martin is my ex-fiancé," she revealed with a shrug. "Besides, I feel like I've already talked your ear off with my tales of woe."

"You haven't."

"My life really isn't that depressing." She got to her feet and began pacing across the gazebo. "I've got my mother and stepfather, wonderful friends, a town house I love and a great business."

"I don't doubt any of that."

"So I struck out in the relationship department," she continued as if she hadn't heard him. "These things happen and I—"

Paul grabbed her hand to make her stop. "Amy, you don't have to justify yourself to me. I don't see you as some poor, pitiful soul." He pulled her back down beside him. "I want you to keep talking to me. I want to know why that message took the smile from your eyes. I want to know about you."

Chapter Five

Amy gazed back at him, speechless. Paul wondered if he'd pushed too far. "You can tell me to mind my own business."

He hoped she wouldn't.

"It's kind of embarrassing." She looked away. "Being jilted always is."

"It happens to the best of us," he said, although it was hard to imagine how any man could leave this bright, lovely and apparently not-so-spoiled rich girl. He encouraged her with a squeeze of his hand. "Don't feel embarrassed."

Keeping her hand in his, Amy took a deep breath before beginning. "This may sound terrible, but I've had to be careful with people. The fact that Thomas Windom is my stepfather tends to have a strange effect on some."

"You mean the kind who take advantage."

She nodded. "I had to learn to keep my guard up at a young age."

"With this Martin fellow, too?"

"At first I did. Jeffrey Martin was—is—an up-and-comer at my stepfather's law firm. Before we met, I had a rule—no dating men who worked at Windom and Hart."

"But it was different with this guy."

"I thought so," she admitted, staring straight ahead. "He seemed so genuine. Even my mother thought the world of him. And let me tell you, that's no easy trick. Eventually, Jeff took me to meet his parents. They own a bakery in Cleveland. They were great. Then, within three months, we were engaged, with announcements in all the papers. There was a huge party, too."

"How long were you engaged?"

"Three months. My mother was pushing us to set a spring date so she could start wedding arrangements. A Windom wedding has to be an event, you know." With a sigh, she slipped her hand from his grasp. "That's when Jeff came clean. He couldn't go through with the wedding. He was still in love with his college sweetheart—whom he apparently left when he met me."

"The boss's daughter." Paul swore under his breath. "This guy actually pursued you to get ahead?"

"I think Jeff was shocked he'd done it himself. But he couldn't live with the lie, although he knew he was putting his position at the firm in jeopardy."

"I hope your stepfather threw the bum out on his ear."

"He wanted to. But I talked him out of it."

Paul couldn't believe it. "Why would you?"

"Because Jeff got in over his head. He never meant to hurt me."

Paul was struck by the lack of emotion as she told him all this. "Weren't you in love with the guy?"

She spun around to face him. "I thought I was."

Did the sudden edge in her voice mean she'd been hurt more than she was willing to admit? Or realized? Paul could identify with that. He used to be an expert at blocking out emotional pain. "I'm sorry it happened to you," he said, curving his arm across her back. "It must have been rough."

"Please. I can do without the pity." Amy pulled away from him and got to her feet. "I've had half of Washington feeling sorry for me for months. The other half probably thinks I'm the biggest fool going."

"I don't think you're a fool. It could have happened to anybody."

She gave him a begrudging smile. "Maybe I'm not that miserable a judge of character. In the end Jeff was honest. He couldn't marry me or anyone under false pretenses."

Paul had to smile. The woman had pride. He liked that.

"Why do you think he called tonight?"

"To tell me when he's getting married."

"How thoughtful."

"Jeff means well. And it can't be easy for him, either. I'm not looking forward to the conversation, though. It's still awkward."

Paul rose from the bench and stood before her. He felt for her and admired her at the same time. "You're quite a lady, Amy Riordan. You know that?"

She didn't answer, but her gaze never left his. Although the scattered ground lights cast a few shadowy beams at the gazebo, it was too dark to read the expression in her eyes. He sensed a loneliness in Amy, or perhaps he was projecting his own onto her. Paul didn't care. He just felt the need to draw her near.

Circling his arms around her waist, he pulled her to him. "All my assumptions about you have been wrong."

He felt a shiver run through her. "It's cold," she said, lowering her face.

Aware only of how if felt to hold her, Paul tightened his embrace to warm her. Or to keep her close.

She pressed her palms against his chest. "Paul—I—"

"Shh. You've got to let me apologize for being so judgmental," he murmured, lifting her chin with his fingers. He felt her body soften as their eyes met, and suddenly his thoughts clouded. Although colorless in the dark, her gaze was wide and lovely, stirring a yearning inside of him, irresistible and warm. He felt pulled into her eyes—into her—closer and closer until his lips brushed hers in a tentative, sweet kiss.

Her moan vibrated against his mouth. He cupped her head between his hands, her fragrant hair thick beneath his fingers. The sound of her, the feel of her, the scent of her propelled him to hold her closer, tighter. He swore he could feel her heart pounding even through their jackets. As he deepened the kiss, Amy curved her arms behind his neck, her lips soft and unresisting.

His mind was in a haze of blossoming passion as her body felt as if it was melting against his. Slowly he caressed her smooth cheeks with his thumbs until she sighed with pleasure, her mouth opening to his insistent tongue. Her feminine warmth engulfed him—he never wanted to stop kissing her. Amy's growing ardor stirred him deeply. It had been so long since he'd felt this alive, and he hungered for more of her and more of these blessed feelings. Sliding his arms down to her waist, he pressed her against his hips, their kiss still unbroken.

With a sudden groan, Amy stiffened and tore herself away.

"This is not a smart thing to do," she gasped, her chest rising and falling with each shallow breath.

"Smart?" He glared at her, bewildered, his breathing as ragged as hers. The abrupt blast of cold night air felt like icy spikes piercing his hot skin and aching body.

"Getting carried away like this—with the night, the gazebo, all the talk," she sputtered, backing away from him. "Discussing a personal experience or two doesn't mean we have to—to—"

"Hold each other? Kiss? Make love?" he said dryly, not sure if he was extremely annoyed, strangely amused or very, very angry.

"I meant we shouldn't take on more than we can handle," she insisted. "Just because you realize you've jumped to some wrong conclusions about me doesn't mean you really know me. And I don't know you."

"Well, wasn't that what we were just doing—getting to know each other better?"

Dismay flashed in her eyes. "Not that way, Paul. I'm the one who keeps her guard up, remember?"

"Now I do." He told himself to cool down. Disappointment shouldn't overshadow his common sense or whatever he had left of it. Perhaps he *had* gotten carried away by his attraction for her.

"Besides, I'm staying here just long enough to settle things with Bernadette. There's no point in you and me getting caught up in—well, you know." She reached out to touch his arm. "You understand, don't you?"

Still reeling from the shock of frustrated arousal, he looked down at her hand on his wrist. "I understand."

But he didn't like it.

* * *

Paul's kiss was the first thing Amy thought of when she woke up the next morning. How hard it had been to pull away was her second. She had wanted it to go on and on; she hadn't wanted the exquisite feelings Paul had aroused in her to stop. Had she ever been kissed like that before? Surely she would have remembered. But she *knew* she'd never responded to a first kiss with such abandon. Contemplating it even now sent her pulse spinning.

Catching herself, Amy realized she'd been right to walk away. Or had she run? That's what it had felt like after she'd told him good-night and scurried back to the inn. Still, to go from verbally jousting with the man on her first night in Tremont to kissing him—passionately—in the gazebo three days later was quite a leap. And way too fast for her. No matter how good it felt to be held in his arms.

But her record in the relationship department was less than winning. Her choices had not always been good ones, and it was especially hard not to second-guess herself after the breakup with Jeff. If she was smart, she'd stay the heck away from Paul Hanley. This was one attraction she had to sit out.

Amy stretched beneath the smooth sheets and heavy layers of blankets, luxuriating in a last few seconds of warmth. She had already discovered the inn's heating system was spotty at best. If the misty ice on the windowpanes was any indication, her body was in for a brisk jolt when she got out of bed.

She washed and dressed quickly, pulling on a red sweater and black jeans, making sure she wore extra warm socks under her ankle boots. Although the smell of fresh-brewed coffee enticed her as she headed downstairs, the thought of the long quiet day ahead of her was daunting. She really had to get down to business with Bernadette soon, or she'd be stuck here till Christmas. Halfway down the stairs, she encountered a work crew on their way to room 16 with ladders, buckets and brushes in tow. Glad to see repairs would soon be under way, Amy hoped Bernadette had begun to recover from yesterday's calamity.

Only a handful of people were breakfasting in the dining room this morning. Bernadette was nowhere to be seen, but Amy spotted Bridget and her two kids sitting at a corner table near the kitchen door. After serving herself a slice of melon and a cranberry muffin from the buffet table, she poured a mug of coffee and made her way across the room. "May I join you?" she asked Bridget.

"If you don't mind putt-putt motor sounds and stray cereal in your lap, I'd love it." Bridget beamed as she pushed Willy's miniature toy cars to his side of the table. Little Jenny was strapped in an old wooden high chair, eating dry cereal with her fingers. "I've just finished checking tomorrow's dairy order for Mama."

Amy sat next to Jenny. "I haven't seen your mother yet, Bridget. She's all right, isn't she? I mean about room 16."

"Oh, she's fine. And thanks so much for looking after her yesterday. It really helped." Bridget reached over to wipe Willy's milk mustache with a napkin. "She's out doing the marketing with Martin right now."

"Will she be back soon?"

"Not until later this afternoon. They're doing major buying today."

"I see." Amy buttered her muffin, disappointed and a tad annoyed. She wouldn't get the chance to talk to

Bernadette at all today unless she somehow managed to corner her after dinner.

"Mommy?" Four-year-old Willy piped in. "Can I go watch them fix the broken room?"

"Honey, I can't let you go up there by yourself," his mother answered. "The workmen are too busy to keep an eye on you. You might get in their way or even get hurt. I'll take you later—when Jenny's napping."

The boy's mouth drooped. "She never goes to sleep."

Amy leaned closer. "Willy, if your mommy says it's okay, I'll go up with you after I've finished my breakfast."

"Can I go with her, Mom? Can I?" His eyes danced with hope beneath his reddish blond bangs.

"Amy, it's nice of you to offer. But you must have something you'd rather do."

"No, I'll be glad to take him," Amy said, tossing Willy a wink. "Except for calling my office later to check on a client's audition, my day is wide open." *Especially with Bernadette gone,* she added silently.

"An audition!" Bridget's eyes widened. She turned to her son. "Amy gets children jobs on TV commercials and in magazines. Isn't that exciting?"

Unimpressed, Willy returned to putt-putting his toy cars around on the table. But his mother was full of questions about the agency. Amy knew people were often dazzled by the perceived glamour and excitement of her business, and Bridget was no exception. Unlike most mothers she'd met, however, Bridget didn't entreat her with a hypothetical query about her little ones' prospects for stardom. For that, Amy was grateful.

When she took Willy up to watch the work in room 16, he was as good as he could be. He watched with open-mouthed fascination for quite a while until he got fidgety and lost interest. Willy agreed to take a walk with Amy, and they spent the rest of the morning touring "downtown" Tremont. By then, Amy had been completely charmed.

Before they climbed the hill back up to the inn, Willy persuaded her to stop at the general store to check out the candy counter. "I'll buy one piece for after your lunch," she called as he ran ahead to the candy cases surrounding the cash register. "And pick out one for your sister."

Following a few steps behind, Amy recognized the tiny gray-haired lady standing by the counter, smiling at her. "Hello, Mrs. Pratt. It's good to see you again."

"Now, I told you to call me 'Janie Lee,'" the woman reminded in her watery sweet voice. "You and Mr. Willy look like you're having yourselves a fine old time this morning."

Janie Lee proceeded to talk a mile a minute, stopping only to ask Amy a polite question every now and then. So when the old woman asked her how Bernadette and she were getting along, Amy was caught short. She didn't think it was any business of Janie Lee's.

"Fine," Amy said with a smile, elaborating no further. She shouldn't have been surprised by the question. Hadn't Paul made it clear that the whole town had heard she was Greg's daughter?

Without missing a beat, Janie Lee continued prattling on about the Blue Sky until an unkempt woman, with scads of bleached curls, burst into the store leading a black lab on a leash. She marched straight to the counter and ordered a carton of cigarettes. Concerned about Willy's safety, Amy edged him farther down along the counter, while the store owner admonished the woman for bringing the large dog inside.

"I can't leave him outside by himself, can I, Ed?" the woman snapped. "Now, how about those cigarettes?"

Janie Lee walked right up the woman. "I heard you were supposed to be quittin' those things, Sandy."

"Yeah, yeah, I'll quit." Sandy waved Janie Lee off. "When I can't afford to buy 'em anymore—which will be real soon, thanks to Mr. Paul Hanley."

"What are you talkin' about?" Janie Lee demanded.

"Haven't you heard? Hanley's threatening layoffs over at the paper. Even my Sam's job is in jeopardy." Sandy tossed a wad of bills onto the counter, muttering all the while. "That Hanley comes riding back into town with bags of money and buys the papers right out from under the Tullys. Why doesn't he use that dough to bail out his business, instead of taking it out of our hides? Tell me that, Janie Lee."

But Sandy didn't wait for Janie Lee to answer. She grabbed the cigarettes and stomped off with her dog. Amy looked down at Willy, still enthralled by the candy selection, oblivious to the woman's harsh words about his cousin Paul. Then she turned to Janie Lee.

"I'm surprised that gal didn't buy a six-pack, too. Usually does," Janie Lee commented, shaking her head. "Don't you pay her any mind, honey. Some people will never be happy, no matter what."

As Amy walked back up the hill to the inn, with Willy swinging his paper sack of candy in his hand, she couldn't help thinking of Sandy's venomous outburst. Was Paul's business really in trouble? He hadn't given any indication of it to her.

Upon reaching the inn, Willy ran ahead, calling to his mother. Inside, Amy found the moist heat from the old steam radiators a welcome relief from the sharp, dry air of early winter.

Bridget emerged from the kitchen to greet them. "Looks like it's getting cold out there," she said, lifting her son into her arms.

He showed her the candy Amy had bought. "And I took Amy to the library and the school where I'm gonna go when I'm five," he revealed. "And we went to the firehouse, but Daddy wasn't there."

"That's because he's not on duty, sweetheart. He's working his carpenter's job today. Remember?"

Confusion flashed across his face, then it was forgotten in anticipation of lunch. Bridget sent him off to wash up.

Amy hung her jacket on the old-fashioned coat rack in the hallway. "Willy was confused because his dad wasn't at the firehouse when we stopped there. I tried to explain to him."

"Greg used to take him down to visit whenever George was on duty. He probably expected his daddy to be there like always," Bridget explained. "I don't think Willy's been to the firehouse much since Greg died."

"My father spent a lot of time with the kids?"

"I'll say. Made up games for them all the time. Took them for walks. Helped George assemble toys on Christmas Eve. And every Fourth of July, he'd take his classic 1952 Buick convertible out of the barn to polish up so he could show off the kids in Tremont's parade." Bridget smiled at the memory. "Of course the kids were very small then, but my George had a ball riding with them."

Although Amy felt a pang of jealousy, she was glad her father had had the chance to be something of a grandpa. She also was glad to learn something new about him. "I didn't know he kept a classic car," she said, "I'd love to take a look at it sometime."

Bridget's expression changed, her gaze lowered to the floor. "Mom sold it not long after Greg died. Although it practically killed her to do it. But there were a lot of expenses, and money's tight around here even now." Then she added quickly, "It was registered in Mom's name, too."

Tension hung in the air. Although Amy wished she could have seen the car, she didn't dispute Bernadette's right to sell it. She also knew about Bernadette's money problems—the inn's money problems. Yet having it expressed out loud had made them both uncomfortable, and Amy didn't like it. She decided it was time for the wall between her and the Ryan daughters to fall.

"Look, Bridget, I'm aware the inn's strapped for cash. That's partly why I had to come here," she said, choosing her words with care. "Let's not pretend with each other anymore."

Bridget's shoulder's sank with relief. She touched Amy's arm. "I hate pretending, too."

"What's for lunch?" Willy cried as he burst back into the hall, his little sister trailing behind him. "I'm hungry."

"Grilled-cheese sandwiches and tomato soup." Bridget turned to Amy. "There's plenty extra. I hope you'll join us."

"I'd love to." The inn did not serve luncheon, so it was kind of Bridget to think of her. Even more, Amy liked being included. She wasn't sure why, but this time it struck the right chord.

Bridget brought out the food while Amy helped the kids get settled at the same table they'd used at breakfast. Both Willy and Jenny dug into their food with gusto. Amy, too, was hungry after her little hike with Willy, and the simple lunch was warm and filling.

"My mother called while you were out, Amy," Bridget mentioned as they ate. "She wanted me to make sure Paul gave you that phone message last night. From a Jeff Martin?"

The mention of Jeff and the reminder of Paul and last night made her skin feel as hot as the tomato soup. Bridget gave her a look that made Amy wonder if she had turned as red, as well. "Yes, he gave it to me." But Bridget continued to stare, compelling her to add, "Jeff's an old boyfriend, that's all. I'll probably call him after lunch."

Amy was amazed she had invoked Jeff as an excuse to cover her discomfort. That was a first.

"You mean you haven't phoned him back yet?" Bridget sounded surprised.

"There's no rush." Amy had planned to call Julie first to hear about Shawna's morning audition. Then she'd call Jeff.

Bridget smiled and shrugged. "I guess not if he's an old boyfriend."

After lunch, Bridget put the kids down for their naps, and Amy returned to her room to make her phone calls. The news was good about Shawna. Julie claimed the ad agency had been impressed with her and would be phoning back. The call with Jeff went pretty much as she'd expected. At the end they wished each other the best and said goodbye.

Lying on her bed, with the pounding of the workmen in room 16 occasionally butting into her thoughts, Amy felt relieved to be finished with Jeff at last. She realized the dull ache that had weighed her down for months was no longer lodged in her heart. When had that happened?

The rest of the day continued in the usual mundane way at the inn: languorous and quiet all afternoon, followed by the frenetic activity surrounding the two dinner sittings. As expected, Bernadette was too busy upon her return to take time for Amy. Bridget left with the children at six, and Maura's shop was opened late on Tuesday nights. That left Amy to sit alone at dinner.

She didn't mind being by herself. The young waiter was charming and solicitous, the food was excellent, as usual, and Bernadette had given her a lovely table near the fireplace. The warmth from the steady blaze soothed her, yet the mandolin's mellow refrains and the candlelight reminded her of the first night she had sat there with Paul. Amy *did* mind thinking about him. But somehow she couldn't stop. She half hoped he'd walk into the dining room and sit at her table. She was half afraid he actually would.

After finishing her meal, Amy decided to turn in early and attack the historical novel she'd tried to start yesterday. She was on her way upstairs, when she heard Bernadette calling her from the main hall below.

"You're going to bed already?" the older woman asked. "I thought we might talk over a glass of wine after I finish up in the dining room. Shouldn't be more than ten or fifteen minutes."

Amy couldn't believe her ears. "That would be great," she said, coming back down the stairs. "I'll wait for you in the Pub Room."

The cocktail lounge wasn't very busy, reflecting the inn's midweek occupancy. Amy sat at the bar and chatted with Bud while he filled drink orders. By the time Bernadette appeared, Amy was showing Bud how to mix an obscure exotic drink a guest had ordered. "Where on earth did you learn to make those?" Bernadette asked.

"I tended bar at Rehobeth Beach the summer after I graduated from college. It was an extremely long summer, but I learned them all."

Stepping behind the bar, Bernadette reached for two white wine goblets. "Your mother allowed that?"

"Well, she wanted me to go to Europe with some sorority sisters."

"But you had a mind of your own, I see." Bernadette chuckled. "Just like your father, God rest his soul."

Stunned, Amy followed the older woman to a table across the room. In her entire life, no one had ever compared her to her father. No one.

Unnerved by her remark, Amy watched Bernadette sip her wine. Lovely pewter teardrop earrings dangled along her strong jaw. She was a handsome woman with a free grace and style that was so unlike her mother's polished beauty and rigid ways. Greg Riordan had gone from one type of woman to a total opposite. Amy wondered why.

Bernadette put down her glass. "I called Paul this afternoon and asked him to come this evening. I thought you might have liked some company during dinner."

"You didn't have to do that," Amy said, being careful not to sound as flustered as she felt. Thank goodness he hadn't come, she thought with relief, choosing to ignore a pesky stab of disappointment.

"It was no trouble," Bernadette replied with a shrug. "Unfortunately, he couldn't get away. Said he had a lot of work to catch up on."

Paul's lame excuse told Amy what he thought about last night and what he thought of her. If he didn't want to be bothered, that was fine with Amy. As far as she was concerned, he was doing them both a favor.

"But maybe he can come tomorrow," Bernadette suggested. "I'll call him again to arrange it."

"No. Don't," Amy blurted out. "I mean, we shouldn't pressure him if he's so busy."

"I suppose you're right." Bernadette looked perplexed as she leaned back in her chair. "But maybe in a few days..."

Amy said nothing, hoping her silence would spur Bernadette on to a different topic. She wasn't disappointed.

"I don't suppose you know how Greg came to buy the inn," Bernadette said.

"I know virtually nothing about my father's life after he and Mother split up. We had little contact."

"Apparently he never stayed in one place too long," the older woman revealed. "He had worked a variety of jobs at motels and small hotels all around the country."

"How did he end up in Tremont?"

"When he got a job at one of the chain motels in Winchester, he rented a room at the old boarding house across from the general store."

"You mean the house that's the bed-and-breakfast now?"

Bernadette nodded. "I worked there at the time, cooking and cleaning. That's how Greg and I met, and after about a year we decided to move in together. Right about that time, the Stanley House—this inn—came on the market. Your daddy wanted it badly—as a business and for a home for us." She went on to explain how Greg had gone about raising the necessary money to add to the sizable nest egg he'd saved during his years on the road.

Amy drank in every word, learning about a Greg Riordan who had craved a home after years of drifting, and who was resourceful enough to make the dream happen. How different this was from the picture her mother had painted of him!

"You changed the inn's name?" she asked, her throat tightening as she broached the subject that had convinced her to come to Tremont.

"Greg insisted, and I saw no reason not to. Stanley House held no significance for us, or for anyone, really. Stanley is the name of the man who owned it before us."

"I see," she murmured, trying to keep the emotional connotations of her next question from weakening her voice. "Then why Touch the Blue Sky?"

"Greg thought of it," Bernadette replied lightly. "Different, isn't it? But pretty."

"That's all? He didn't say *how* he thought of it?"

"It seemed to fit, what with the mountains and the gorgeous vista and all," Bernadette explained. Lifting her wineglass to her lips, she paused before drinking. "I did ask him where it came from. He just shrugged and smiled with this faraway look in his eyes. He liked the way it sounded—said it reminded him of happy times."

"He said that?" Amy gasped with astonishment. "My father really said that?"

Bernadette stared across the table at her, puzzled by her reaction. "Why, yes. I remember it like it was yesterday. That's exactly what your daddy said."

Chapter Six

Amy went to bed filled with thoughts of her father. Although Bernadette didn't know it, she had confirmed a connection between the inn's name and Greg's memories of Amy. It was something, however slight, for Amy to latch onto. As for Greg's will and the running of the inn, Bernadette had been as unforthcoming as ever.

"It's like pulling teeth with that woman," Amy mumbled on her way downstairs to breakfast the next morning.

At the front desk she found a message from Maura inviting her to the shop in Winchester, followed by lunch with Bridget. With the prospect of a break in an otherwise uneventful day, Amy was delighted to call Maura with her acceptance. After a week in Tremont, she no longer found it daunting to be surrounded by Ryans.

Although Maura's directions seemed scattered when Amy jotted them down, they worked. Amy drove through the rolling countryside to Winchester and had no trouble finding the shop in a neighborhood near the Shenandoah University campus.

New Worlds was attractively laid out with huge decanters of potpourris and herbs, ethereal artwork on the walls and an array of wind chimes dangling from the ceiling, and shelves of essential oils and books about everything from walking with angels to the power of Zen. Maura showed off the shop with pride as she and Amy discussed what might need improving.

When it was time to meet Bridget for lunch, Maura insisted on driving Amy in her Jeep. "After eating fancy meals at the inn all week, I thought you might enjoy the Blossom Diner. The food is simple, but good. Even a vegetarian like me can fill up on some great dishes. And they make the absolute best fruit pies."

Maura drove to the classic 1950s road diner at breakneck speed. "I don't see Bridget's car," she said, sliding out from behind the wheel. "Let's go in and wait."

Amy followed the younger woman inside, where country music twanged on the jukebox, every stool at the long counter was occupied and pink-uniformed waitresses swept past quickly. Maura craned her neck in search of a vacant booth. When she spotted one, she tugged at Amy's coat sleeve.

They wove their way past a quartet of departing truck drivers and then Maura stopped short. "Well, hey, Cuz."

"Hello, ladies."

The rich voice made her heart skip a beat. Excitement clashed with wariness. Amy stepped up behind Maura. "Hello, Paul."

He was sitting beside a well-dressed blonde and across from an attractive, dark-haired man. The woman looked exquisite in a winter-white wool suit; her golden blond pageboy was beautifully cut and styled, her skin tawny peach. She would have fit right in at a power lunch on Connecticut Avenue in D.C. Amy wrapped her jacket tighter over her poor-boy sweater and jeans, wishing she had given more thought to her attire that morning.

Paul stood up to introduce Amy to his lunch companions. The blonde, Lynette Devroy, nodded and smiled. The man, Dirk Campbell, made a point to stand when he shook her hand. "Finally I get a chance to meet you, Amy. My buddy here has been very secretive about you."

From the look Paul shot his friend, Amy couldn't tell if Dirk had been serious or not. She wondered if Paul was afraid his lady friend might get the wrong idea. She wondered if he regretted kissing her the other night.

"Dirk is the business manager for the News Group," Paul said, sitting again. His voice sounded strained, his eyes watchful.

"Why don't you join us?" Dirk asked, clearly more at ease than Paul. "There's plenty of room."

"Actually, it looks like you're just finishing up," Maura piped up quickly. "We should probably grab that last empty table before somebody else does. Come on, Amy."

Maura jerked Amy away before she could utter anything more than goodbye to Paul and his friends.

"Why did you do that?" Amy asked when they reached the booth.

"I don't really need to spend my lunch hour with Dirk Campbell."

"Why not?" Amy certainly didn't want to join Paul's party, either, but she was curious about Maura's resistance. "He seemed nice enough. And not bad looking, either."

"He's all right, I guess." Maura began perusing the laminated menu. "We just don't see eye-to-eye on most things—like the kind of business I'm in. Some people around here aren't particularly forward thinking."

Amy felt there had to be more behind Maura's agitation than that, but thought it best to drop the subject. Besides, something else was on her mind. "Are Lynette and Paul an item?" she asked with as much nonchalance as she could muster.

"Hardly. She's his accountant," Maura said, her attention still glued to the extensive menu. "I think she's practically engaged to some big shot in county government."

"Oh, I see." Amy chided herself for feeling relieved. Paul's personal involvements shouldn't concern her. Yet she couldn't help keeping an eye on his table until he and Lynette left—without Dirk. Again she had to quash her inner dismay.

Dirk came over to Amy and Maura's table. "You haven't ordered yet?"

Maura scarcely looked up from her menu. "We're waiting for my sister."

He asked Amy if he could join them, and she thought it would be rude to refuse. Although Maura ignored him, Amy found him quite nice and enjoyed hearing his story about the diner's colorful owner. But both Dirk and Maura became noticeably tense when a fleshy, middle-aged man wearing a wrinkled sport coat and too much cologne passed by their booth on his way to the cigarette machine.

The man stopped on his way back. "Taking some time off in the middle of the day, Maura?" he said after an archly polite greeting. "Business must be a little slow, eh? Maybe you should meditate yourself up some customers. Or even better, conjure up an aphrodisiac potion with those herbs and aromas of yours. That would be a surefire seller.''

''Wouldn't do *you* one bit of good, Todd Tully,'' Maura snapped as Dirk got to his feet.

Amy saw that Dirk's brown eyes were stone cold as he stared down at the other man. She remembered hearing the name Tully before.

''You know, Todd, a man who bets on horses all day has no call insulting a woman who works hard at an honest living.'' Dirk's tone was sharp, but his voice was calm and low.

''Dirk, I believe you have a point. At least, she's honest,'' Tully agreed with a sappy smirk. ''She wouldn't use the good-old-boys around here like her cousin Paul does. She wouldn't take away my pa's company by promising the employees the world and then proceed to do away with their jobs a few years later.''

''That's a damn lie,'' Maura shouted, her face beet red. ''Your pa sold the papers to Paul fair and square, while he still could get a decent price after running them into the ground for years. And if he hadn't, you wouldn't be wearing those disgusting diamond pinkie rings or spending every day at the Charlestown track. My cousin saved your pa from bankruptcy!''

''Yeah? That's what he tells you,'' Tully yelled back. ''And who's gonna save Paul Hanley when the papers go under?'' With that, Todd Tully walked out.

Dirk sat back down. ''Good going, Maura—flying off the handle like that, attracting everybody's attention.''

''Oh, please, he deserved it.''

''But Paul didn't, and neither did the company,'' insisted Dirk. ''We're having a hell of a time keeping the lid on rumors. You shouldn't have let him goad you like that."

Maura's brown eyes flared. "Sometimes all you good-old-boys are just a little too good. You know what I mean?" Picking up her menu, she buried her nose in it.

Dirk apologized to Amy for the ruckus, adding he hoped they would meet soon under better circumstances.

After he was gone, Maura lifted her head from the menu. "To think I had a crush on him when I was eleven and he was the college lifeguard at the lake," she muttered. "Mom thinks the world of him. Can you believe it?"

"He did defend you to that Todd Tully," Amy reasoned.

Maura was having none of it, and turned her attention, instead, to her sister's tardiness. Just as she was digging into her purse in search of change for the pay phone, Bridget arrived.

"Sorry I'm late." Bridget slid into the seat next to Amy. "I had to stop in town and pick up the Santa suit for George."

Amy was curious. "Santa suit?"

"For Safety Santa night," replied Bridget. "That's when one of the volunteer firemen dresses up as Santa a few nights before Christmas and visit families with small children to stress fireplace safety rules. He also delivers small gifts and checks the fireplaces to make sure they're clear and safe for the real Santa."

"The kids must love it."

"They do, and so does George. Safety Santa night is practically sacred to him. He just can't bear the thought of disappointing one single child." Bridget reached for her menu. "So, have I missed anything?"

Maura looked at Amy. "Not much, sis," she said with a breezy air. "Paul was here with Lynette Devroy and Dirk Campbell. Amy wanted to know if Lynette was Paul's girlfriend."

Bridget turned to Amy. "She's not his type at all. I wouldn't worry."

"I'm not worrying," she protested.

"Plus Dirk started putting the move on Amy," Maura continued. "And then Todd Tully and I had a screaming match in front of the whole diner."

"Shoot!" Bridget flopped against the cushioned seat back. "I always miss the good stuff."

As their luncheon progressed, Amy grew increasingly relaxed with the two sisters. They gabbed, laughed and shared ideas, never failing to draw her into the conversation. By the time their apple pie à la mode was served, Amy felt comfortable enough to express her frustration about Bernadette's unwillingness to discuss the will. They both urged her to give it more time.

"Mom may be dragging her feet on purpose," Bridget volunteered. "Could be she wants you to really know the place before you make a final decision."

"The inn is her lifeline now that Greg's gone," added Maura. "I think she'd wither on the vine without it."

Although Amy reminded them that her business, family and home were firmly planted in Washington, the sisters stood their ground on the matter. One way or another, they wanted Amy to become an active co-owner of the inn—as her father had intended by his bequest.

"It would be great having you around here—even on a part-time basis," Bridget assured her between bites of juicy pie. "And I bet Paul would like it."

"I doubt that." Amy shifted restlessly in her seat. Why did Bridget imply a more than casual interest between her and Paul? Had she somehow caught wind of what had happened the other night?

"Well, I admit it may be hard to tell with him sometimes. He keeps a lot to himself," Bridget said, pushing her dessert plate aside.

When the waitress returned to refill their coffees, Amy decided to risk further speculation by asking about Paul's marriage and divorce. That's how much she wanted to know.

"It's really sketchy," Maura said. "He's never talked about it to me. How about you, Bridget?"

Shaking her head, Bridget turned to Amy. "For a time—after he moved out West—Paul really wasn't a part of our lives," she explained. "He kept in touch with Mom, sending her money now and then, but we never saw him."

"He was probably just too busy living it up," interjected Maura with a laugh. "After Tremont, who could blame him?"

"He's more than made up for it since he came back, though," Bridget offered.

Maura agreed. "He's been a rock for Mom."

Amy sat back, mulling over this information. "You've never met his wife?"

The two sisters shook their heads.

"All I know is she worked at the TV station with him, and it was kind of sudden," Maura told her. "I was about to go away to college when it happened, and I overheard Greg and Mom discussing it. I got the impression that a baby was on the way and Paul *had* to get married."

Bridget scoffed at her sister. "You must have dreamed that one, Maura. If Paul had a child, where has it been the past four years?"

"I said it was just an impression."

Trying to make sense out of their vagueness, Amy looked to Bridget. "How long was he married?"

"Maybe three years," Bridget replied. Leaning closer, she lowered her voice. "I think another man might have been involved in the breakup. Mom knows, but she won't talk about it."

"And he's said nothing himself?" Amy asked, alarmed and puzzled by what she was hearing.

"I asked him about it once," admitted Maura. "He said it was over and done with, and he saw no point in dredging up the past."

"That's Paul," Bridget claimed with a knowing nod.

Yet Amy was bewildered. Paul was even more of a mystery to her now. Fuzzy speculations about a probably nonexistent child and a marriage broken by a third party just didn't fit with her image of the man. The possibility that he could desert a child was too abhorrent for her to imagine, never mind accept. Paul had listened to her talk about her father's abandonment without any indication of discomfort or distress. He'd been much too kind and sympathetic to be guilty of a similar sin. Clearly Maura's "impression" was way off base.

Yet she couldn't shake the implications inherent in Bridget's and Maura's hazy remarks about Paul. They nagged at her for days afterward until Amy decided enough was enough. She was thinking about the man too much. His continued absence from the inn heightened her curiosity about him and aggravated her concern about the reason behind his distance. She had to resolve the questions and her feelings.

Realizing how much she wanted to see him again, Amy finally tried calling Paul on Friday morning. Unable to reach him, she left a message on his answering machine at the Valley News Group office and on the one at his home.

When Paul hadn't returned her calls by the next day, Amy couldn't help feeling hurt. She was also feeling at odds with herself. Why was she wasting her valuable time moping about Paul Hanley when she hadn't even begun settling her business with Bernadette? After all, she had a life to get back to. She couldn't afford to lose focus or to be distracted by an inopportune attraction.

And she couldn't afford to be put off by Bernadette any longer, either. Wasn't her preoccupation with Paul pure proof of that?

Armed with renewed purpose, Amy cornered Bernadette after breakfast and insisted they sit to discuss the future of the inn *today*.

"Of course, dear, you're right. We shouldn't put it off any longer," Bernadette concurred without hesitation. "Right now I'm up to my eyeballs getting ready for tonight's dinner crowd. Saturdays are always booked solid. But I'll set aside some time before the first sitting so we can have a good talk."

They agreed to meet in the front office at five o'clock.

"Paul the conqueror is back at last," Dirk Campbell declared as Mr. Snead barked and yelped with excitement. "With a big fat check in hand, I hope."

Paul dropped his overnight bag on the table, not surprised to find his colleague in his kitchen in the middle of the afternoon. Dirk had looked after the dog while Paul was away in Richmond attempting to drum up short-term business loans.

"We're getting the money. But I had to put the house up as collateral this time."

"I was afraid of that." Dirk shook his head. "It is going to be tight. Just try not to worry—we'll make the payments."

"We have to. I can't lose this house." It was the one solid thing in life, the one and only home that had ever been completely his. Planning and building the house had been a merciful distraction when he had most needed one. Living here in splendid isolation between the rolling hills and breathtaking valley vistas had long been his solace.

The panting golden retriever pressed against Paul's leg in a play for attention. "Did Snead behave?" he asked, ruffling his pet's long, reddish coat.

"He did his usual moping each time I walked through the door instead of you. And he didn't eat very much."

He gazed down into his dog's golden brown eyes with affection. "Poor Snead. Alone all day while I'm working. You lead a lonesome life out here, don't you, boy?"

"He's very playful for a dog his age," Dirk noted. "Too bad there aren't any kids living around here. A couple of little boys to help him run off all that energy would make Snead a happy fella."

Paul winced at his friend's comment. Snead did indeed love children, and had since he was a puppy. Snead was also the only remnant left from his life in San Francisco. Because Shelly's new mate had allergies, there had been no place for Mr. Snead in her new life. Paul had tried to locate a good home for the dog before moving East, but found the prospects unacceptable. And turning such a great pet over to the animal shelter was out of the question. So Snead came with him to Virginia.

"Maybe Bridget might like him now that Willy is older," he mused. "Snead would adore that kid."

After Dirk went home, Paul dialed his office answering machine. He was startled to hear a message from Amy Riordan. He was even more surprised to hear her message repeated on his home machine. But the sound of her voice brought back the sense of excited anticipation that had bedeviled him since the day she had arrived in Tremont. Hoping to suppress this very feeling, he had tried to keep his distance from her.

Lord, how he'd tried.

Yet the enticing possibilities of their passionate kiss had kept Amy in his thoughts, tempting him to seek her out no matter what the costs. He wanted her to acknowledge the electrifying desire they had ignited out on the gazebo. He wanted to know why she had run away from him that night. He wanted her to tell him she was as astounded about their evolving fascination as he was. He wanted . . .

He wanted too damn much.

Which is why—after seeing her at the Blossom Diner—he'd taken off for Richmond. Sure, his company needed cash. But more than anything else, he needed space to think. This was hitting him too hard to be just a passing attraction, yet the answers to why her and why now were elusive, even from miles away.

Amy Riordan didn't belong in a mountain backwater town like Tremont, Virginia. She couldn't possibly have any interest in the kind of life he'd come home to find. And he doubted she would maintain a permanent connection with the inn—not with all the emotional dynamite it held for her. Although Amy was not the spoiled, rich brat he had expected, her life seemed to be very much wrapped up in the whirl of Washington, D.C. He was not part of that, nor did he want to be.

No question about it, he'd be asking for trouble if he pursued the attraction further. He felt it in his soul.

His marriage to Shelly had proven his gut feelings were worth heeding. Maybe everything would be hearts and flowers at first. Then, two, three, four years down the road, conflicts and complications would float to the surface—there would be hell to pay. But he had already paid his pound of flesh. He'd lost more than most could imagine. He'd be crazy to get caught up in another tangled mess. Perhaps Amy had similar trepidations, and that was why she'd pushed him away the other night. Perhaps she had a hell of a lot more sense than he.

But why did she want to talk to him now?

Snead barked once and paced restlessly, showing he was ready for his dinner. Filling the dog's food and water bowls, Paul glanced at the kitchen clock. It was just past five o'clock. Should he call Amy now? he wondered. Or should he go over to the Blue Sky and speak with her face-to-face?

"Brilliant idea," he muttered with derision as he placed the two dog bowls on the floor.

His strategy had been to keep his distance from Ms. Riordan for his own good. It was the smart thing to do. But damn, what he really wanted was to hightail it over to the inn to see her. And, at this point, desire had a definite edge over straight thinking.

The telephone rang, interrupting his deliberations.

"Oh, Paul, thank goodness you're back from Richmond," Bernadette declared in a breathless rush. "You've got to come to the inn right away. We need your help desperately."

Chapter Seven

Amy waited in the front office for Bernadette, nervous, yet anxious to be done with it all. This crucial discussion about the inn was overdue. The time had finally come.

Actually, the time had come and gone. Bernadette was late.

True, she was just a few minutes late, but Amy couldn't help feeling uneasy. Bernadette had been so slippery about the entire matter Amy wouldn't put anything past her at this point.

"Amy, Amy, I'm so sorry," Bernadette exclaimed when she dashed into the office at last. She was out of breath and clearly agitated. "I didn't mean to keep you waiting, but I'm in a jam."

"Good heavens, what happened?" Amy was regretting her suspicions already.

"Bud had a family emergency. He called in not more than twenty minutes ago—something about his mother-in-law taking ill," Bernadette revealed, gasping to catch her breath. "I can't find anybody to fill in, so I've been stuck behind the bar fixing drinks. I even tried calling Paul, but he's not back from Richmond yet."

"Paul went to Richmond?" Amy's mind reeled with surprise. That must have been why he hadn't returned her calls.

The older woman nodded. "Both of Bridget's kids are sick with the flu, so she can't come. George is on duty at the station, and heaven knows where Maura has gone off to tonight. I can't find her. Anyway," she continued, "I've got to get back to the Pub Room. We'll have to postpone that talk we planned because I'll be running back and forth between the dining room and the bar all night."

By now Amy knew the inn was a zoo on Saturday nights. Bernadette couldn't cover both areas. "I'll man the bar tonight."

"I couldn't ask you to do that."

"Do you have any other experienced bartenders hanging around here?"

"Why, that's right. You used to tend bar, didn't you?" the older woman recalled. "But are you sure you can handle it? We'll be very busy tonight."

"I'll handle it," she said, halfway out the office door. "Don't worry."

"I'll try Paul again, anyway," Bernadette called after her. "You might need an extra hand."

Amy hurried into the Pub Room and took up station behind the bar. Finding a clean, white apron hanging on a hook near the sink, she wrapped it over her white, silk blouse and black stirrup pants. She rolled up her sleeves

and took a quick survey of the lounge. Most of the patrons were still nursing the drinks Bernadette had served
them, allowing Amy to take a few minutes to familiarize
herself with the bar's layout and the cash register. Luckily she had seen Bud tabulate a few bills the other night,
so she had some idea of how the system worked.

The first half hour was frenetic as she tended the bar,
waited on tables and filled drink orders for the dining
room when it opened. Juggling these tasks was a challenge, yet gradually the work became routine.

The steady stream of customers in and out of the pub
kept her hopping. Several were townspeople she'd met in
previous days, who now greeted her with friendly hellos
and inquiries about how she was doing. They were also
patient about delays. Some even helped by delivering
drinks to tables, refilling nut dishes and fetching extra
napkins and swizzle sticks from the storeroom.

In the midst of this chaos and cooperation, it dawned
on Amy that few people knew or cared that she was the
stepdaughter of one of Washington's most powerful private citizens. In this tiny Shenandoah hamlet, the Windom name and wealth held no significance. To some
townspeople she was Greg Riordan's girl, to others she
was just Amy. She'd been sensing this acceptance all week
long, but now the reality of it hit her with a liberating
force. Her spirit soared.

Buoyed by this new realization, she picked up some
speed and really began enjoying the job. She was catching up with another round of dining-room orders, when
Paul entered the room. Bernadette had reached him after all, Amy thought with inexplicable relief.

She drank him in with her eyes. He headed her way, tall
and lanky, longish blond hair blown askew by the night
wind, vital and handsome as all get out. Excitement rip-

pled through her. Yet Amy wasn't sure what to expect from him. They had barely spoken since she had run from his kiss that night on the gazebo.

"Your reinforcement has arrived," he said, taking a look around the room. "Although it seems you're doing just fine on your own. Bernadette was sure you'd need rescuing."

"I've managed to hold on. But believe me, I need all the help I can get."

Amy's heart thrummed madly as Paul joined her behind the bar. Her awareness was at high voltage now that he stood so close. A gray-blue crew-neck sweater hugged his broad, muscled shoulders, his tight, flat waist tapered into charcoal wool slacks. He smelled of sandalwood soap and the cold evening air—an earthy combination that made her feel weak in the knees.

"You're in charge, ma'am. What do you want me to do?"

"Would you mind waiting on the tables?"

He scanned the array of tables surrounding the bar. "I worked a lot of different jobs to support myself after I left the army. In college, too. But I have to admit I've never been a cocktail waitress."

"Call me an equal-opportunity employer."

"Just don't expect me to split my tips," he said, his tone wry. Then, grabbing a tray and throwing a clean dish towel over his shoulder, Paul wove his way among the tables.

Although he said little, his presence eased the pressure considerably. Not only did Paul wait on tables, but he got behind the bar to help her pour beers and mix drinks whenever time permitted. For Amy, the hectic hours flew by as they worked around each other.

Patient and charming, Paul was a champ when it came to waiting on guests. He was raking in the tips, too. The empty nut jar he'd rustled up to hold his earnings was on the counter behind her, filling up fast. When Paul mentioned he planned to give the jar's contents to Bernadette to distribute among the dining room employees, Amy threw her tips into the kitty, too.

Once the dining room closed for the night, business in the Pub Room began to wane. Only three people sat at the bar: a college-aged couple on their first date and Hal, a middle-aged guest of the inn whose wife had already retired to their room with a migraine. He'd been nursing beers for the better part of the evening, casting sheep's eyes at Amy and making leading comments. She did her best to ignore them.

With the late-evening lull, she had time to observe Paul serving what seemed like the umpteenth round of white-wine spritzers to three ladies sitting near the fireplace. This was one instance where she thought he was performing his job a little too well. The women—all attractive and clearly younger than her—had been ogling him and flirting with him all evening. Amy didn't know which she found most irksome—Paul's unimpeachable charm, the women's frivolous behavior or the extent of her own chagrin about it.

These ladies, staying long after last call, eventually were the only customers left in the place. Except for Hal. Amy wondered if he'd give her trouble about leaving.

Paul came up beside her. "Your friend's been hanging out here a long time," he remarked, as if he'd been reading her thoughts.

"Not as long as your three chums over there." She nodded at the corner table.

A devilish grin crossed his lips, as sexy as it was vexing. "They're just making the most of their girls' night out."

Hal interrupted them by rapping his empty beer glass on the counter.

"Amy honey, bring me another, will you?" His rakish grin and oozing tone intimated a thirst for something more than beer.

Paul's smile vanished and Amy noticed his hands had tightened into fists. "Has that jerk been coming on to you?" His voice was low, but tense.

"He's harmless, Paul," she assured him. "Besides, his wife is right upstairs."

Announcing that they were ready to leave, the women at the corner table beckoned Paul to come with their check.

"Go. Take care of the ladies," Amy urged. "I'll tell Hal to run along."

He cast a doubtful glance at Hal. "Are you sure?"

"I can handle him. Don't worry."

She moved to the end of the bar to confront Hal. "Sorry, but it's closing time," she said, placing his entire night's tab in front of him.

"But, darlin', we still need to get better acquainted."

"Would you like to pay this now? Or shall I put the charges on your room bill?"

He dug into a back pocket for his wallet. "How about you and I find a place with soft music and—"

"I'm sure your *wife* is wondering where you are."

Hal dropped several twenties onto the counter. "She'll never miss me. Sleeps like the dead when she takes her headache medicine."

His punctuating wink made Amy want to gag. "I'll get your change."

"No, no, sweetheart." He grabbed her arm to stop her. "You keep the extra."

"It's too much." She jerked her arm away and went straight to the cash register.

Hal persisted, however, when she returned with the change. "Tell you what, sweet thing," he drawled as he slid a crisp one-hundred-dollar bill from his wallet. "Use this for the very best champagne in the joint, and then we can take it over to your place and have us a fine old time."

Grasping her hands, Hal pushed the money into them. His expression had gone from rakish to unabashedly suggestive. She tried to pull away, but he held firm. Disgusted and angry, Amy was about to deliver a tongue-lashing the creep would never forget, when Paul rushed up behind him.

"Take your hands off her," he growled, grabbing Hal by the shoulders, yanking him off the bar stool. Paul shoved him toward the door. "The bar is closed."

Although Hal was worse for the number of beers he'd downed, he stood his ground. After directing a string of stinging invectives at Paul, he turned to Amy. "Tell this clown to get lost, honey. We're gonna go party, right?"

"That's it, buddy." Paul's face burned with rage. Taking a menacing step closer, he loomed over Hal. "Get out of here before I throw you the hell out."

Hal shrank back. "What a fine way to treat a good paying customer. I'll have a word with your boss in the morning, fella. You ain't gonna have a job tomorrow night." Turning on his unsteady heels, he headed out the door, muttering with indignation.

Stunned by this vehement confrontation, Amy looked at Paul. She didn't know what to say. His rescue wasn't really necessary, she could have dealt with the pugnacious twirp on her own. Yet, in all truth, Paul's intervention pleased her, as did his male protectiveness. She supposed that wasn't very independent of her, but she didn't care.

"Thank you," she murmured.

Paul's eyes, no longer dark with anger, held her gaze for a long, silent moment. His deep, searching expression sparked a surge of mixed-up emotions within her, emotions ranging from apprehension to intense attraction. He seemed to be waiting for her to say more. But her thoughts and feelings were in such turmoil, she couldn't speak. She was afraid she'd give herself away.

"I better put out the fire," Paul finally said, turning toward the fireplace.

As he leaned over the old marble mantel, stoking the dying embers with a black iron poker, she noted the play of muscles across his strong, broad back. It was a pleasure to watch him like this. It also made her want to get closer. Amy came out from behind the bar and slowly approached the fireplace. Her footsteps on the bare wood floor echoed in the empty room.

Paul did not turn around, but continued to poke at the smoky ashes. "I just got your messages this afternoon. I've been out of town."

"So I heard," she said, standing by his side now.

"What did you call about?"

"I wanted to talk." Pausing to screw up her courage, Amy took a deep breath. "About what happened the other night . . . at the gazebo."

Paul stopped what he was doing, yet continued to stare down at the smoldering ashes. "Why?"

"I can't stop thinking about it." She wished she could see his face.

"Which part, Amy?" He turned to look at her at last. "Which part can't you stop thinking about?"

His blue gaze was intense—unrelenting, really. Amy could see Paul wanted answers. But more important, she saw that their encounter on the gazebo had affected him as much as it had her. It had meant something to him.... *She* had meant something.

As his eyes held her captive, her heart began to pound wildly. She could almost hear it. Paul was waiting, and this time she had to speak.

"I think about our talk, the painful things I told you about Jeff. And I think a lot about the way we kissed."

His eyes closed for a brief second. "So do I," he whispered.

"I've asked myself why I made you stop."

"Why did you, Amy?" his voice and gaze implored.

"Because I was afraid of how it—how you—made me feel."

Paul's expression softened into a slight smile as he rested the iron poker against the fireplace. "You shouldn't be afraid of that."

"You don't know my history with men. What happened with Jeff was the worst, but I've had other failures," she explained. "As a politician would say, my record speaks for itself."

"I see." Paul leaned against the mantel, studying her face for an uncomfortable minute or two before he spoke again. "So, which one of us don't you trust? You or me?"

"Both." Amy grimaced as Julie's countless reprimands came to mind. "I have a friend who thinks I subconsciously make a point of choosing the wrong men. Something to do with my father deserting me as a child. Maybe she's right."

"Do you think I'm wrong for you?"

"That's why I practically ran out of the gazebo the other night."

Her frankness made him wince. "That would explain it."

"But that's what I *think,* not how I *feel.* Which is why I didn't want the kissing to stop."

"This is crazy," Paul said, shaking his head. Then he smiled and took her hand. "You and I have been doing way too much thinking."

He drew her to him, his arms curving around her waist, holding her close. His chest felt rock hard against her breasts which tingled with shameless excitement. His embrace was strong and firm. Her breathing quickened as his gaze swallowed her into its dark blue depths. Caught in this whirlpool of sensation, Amy's mind spun with dizzy delight.

Finally, Paul lowered his face to hers until she could feel his warm breath on her mouth. Her lips quivered in anticipation. This felt good. Too good. She uttered his name in weak protest. But she didn't mean it. And Paul's eyes told her he knew it.

"I brought you two something to eat," Bernadette's voice suddenly trilled across the room. "You're probably starving."

Amy sprang back from Paul as he cursed under his breath. They both turned to find Bernadette backing into the Pub Room, pulling a tray cart through the door. Had she seen them embracing? Amy wondered. She stole a glance at Paul. He looked as glum as she felt.

"You're good souls to help me out on such short notice, missing dinner and everything." Bernadette pushed the cart toward them, its wheels squeaking as they rolled across the old floor planks. "I had Martin put a couple of trays together before he went home. His chicken was superb tonight. You'll love it."

Although her stomach was indeed empty, food was the last thing on Amy's mind. She wanted to be alone with Paul. The final few moments between them had been steeped in emotions mysterious and magnetic, romantic in a way she'd never known. After this interruption, Amy feared they'd never get those heady emotions back.

"This really isn't necessary," Paul said to his aunt. "It's late—you must be tired."

"Of course it's necessary. You've got to eat, don't you? Besides, it's no trouble." Bernadette unfolded a white, linen cloth and tossed it over a table in front of the fireplace. "Oh, what a shame. The fire's gone out."

"We were closing up, so Paul put it out," Amy told her.

"Never mind. I've got an idea." Bernadette plucked one of the pewter candlesticks from the mantel and placed it in the middle of the table. Pulling a book of matches from her apron pocket, she lit the green bayberry taper before finishing off the table with napkins, silver and wineglasses.

"There, that's more like it," she remarked when finished. "Now, sit and enjoy."

Amy was amazed, and a tad amused, by the older woman's attempt to create a cozy dinner for two. One look at Paul told her he felt the same way.

He pulled out a chair for her. "Shall we?"

"Don't worry about cleaning up when you're done," Bernadette said as she ceremoniously uncorked a bottle of white wine. "I'll take care of it in the morning."

She poured the wine and left, closing the Pub Room's wide double doors behind her. Paul gazed across the table at Amy, his eyes dancing. "Perhaps it's just my imagination, but I think my aunt has ideas about us."

"Let's see, candlelight, crystal, wine, closed doors..." Amy shook her head. "I don't think it's your imagination."

"Think she was spying on us?"

"Either that or she's psychic."

"Knowing Bernadette, it could be a little of both," he said, entranced by how lovely she was in the warm glow of candlelight. Her sapphire eyes sparkled and her skin looked so creamy and soft his fingers ached to touch it.

"She's right about one thing."

"What's that?" Unable to resist, he reached across the table for her hand. It felt smooth and warm and delicate in his grasp.

"I'm really, really hungry. Whatever is under these warmers smells delicious."

With his free hand, he lifted the silver insulated warmer off her plate. He watched her breathe in the mouth-watering aroma wafting through the air, her eyes closed, her lips slightly parted and her expression blissful. Paul swallowed hard. The desire that had been simmering deep inside all evening now roiled in his blood with a fury. No matter how long it had been since he'd last eaten, Amy was a hundred times more delectable than any dish Chef Martin could create. And oh, how he hungered for her.

"You should eat before you faint," he said abruptly. He let go of her hand, hoping he hadn't sounded too gruff.

Smiling, Amy picked up her fork and dug into the golden chicken on her plate. Paul ate, too, yet he barely tasted the food. All his senses were focused on the pretty woman sitting across from him. Eventually, Amy pulled him back into real time when she began discussing their evening of service in the Pub Room. Comparing notes and laughing about the experience eased the tensions slicing through his body.

He was thankful for the respite. The fierce feelings building up inside him would have scared Amy off for sure. That was the last thing he wanted.

When they were finished with the entrée, Amy insisted he sit while she cleared the dinner plates and served the apple pie and cheese Bernadette had left on the cart. This display of feminine caring touched him. He'd never been the kind of man who expected—or even wanted—a little lady to wait on him with pipe, slippers, gourmet meals on the table. But he did miss the snug warmth and quiet grace that only a woman could provide for a man. He just never knew how much until now.

Admitting to a wicked sweet tooth, Amy raved about the pie. She ate with gusto, while Paul picked at his piece. Although he enjoyed her fresh enthusiasm and the wit she playfully turned on herself, all this vibrancy made him want her more. He wondered how to get Amy into his arms without scaring the daylights out of her.

"I know what's missing," he blurted out the moment he'd hit on an answer.

Amy's eyes widened as he bolted from the table. "Where are you going?"

"We need music." He went behind the bar and began flinging open cabinet doors. "Bud plays tapes sometimes when it's not too crowded and noisy. I know he keeps them back here somewhere."

"Try the middle cabinet under the bar. I saw a boom-box in there when I was hunting for the blender."

Paul took a look. "Bingo," he cried, pulling out the stereo cassette player and Bud's small stash of jazz tapes. He set the box up on the counter and quickly looked through the cassettes until he found a title he knew. As soon as the low, dulcet tones and smooth beat flowed through the player's speakers, Paul smiled. "Perfect."

Amy's brow wrinkled with uncertainty. "Perfect for what?"

"Dancing," he replied, returning to their table. "I can't think of a better way to complete Bernadette's picture."

"I'm not sure she had dancing in mind."

Longing to draw her into his embrace, Paul held out his hand. "Come on. A few turns around the room can't hurt."

Amy hesitated at first, then rose from her chair and walked straight into his arms. Wrapping them around her before any second thoughts could interfere, Paul caught the alluring glimmer in her eyes. Maybe he didn't have to worry about her pulling away after all.

As they moved with the music's mellow beat, Amy's silky hair caressed his chin, and her body molded softly, perfectly, into his. Her breasts pressed against his chest, stirring his blood into a quickening boil. Feeling her warm breath on his neck, Paul tightened his embrace. "You're so beautiful," he whispered in her ear.

Suddenly, she stopped and lifted her gaze. Her dark blue eyes, wide and searching, held him spellbound. Although his pulse was pounding in his ears, his mind was focused on her moist lips and how much he wanted to taste them. Unable to hold back, he lowered his head, drinking in her moan as his mouth covered hers.

No longer hesitant, Amy gave herself up to the kiss, her lips yielding to his tongue's urgent prodding, welcoming him inside her honeyed warmth. An electric ache burned within him, low and intense. He groaned as he deepened the kiss, his hands roaming along her smooth, angular back down to her curvy hips, again and again.

He was lost in the moment, lost in her.

Paul couldn't remember when he had last felt so connected. The losses of the past had taken their toll; his life had been marked by shattered ties and empty promises. After his divorce, he'd figured he was meant to go it alone. And, for the past four years, he'd been content to do just that.

Amy combed her fingers through his hair. As her hands slithered over his ears and down his neck, he finally broke the kiss to glory in the sensations of her touch. "Oh, what you do to me, Amy," he growled, before planting light kisses on her eyes, her nose, her cheeks.

What was it about Amy Riordan that made him yearn, made him hunger like never before? After years of keeping other women at arm's length, why did he want to hold *this* woman as close as possible? Paul kissed her mouth again, long and slow and hard, until his body was on fire. He wanted to take her back to his house and make love to her. Surely the answers he needed would be found in their shared passion.

Paul broke off their kiss while he still had some semblance of self-control. "Amy, wait," he rasped, ready to ask her to come with him right then and there. "I want you. I want to—"

The look on her face made him stop.

Although her own passion was unmistakable, so were the questions in her eyes. Paul understood these all too well, for they were the same as the ones in his heart. What was happening to them? And why?

There was something else in her deep gaze—a vulnerability that gave him pause. He doubted if Amy was even aware of it. Yet the inner conflicts he detected—passion and uncertainty, yearning and fear—convinced Paul to take a step back.

It took all his strength to pull away. "I'd better go."

"Go?" She clutched his arms to stop him, her expression tearing at his heart. "But I thought . . ."

"Just for now," he reassured, cupping her face with his hands.

"It's happening too fast between us, isn't it?"

"Maybe." He kissed her forehead.

Amy looked down at their entwined arms. "Paul, I'm not going to be here forever. I don't want to leave with any regrets."

"I don't want you to, either," he implored. "That's why I should go now."

"But you'll come back?" she said, sounding unsure as she searched his gaze. "You won't go dashing off to Richmond again or anything like that."

Chuckling, he shook his head. "That tactic didn't work. All I did was think about you."

She smiled with obvious pleasure. "Good."

This feminine grin had a mesmerizing effect, reminding him of all the things he found irresistible about her. "Don't worry, I'll be here for you. I'll come back tomorrow afternoon—if you'd like."

"I'd like."

The provocative gleam in her eye, the seductive shadings in her voice stirred his desire anew. Leaving her was twice as hard now. But when he finally managed to drag himself away from the inn, Paul felt an optimism that helped soothe the unrequited burning in his loins. Feeling for all the world like a goofy, infatuated kid, he hopped into his pickup and gunned the engine. He couldn't wait until tomorrow.

After years of keeping the pain of personal loss at bay, Paul found it exhilarating to be looking forward for a change. All he could think about was seeing Amy tomorrow, and the next day, and the day after that. Of course, Amy's stay in Tremont was limited, as she had pointed out herself. But he didn't care. Who knew better than he that nothing lasted forever? He'd take this time with her, without reservation, for however long it was meant to last.

He was happily humming a tune from Bud's jazz tape when he pulled into his driveway. Snead, barking and squealing, dashed out the door as soon as he unlocked it. While the dog attended to his business outside, Paul went into the kitchen for something cold to drink. As he opened the fridge, the pile of mail Dirk had collected caught his eye. He chuckled at the neat stack on the counter, with catalogs and magazines on the bottom and the envelopes arranged in order by size. His buddy was a supreme organizer.

Cracking open a can of cola, he began flipping through the Christmas cards and bills. At the bottom of the pile was a pale blue vellum envelope inscribed with a stylish handwriting he recognized all too well. It belonged to his ex-wife. Yet this was not Shelly's annual family Christmas card—which she had dutifully sent him for the past four years. This looked like something else altogether, and it made him uneasy.

He started to tear open the envelope, but his fingers froze when he noticed the return address scrawled on the back flap. Paul was stunned. This letter had not come from Southern California, where Shelly and her family had been living for years. No, she had mailed this from a new address—an address in Washington, D.C.

Chapter Eight

Paul read Shelly's brief note with disbelief.

Her husband, Bob Wickwire, had been promoted to the network's Washington bureau, and they had recently moved to the city with their two boys. Shelly suggested they should all get together after the holidays.

All get together? He crumpled the note in his fist, unwilling to grapple with the cause for the Wickwires' change of heart.

Mr. Snead barked outside the door. Paul let the dog in, tossing the pale blue wad of paper into the trash can. He wished he could trash the sudden flood of memories as easily. But they gushed over him with the megaton force of a broken dam. God, how he hated remembering that time.

The divorce had been so painful, so brutal, he had had to move a continent away in order to put it behind him. Even then, Shelly's tearful pleadings, the bitter arguments with Wickwire and the sad, final goodbyes had all haunted his sleep for months. The fact that he'd been a popular local TV newsman at the time had added to the mess considerably. The responsible San Francisco newspapers' coverage of his divorce was difficult enough. But the tabloids' screaming headlines about love triangles and legal maneuvering plus the gossip media's relentless hounding had shattered his privacy.

Paul plunked the empty soda can on the counter. "Don't get sucked back into the past," he admonished himself.

Not tonight of all nights. Not when he and Amy were just opening up to each other.

Mr. Snead followed him into the bedroom, gazing up lovingly as Paul kicked off his leather boots. Reaching down to rub the golden retriever's neck, Paul decided not to answer Shelly's note. Tomorrow he'd go back to the inn and arrange to see Amy as much as possible.

"The past is over and done with, Snead," he said, giving the dog one last affectionate pat for the night. "We're moving on."

Amy sat in the dining room, nibbling at her breakfast as she reexamined what had happened last night with Paul. His fervent kisses and caresses had aroused in her an intense need to express her budding passion. She had never felt such a powerful rush of desire before—not even with Jeff.

And it scared her half to death.

She sipped hot coffee to warm herself against the room's drafty chill. It was bitter cold outside as sporadic flurries sifted through the dreary, gray sky. The weather fit her mood to a tee. Because as much as she wanted to see Paul again, lingering doubts overshadowed her excitement. She couldn't help if mistrust was ingrained in her nature. Amy had told him that about herself, and a whole lot more. But when all was said and done, what did she really know about Paul Hanley?

"Good morning, Amy. I hope you enjoyed your dinner last night." Bernadette, dressed in Sunday-church clothes, sat at Amy's table. "I can't thank you enough for taking over in the Pub Room," she added. "What a scare."

"How's Bud's mother-in-law?"

"Mother-in-law... You mean the emergency?" Bernadette declared after a moment's befuddlement.

"Is she all right?"

"Yes, yes. Everything seems to be fine. Bud will be back tonight."

"If he needs more time, I don't mind filling in again."

"You're a peach to offer. I'm sure you worked your you-know-what off last night." Bernadette shuffled her chair closer to Amy's. "You and Paul made a great team."

Amy stiffened, wondering what, if anything, Bernadette had seen the night before. "He was a great help."

"I'm glad you two are hitting it off so well." Bernadette's grin was of the Cheshire-cat variety.

"You think we are?"

"It looked that way to me." The smile faded. "Am I wrong?"

Amy eyed the other woman thoughtfully. Perhaps Bernadette could help quiet her fears. "I like Paul," she admitted. "Still, I don't feel I know him. He says so little about himself."

Bernadette nodded. "He tends to hold things inside. He always has."

"I know he was married. Bridget and Maura have given me the impression it ended badly."

"It did. And he's been alone ever since." The motherly compassion in the woman's voice touched Amy.

"Bernadette, I have to ask you. Does he have a child?"

"Did Maura tell you that? She has no idea what she's talking about, you know."

"Then there were no children from the marriage?"

Bernadette looked uncomfortable. "You should be asking Paul these questions."

She was probably right, but Amy couldn't stop now. "I'm asking *you.*"

Bernadette shook her head. "If Paul had a child, I'd know about it, wouldn't I?"

An awkward silence followed. Amy didn't know what to say. Although she believed Bernadette, she felt something wasn't quite right. She just couldn't put her finger on what.

Finally, Bernadette cleared her throat with a nervous cough. "Why don't you come back with me to my cottage?" she suggested. "I have some things I'd like to show you."

Amy was startled by this sudden shift. "What things?"

"Things you should have seen a long time ago."

Bernadette urged Amy to grab a jacket for the short walk to the innkeeper's cottage behind the inn. "Winter is here to stay. The weatherman on the radio says a big storm may be headed our way later this week. Hope you like snow, Amy. We get a lot of it out here."

Despite her coat, the wind whipped right through Amy as she and Bernadette traversed the footpath leading to the ivy-trimmed clapboard cottage. With teeth chattering more from nervousness than from the cold, she stepped inside her father's last home. The small rooms were attractive and toasty warm.

"Greg always teased me about keeping the furnace turned up so high. He'd say I had ice water in my veins." Bernadette turned to her with a revealing glint in her eyes. "But he knew better."

Bernadette's candid comment startled her, yet touched her, as well. Clearly Bernadette had loved Greg very much, and it comforted Amy to know her father had not died a lonely man.

"Let's go into the study," Bernadette suggested after taking her coat. "Most of his things are in there."

Amy followed her into a comfortable-looking room paneled in rich cherry. The worn leather sofa and chairs fit in well with the big fireplace and old-fashioned, multipaned casement windows. "This is very nice."

"Your father loved this room. If he wasn't at the inn, this would be where you'd find him."

Drawn to the arrangement of framed photographs on the credenza, Amy studied them for a long time. The pictures were mostly of family—the Ryan family. One shot was of a younger Bernadette sitting on the hood of Greg's old shiny Buick. She recognized school pictures of Maura and baby pictures of the grandchildren. And there were formal and candid shots from Bridget's wedding. Apparently Greg Riordan had given the bride away.

Amy bit her lip and looked away. These photos were visual testament to a man's rich family life—a life in which she had no part. Seeing them displayed this way in her father's beloved inner sanctum felt like an unspoken affront.

Unnerved, Amy glanced up to find the older woman rummaging through a small closet. She soon emerged with a charcoal tweed jacket folded over her arm.

"This was Greg's favorite piece of clothing. He had it sent from a shop near the Riordans' ancestral home in Ireland." Bernadette sighed as she sat on the old, leather couch. "He looked so handsome in it, Amy."

"Did he?"

Nodding, Bernadette beckoned Amy to sit beside her. "Feel how fine the wool is."

Amy's hand skimmed over the wool tweed spread out on the woman's lap. "It's an excellent weave," she whispered.

"It still smells like him a little," Bernadette declared, lifting the jacket to rub against her cheek. Then she held it up to Amy. "Here, see for yourself."

She hesitated for a moment, but Bernadette pressed the sport coat into her arms. Slowly she raised the fabric to her face until the subtle, lingering traces of wood smoke, peppermint and mellow tobacco filled her head. Tears of regret smarted in her eyes. She had no memory of this scent, this essence of her father. Yet it was as close to him as she would ever get for the rest of her life.

Blinking back her tears, Amy said the first thing that popped to mind. "He smoked a pipe?"

"Oh, yes, he enjoyed a good tobacco. And he loved collecting those pipes." Bernadette pointed to a rack of carved pipes on top of the mantel. "They're yours now, you know. This jacket, too," she added. "And any other personal items you'd like to keep."

"You don't have to do that," Amy said, taken aback.

Glancing around the room, she couldn't imagine picking out keepsakes of a man she had scarcely known, a man who'd known next to nothing about her. When her glance came to the offending display on the credenza, she couldn't bridle her resentment. "Surely your girls would like to have these mementos of my fa—of Greg."

"But they rightly belong to you, dear."

"I'm not so sure about that, Bernadette. Bridget and Maura are the ones with the special memories," she insisted. "Greg's things will mean more to them."

Bernadette sat back in dismay. "If that's the way you feel."

Handing back the tweed jacket, Amy started to rise from the couch.

"Wait." Bernadette tugged her back down. "I have something very important to show you."

Although she was reluctant to deal with any more artifacts from her late-father's life, she remained seated while Bernadette fetched something from the handsome antique desk near the credenza.

"You'll have to keep *this,*" Bernadette told her when she returned to the couch. She was clutching a full-size, leather-bound photo album.

Amy watched in silence as Bernadette opened up the album on her lap. Turning to the first page, the older woman looked over at her. "Do you recognize the picture?"

Did she recognize it?

Her heart was in her throat as she gazed down at the photo of a giggly, pigtailed girl not more than five or six, sitting on the rugged shoulders of a dark-haired, smiling young man. He was standing beside a wooden-seat swing hanging from a thick-limbed old maple tree.

"Yes, I remember," she murmured, unable to pull her eyes away the photograph. "I think it was taken after my father put the swing up for me in our backyard."

"It's a marvelous picture of you both. And you looked like him even when you were a baby." Bernadette turned the page. "See."

Amy stared hard at the pictures of her in the various stages of babyhood. She shook her head. "I had no idea he'd kept these."

"Oh, Greg kept many, many pictures of you, dear." Bernadette shifted the album onto Amy's lap. "Here, see for yourself."

Time seemed to stop as Amy leafed through the pages of the photo album. She was amazed to find that it was totally dedicated to her. Surprise soon burgeoned into shock, however, when she realized the photographs went beyond her early-childhood years.

Included in the dozens of pictures were shots of her wearing her first-Communion dress; diving into the lake; dancing at her sixteenth birthday party; posing for her high school and college graduation portraits. She found the final few items even more stunning—snapshots from her agency's grand opening party and of the day she moved into her own home.

"I don't understand," she gasped, her head spinning as she tore through the pages again. "My mother couldn't have sent these pictures to him...she wouldn't."

Bernadette bristled. "Certainly not."

"Then where did he get all of these? How did he get them?"

"You don't have a clue, do you?"

Amy shook her head. How could she even guess? The album sitting in her lap defied belief.

"It was your stepfather—Thomas Windom. He's been sending pictures to Greg for years."

Amy gaped at the other woman in astonishment. "I can't believe it. He never said a word to me."

"Maybe he thought you wouldn't want to know. And I bet he didn't want your mother to know what he was doing."

Bernadette's point was well taken. Her mother would absolutely not abide any contact with Greg.

"Why would Thomas do it?"

"Your father called him a few months after he'd written to you about the inn," Bernadette revealed. "Mr. Windom, bless his heart, tried to help Greg understand why you hadn't answered his letter. After that, he started sending the pictures. First, it was a big package covering all the years Greg had missed. Then, over the years, they'd come in dribs and drabs, but Thomas Windom never forgot. He's a good man, your stepfather."

"The best," Amy assured her. "My mother and I are lucky to have him." Looking through the last few pictures in the album, she wondered why Thomas hadn't sent the engagement picture of her and Jeff.

"I'm sorry I've never met the gentleman. But Greg was very grateful to him. It meant a great deal." Bernadette sought Amy's gaze. "I know you'll find this hard to believe, but these photographs meant the world to him. He held them—and you—close to his heart to the very end. That's why he left you half the inn—to *keep* you close."

Amy couldn't speak. Her tongue felt like lead; her heart felt even heavier. Bernadette had just told her something she had longed to hear almost all her life. She knew now that her father had really cared, yet this coveted knowledge was painful to absorb.

"Greg kept a copy of the picture of you two together up in our bedroom, along with his parents' wedding picture. I'll make sure you get them," Bernadette said.

Amy didn't hear. She sat stone still, her fingers gliding gently over the photo album's leather cover. Her sense of loss was immense.

"Amy, dear? Are you all right?"

She turned to Bernadette, her lips quivering. How could she be all right when her heart had just been smashed into bits as a result of her own fearful pride?

"I turned my back on him," she finally said, her voice trembling. "Why would he have still cared?"

"You cared about him all those years he was drifting, didn't you? Deep down, I mean—even though his leaving hurt you."

Recalling the many nights she had wished on a star for his return, Amy nodded.

"Well, it worked the other way, too," continued Bernadette. "Your staying away didn't change his love for you. He always held out hope. And look, here you are."

"A little late, wouldn't you say?" She pounded a fist on her thigh as frustration and anger roiled inside her. "I shouldn't have kept myself away like that—refusing to see him or even talk to him on the phone. Even after all these years, I never tried."

"And neither did Greg. Not after that first letter," Bernadette stated flatly. "You shouldn't blame yourself because Greg couldn't swallow his pride and try contacting you again. I begged him not to give up."

"You did?"

"Of course. You were his one and only child and he should have tried harder. But Greg could be so darn stubborn. And proud!" Bernadette shook her head at the thought. "He was convinced your mother had brought you up believing you were better than anybody else— most of all him."

"That's not so."

"I know. I saw it for myself the day the ceiling collapsed in room 16. In my prayers that night, I told Greg how wrong he'd been."

"Looks like we were both wrong."

"You are your father's daughter, after all." Bernadette reached for Amy's hand. "I know you were reluctant to come to Tremont. But you did. And now you've seen the inn and the life your father had here. That's what matters."

"Still, I wish things had been different."

Giving Amy's hand a pat, Bernadette rose from the couch. "You and I have decisions to make, and I've been putting you off for days."

"We do have a lot to talk about." Amy leaned back against the sofa cushions, emotionally drained.

"You don't look like you're up to it now, though. Shall we wait another day or two?"

Amy agreed that would be best. The conflicting information and feelings she'd experienced this morning were like so much scrambled egg in her head. She had to sort it all out. With Greg's photo album tucked under her arm, Amy left the cottage and started out on a brisk walk through town.

Although she appreciated Bernadette's reassurances, Amy still felt terrible. She walked and walked, trying to resolve today's revelations in her mind. Intellectually she could understand Greg's actions over the years, and her own, as well. Yet her heart remained in confusion. How could she begin to reconcile the resentment and guilt, the anger and sadness? She wiped a warm tear from her cheek.

At that moment, Tremont felt like a lonely cage. She wasn't ready to go back to the inn, but taking off in her car was no remedy, either. She'd still be alone with painful thoughts. As she slowly walked back up the hill toward the inn, the photo album close against her chest, Amy thought of Paul. He was the one person she could talk to about all this.

Her heart lightened as she rambled up the rest of the hill. She no longer felt the cold. Remembering it was Sunday, Amy realized his office would be closed and she'd have to track him down at home. But she was sure someone at the inn could give her directions.

Amy was so intent on getting to Paul that she didn't see the person standing in the gazebo when she passed by.

"Amy, wait, I've been looking for you."

The deep, rich timber of the caller's voice felt like balm on her aching heart. Yet her emotions were in such a jumble, she didn't know whether to laugh or cry. As she turned around, Paul was hurrying down the gazebo steps to meet her.

His smile of delight vanished into concern. "What happened? You look like you've just lost your best friend."

"No, I—I—" Pausing to still the trembling in her throat, Amy peered up into Paul's sky blue eyes. They encouraged her to go on. She took a deep breath and held up the photo album. "Actually, I've found my father."

"This is Greg's?" He took the book from her. After a quick perusal of its pages, Paul let out a long, low whistle. "This must have been a shock," he said, putting an arm around her shoulder.

His tender gesture was almost enough to undo her. She steeled herself against the emotions rumbling within her, and squinted hard to keep errant tears at bay. The situation was ridiculous. Never having cried in front of a man before coming to Tremont, Amy couldn't believe she'd already wept once in front of Paul. If it happened again, he'd be convinced she was a blithering crybaby.

Although she managed to hold back the tears, Amy couldn't keep her shoulders from shaking or her lips from trembling. Paul held her close to his chest.

"Let's go inside where it's warm," he said gently. "Then you can tell me what happened."

"Not there." She pulled back. "I can't deal with the inn right now."

"Then you don't have to." Paul looked down at her, the concern on his face deepening. Clutching her hand, he started down the hill. "Come on. I know where we can go."

Moving at a brisk clip, they reached the town center quickly. Paul led her past the general store and the school before turning onto a side street near the tiny post office. Finally, he stopped at a two-story brick building that was of a vintage more recent than the quaint structures lining the main thoroughfare. It was probably only forty or fifty years old, Amy thought wryly as she read the sign hanging out front.

"Valley News Group." She turned to Paul, who was searching his pockets for keys. "Your company?"

He nodded. "And it's closed up tight today. So you'll have all the privacy you need."

Paul apologized for the drafty temperature as they climbed the stairs to his second floor offices. "Shutting down completely on the weekends is our newest cost-saving measure."

When they entered his icy cubicle of an office, Paul switched on the space heater and put on a pot of coffee. Making sure she was warm enough and comfortable in his leather desk chair, he pulled up another chair for himself when the coffee was ready. The hot mug he gave her warmed her hands; his amiable banter and kind gaze helped ease her anguish. She no longer felt on the verge of tears.

Opening Greg's album on his desk, Paul looked through it more carefully this time, while Amy described what had been happening in a few of the shots. When he reached the last picture, of Amy playfully leaning on the Sold sign in front of her new home, he shook his head with amazement.

"How in the heck did Greg get his hands on these?"

Once she started explaining about her stepfather's secret endeavor, the rest of the story soon came tumbling out.

"I'm just so confused about how I feel," Amy admitted, gripping the coffee mug between her palms. "On the one hand, I'm sad about what my father and I missed, and I'm moved by this unbelievable photo album. But I'm angry, too. What kind of man would desert his child in the first place? And if he loved me, why didn't he try harder to get me back?"

Her words seemed to trouble Paul. "Amy, that doesn't have anything to do with how much he loved you," he protested. "You can't know what kind of turmoil he was going through."

"Do you?"

Paul's shoulders stiffened, but he did not reply.

"I'm sorry," she offered quickly. "I didn't mean to snap at you. But if my father was in turmoil, he still somehow managed to meet Bernadette, buy the inn and raise her daughters.

"You know, I'm ashamed to admit it," she continued, feeling somewhat sheepish, "but I'm jealous of Bridget and Maura and the life they shared with him."

"I'd say that was a fair reaction—nothing to be ashamed of. Don't be so hard on yourself, Amy. You've had a rough time," Paul insisted. "And besides, Bernadette shouldn't have dumped all this on you without any warning."

It was the first time she'd heard him criticize his aunt.

"She didn't know, Paul. She thought she was help-ing," Amy assured him. "I'm glad I know about the photo album, and about the hand my stepfather had in it."

"You never had any inkling about that?"

"None." Amy put her empty coffee mug on the desk. "After my mother, Thomas Windom is the last person I would have expected to be involved. That's the irony of the whole thing."

"I take it there was no love lost between your moth-er's husbands."

"One would've thought so," she said with a shrug. "You see, Thomas tried to legally adopt me after he married my mother."

"Tried to?"

"My father put up a huge fight—even went into debt to block it. At the time, he told me I would always be his little girl and nobody else's. Of course, that was a few years before he took off."

"Windom didn't try again after Greg disappeared?"

Paul's question startled her because she'd never given it much thought. "Thomas was disappointed the first time around, I know. And then, he and my mother tried to have children of their own, but couldn't. To tell the truth, I'm not sure why he didn't give it another try."

"Maybe he was afraid Greg would show up and cause more trouble," Paul offered as he reached for the cof-feepot. "Want some more?"

She held out her mug to him for a refill. "Now that I think about it, Thomas never said a negative word about Greg. In fact, he used to bend over backward to help me understand him."

A thoughtful look came over Paul's face. "He seems like a great guy."

"Thomas has always been good to me. But that doesn't make up for the way I lost my real father."

"No. Of course it doesn't," he agreed. "But tell me, where does your mother fit in all of this?"

She couldn't help the rueful chuckle. "My mother never said a positive word about my father. And she still doesn't."

"She sounds bitter."

"Extremely."

Paul pushed aside their coffee mugs and took her two hands in his. "Mind if I make a suggestion?"

His reassuring touch made her skin tingle. His discerning gaze was so compelling, Amy nodded without so much as a second thought. Paul had been there for her without question, listening without judging as she confided to him the trouble in her heart. She placed a high value on that kind of support.

He squeezed her hands warmly. "Talk to your mother, Amy. Get her to tell you what really happened with Greg all those years ago."

"Paul, I've tried. Many times."

"Try again," he urged. "She may give you some clues to what this sadness and bitterness in your family are about."

"I thought I'd find those answers at the Blue Sky."

"Instead, you just found more questions."

"I'm sure some wise soul along the line told me there are no easy answers," she mused. "My visit here proves it."

"Are you sorry you came?"

"Is that a leading question?"

"You bet," he replied, a sly, teasing gleam lighting his eyes.

Amy tried to think of a snappy retort, but the way his thumb caressed her hand was distracting. After the morning's intensity, she was happy to focus on his touch, his smile and how good he made her feel.

"I'm glad you happened by this morning. I don't know what I would have done—"

"I didn't just happen by, Amy. I told you last night I'd be back." His eyes narrowed as he leaned back in his chair. "Didn't you believe me?"

"Yes, I believed you."

Amy meant it. Last night, his kisses had made her want to believe everything about him. After he'd gone home, however, a tiny bedeviling part of her had questioned his sincerity, his motives. It was foolish, of course, an automatic reflex undeserving of attention. She had no reason to doubt Paul.

"I want to spend the day with you, Amy. We can do anything you want."

What she wanted was to be in his arms again, on the receiving end of his dynamite kisses. But she suggested a tour through the valley, instead.

"And dinner afterward," he added, getting their coats. "Just not at the inn."

Amy brightened. "I loved Fred's Bar-B-Que Bash."

Helping with her jacket, Paul laughed. "I had something more atmospheric in mind for tonight. But I'll take you back to Fred's soon. Promise."

Atmospheric. All sorts of pleasant possibilities prickled Amy's imagination as they headed back to the inn. Although the weather was cold and gray, she sensed her day with Paul would continue to glow with warmth. Having him all to herself—away from Tremont, Bernadette, the inn—was an enticing prospect.

She couldn't wait to get going.

When they reached the crest of the hill, they began discussing whose vehicle to take. "My car will be much more comfortable than your pickup on a long drive like this," Amy asserted.

"I don't know. Some of the back roads around here are rough." Paul glanced up at the murky sky. "Besides, it's going to rain—we'll probably hit some icy stretches. The truck will handle it better."

Amy followed him into the inn's parking lot. "My car has top-of-the-line, all-weather radial tires, and antilock brakes, too."

At that moment, a person ran out of the inn. A compact figure dashed toward them, and Amy immediately recognized the auburn head popping up from the folds of an overstuffed purple, down parka. It was Maura calling Amy's name.

"You're finally back," Maura gasped, nearly out of breath, looking annoyed. "Mom didn't know you were with Paul. And I've been waiting forever."

Amy was puzzled. "Were we supposed to get together?"

"No! I've just come from Bridget's. Everybody's got the flu out there."

"Bridget, too?"

Maura shook her head. "She's fine. Well, as fine as anybody can be under the circumstances. But she could use a hand."

"She needs my help?" Amy asked.

"That's why I came. She needs you to do something for her." Maura cast a nervous glance at Paul before turning back to Amy. "I'll take you there right now."

Chapter Nine

Paul stepped in between Amy and his cousin. "Are the kids okay?"

"Don't worry. They seem to have a mild case. Cabin fever is their biggest problem right now. George came home from work last night sick as a dog, though," Maura said, moving around him to put her arm through Amy's. "Come on, Amy. Bridget wants to see you."

Ignoring Paul, Maura started tugging her toward the Jeep. Amy wasn't sure what to do. She had her heart set on going with Paul, although she was concerned about Bridget, too. Of course, if she thought Bridget truly needed help she'd go there in a flash. Yet something about Maura's story didn't ring true.

"Paul and I were just about—"

"You can call him later, I promise."

"Well, if you're sure Bridget really wants me . . ."

Paul was right on their heels. "Maura, what the heck are you up to?"

"Gee," Maura muttered, stopping in her tracks. "I'm just trying to do a favor for my poor sister—your cousin—who's been alone for days with two sick kids. And now her husband's sick. Don't you think she deserves some company?"

"If that's what this is all about, why don't I come along, too?"

"I give up!" Maura threw up her hands. "Fine, Paul, suit yourself. But I have room for only one other person in the Jeep. You'll have to follow in your truck."

Before Amy had a chance to say anything, Maura yanked her away.

"I'll meet you at Bridget's," Paul called after her.

As she climbed into the Jeep, Amy didn't know whether to yell or laugh. This stunt of Maura's was totally absurd.

"You're nuts, absolutely nuts," she said as Maura started up the engine. "Bridget's not really in such dire straits, is she?"

"Hey, I did my part," Maura replied, peering over her shoulder as she backed out of the parking space. "This is her baby now. But she's sure gonna be surprised to see Paul."

She glared at Maura. "You're not going to tell me what this is about, are you?"

"You'll know soon enough. Trust me."

"Maura!"

"Look, I'm sorry if I spoiled whatever plans you had. But Bridget had me backed into a corner. She told me it was either you or Dirk Campbell. And I'd rather eat raw meat than go to him."

Because Maura was a vegetarian, Amy knew she meant business, so she dropped the subject. Still, she remained mystified.

Within minutes, they were pulling into the long, unpaved driveway leading to Bridget's house. Glancing through the rear window, Amy saw Paul following close behind in the red pickup.

"Here we are at the sick house," Maura announced, stopping at the front door. "Hope you've had flu shots."

"Get them every year—I work with kids."

Amy waited for Paul to catch up and went inside with him. Bridget's eyes widened when she saw Paul, but otherwise she acted pleased to see them both. She looked a little tired, but not nearly as decimated as Maura had initially described. Amy was not surprised.

Her husband, George, was upstairs in bed, too ill from this flu to lift his head, according to Bridget. Little Willy, padding around in pajamas, appeared to be recovering nicely, and he soon was all over Paul, begging him to set up his toy-train set. Jenny, still a little wan and glassy eyed, was on the couch cuddled beneath several layers of handmade afghans, watching cartoons on TV.

The house had been recently built and was contemporary in style. The first floor was practically one big room, with the kitchen and dining area opening onto an expansive family room. Toy cars and trucks, dolls and stuffed animals were scattered about, a sewing machine sat open on the kitchen table and a rustic-looking wood stove was spewing supplemental heat.

Amy couldn't remember the last time she'd been in a house this *lived in*. The homes of friends in her circle tended toward the expensively designed and coordinated abodes pictured in glossy coffee-table magazines. Still, she liked the comfortable family feel of Bridget's attractive home.

When Bridget insisted they eat the sandwiches she'd prepared, Amy and Paul exchanged glances. The dining-area table—all set and ready for guests—was one more confirmation that Maura had misrepresented Bridget's "crisis" situation. Yet Maura behaved as if nothing were askew, eating most of the sizable salad and chatting gayly during the entire luncheon.

They'd both been snookered by the Ryan girls. Thinking glumly of what might have been with Paul this afternoon, Amy wanted to strangle both Ryan sisters. One look at Paul's face told her he was feeling similarly inclined.

"So, Bridge, Maura says you're having a rough go of it," Paul said, helping to clear the table after lunch.

Her face turned pink. "I was going a little stir-crazy, especially when the kids were at their worst. That's why I'm glad to have some company."

Busy stacking the dirty plates, Amy wondered when she'd find out the real reason Bridget wanted to see her. She had the distinct impression Paul wasn't supposed to be part of that picture. Yet he was close by their sides, helping out in the kitchen.

Paul took the sponge from Bridget's hand. "The three of us will finish up in here. You should lie down and relax a bit while you have the chance."

"And miss this opportunity for adult conversation? No way."

Bridget sat on one of the counter stools and began chatting with them while they worked. She discussed her erratic newspaper delivery with Paul and asked Maura if she was getting many Christmas shoppers at New Worlds.

Then she turned to Amy. "I've been out of touch with Mom and the inn these past few days," she said as Amy loaded the dishwasher. "Have you decided what to do about the Blue Sky yet?"

"Not yet," Amy replied. So much had been happening, so much had changed from day to day. She'd come to Tremont with every intention of unloading her half of the inn, one way or another. Now, she realized, the path ahead was no longer quite that clear.

Maura handed over one more dirty glass for the dishwasher. "For what it's worth, Amy, I'm still on Mom's side. Stick around, help her keep the inn going."

"I'll keep that in mind, Maura."

"You told Mom you'd be leaving by Christmas," Bridget reminded her. "That'll be here before you know it. You're going to decide before then, aren't you?"

"Or will you stay here through Christmas?" Maura chimed in hopefully. "Wouldn't that be great, Paul?"

"Wait a minute," Amy interjected before Paul could react. "I promised *my mother* that I'd be home in time for Christmas. And my partner will have my head if I don't get back to the office after the holidays."

Actually, Julie and the agency were doing just fine without her, and Amy had begun to feel the daily phone calls were pointless. Although she cared about her pint-size clients, feeling temporarily dispensable didn't bother her that much. Her business life seemed so disconnected from the emotional cyclone she'd been caught up in these past weeks.

"But, Amy, you must be leaning one way or the other by now," Bridget prodded.

"And haven't you and Mom been discussing this?" added Maura.

"Come on, you two, leave Amy alone," Paul said, stepping into the fray. "She'll decide when the time is right for her. Okay?"

With an incredible mélange of emotions welling inside her, Amy gazed at Paul with grateful eyes. This man, this self-appointed guardian angel of the Ryan women, this very same tall, gorgeous hunk of man was defending *her* now. Over the inn yet! Things were changing very fast indeed.

As Paul winked at her from across the room, Willy crept in, pushing a bright blue plastic storage box on the floor. "Are you done eating your sandwich, Paul? Can you fix my train now?"

"Let's check with your mom," Paul said, turning to Bridget. "He told me George had promised to set it up before he got sick. Do you mind if I do it?"

"Are you kidding?" Bridget hopped off the stool. "I'll be forever in your debt. He's been dragging that box around for two days."

"Where do we put it?" Paul asked. "In the family room?"

"We usually set it up in there by the bookcases."

As Paul stooped to pick up the heavy storage box, Amy caught Maura poking an elbow into her sister's ribs. Then Maura pointed to the upstairs as Bridget nodded. Amy kept a straight face, pretending not to notice the sisters' antics. Her curiosity, however, was aroused.

"On second thought, Paul," Bridget said quickly, "Maybe you should set it up in his room. We'll be putting up the Christmas tree in the family room soon—that train will just be in the way."

"Upstairs it is, then. Come on, pal."

Willy started bouncing with excitement. "Wait till you see my train, Amy."

"Maybe Amy would like to help us," Paul said to Willy while looking directly at her with smiling eyes.

The sexy gleam in his eye sent little shivers down her spine, provoking her to return the smile. "I'd love to," she murmured.

"But let me show you the house first," Bridget declared, clamping her hand on Amy's arm. "It won't take long."

Maura tossed her dish towel onto the counter. "I'll help the guys."

Paul looked from one sister to the other. The two of them were as transparent as plastic wrap. They were cooking something up, all right. Damned if he knew what it was, though.

"Never mind, Maura. Willy and I can manage on our own. I'm sure you don't want to miss the house tour," he added with a deliberate tinge of scorn. Just so they'd realize he wasn't one bit fooled.

"I'll be up soon," Amy called after them as he and Willy headed upstairs.

He glanced back at the lovely, petite brunette standing between his tall, fiery-haired cousins. Heaven help Amy if those two were in their Lucy-and-Ethel antics mode.

Reminding Willy to keep his voice down because his daddy was sleeping, Paul led the boy upstairs to his room. Balancing the blue box in his arms, Paul switched on the light and found dozens of action figures and building blocks strewn across the floor.

"Why don't you pick up your toys to clear a space for the train?" he suggested to Willy, "and I'll start going through this box."

The boy agreed readily and began tossing the wooden blocks into a bin against the wall. Paul put the box down on the floor and sat beside it. As he sorted through the train-set pieces, Willy gathered the colorful action figures into a plastic milk crate.

"Look at this one, Paul," he said, holding up a mouse in alien attire and a jazzy silver motorbike. "Auntie Maura bought me this because I was sick."

Before he dropped each figure into the crate, Willy described each character in detail, from alien mice to GIs to turtles. Paul listened, fascinated by the imaginative attributes the kid assigned to his hero figures. The scamp was all boy, and an articulate one at that.

Paul recalled when he had returned to Tremont. Willy had been maybe two or three months old at the time. Now he was a talkative, rambunctious preschooler—a completely different being from the infant Paul had held in his arms. The change in four short years was startling. But that's how it was with children, he told himself; they and their worlds changed quickly.

He thought about Shelly's letter. After four years of their own momentous changes, why was his ex-wife proposing a visit? What possible good could come out of seeing them again? What would be the point? They didn't know each other anymore.

"All done!" Willy announced. He plopped down next to Paul, stretching out on his belly.

His eagerness made Paul chuckle. "Good timing, pal. We're ready to lay out the tracks." Paul glanced at his watch, wondering how much longer his cousins would hold Amy captive.

Paul had forgotten that setting up a miniature train was so time-consuming. By the time he had wired the tracks and connected all the cars, Willy had grown bored and had hauled out his action figures again. And Amy hadn't yet appeared.

After testing the power box, Paul called the boy over. With Willy nestled in his lap, they pulled the switch together, watching intently as the motor buzzed with electricity.

"All aboard," Paul called.

"Choo-choo-ooh-ooh," Willy sang out.

The tiny car came to sluggish life, gradually picking up speed as it moved forward. Willy let out a whooping cheer. Applause broke out behind them.

Paul turned to find Amy clapping. "It looks great, guys," she said.

"Finally back from your tour?" he teased.

She grinned. "I'll tell you all about it later."

"All?" He shot her a skeptical look.

"Every single word that was said. I promise." She crossed her heart with her hand.

Willy waved her to come over. "Watch me make it go backward, Amy."

She sat on the floor with them, her subtle scent stirring Paul's memories of last night. He watched her watch Willy switch the power into reverse and he listened to her giggle with him over how funny the train looked going in the opposite direction. When Willy handed Amy the controls, Paul felt her delight as she sent the train cruising at breakneck speed.

He gazed at her out of the corner of his eye, an unexpected contentment washing over him. Sitting here, warm and snug with Amy and the child while the cold sky darkened outside, felt right. For Paul, it was a moment lush with belonging—something he'd rarely experienced in his life. He wanted to bask in the sensation while it lasted, because he knew it couldn't last long.

The spell was broken when Maura stuck in her head to say she was leaving. "You'll take Amy back to the inn, won't you, Paul?"

"I had planned to."

A few minutes after Maura left, Bridget brought Jenny in to see the train. By then it was completely dark outside, and rain could be heard pelting the roof. It sounded as if it might be freezing up.

"Paul, you're a natural at this stuff," Bridget noted as he adjusted a derailed caboose. "You should have yourself some kids."

Her comment zinged a nerve. Yet in a way he was glad, because it snapped him back to reality. Willy and Amy were not his. Being with them like this had been sweet, but he should have known better than to drift too long in this fantasy of belonging. He'd given up hope of that long ago.

Bridget invited them to stay for supper, but he and Amy agreed they should leave. The weather had taken a turn for the worse, and now it was sleeting heavily.

"I should get you back to the inn right away," he said as they carefully walked the few slick steps between the house and his truck. "These narrow backroads around here ice up fast."

"Then I am glad we have your truck instead of my car." Amy winked before climbing into the truck.

Although the drive back to the Blue Sky took longer than the usual five minutes, Paul had little trouble steering his truck up the slippery, steep hill leading to the inn. Still, they both breathed easier when they pulled into the parking lot.

He turned off the engine and turned to Amy. "Now, I believe you promised to tell me all about your so-called house tour."

"So-called?" she echoed with a laugh. "I told them you weren't fooled."

"What are those two plotting?"

Amy put a hand on his shoulder. "Paul, it's a long story. How about I buy you a hot chocolate? Then we'll talk."

They walked arm in arm through the main hall into the Pub Room. There were plenty of guests milling about, kept in by the ice storm. The Pub Room was buzzing with business. Paul noticed that Joey, the regular Sunday-night bartender, had brought his brother along to help.

"I guess our services won't be needed tonight," he murmured in Amy's ear.

She went up to the bar to order hot chocolates while he snagged one of the few remaining tables. He looked around the crowded room. What an apt ending for a day he had hoped to spend alone with Amy, he thought dryly. He hadn't counted on two plotting cousins, an ice storm and a packed house. Fate had not been kind.

Yet as he watched her carry two steaming mugs across the room, her pert body maneuvering through the crowd with agility, Paul figured he was still the luckiest man in the room. Fate be damned. He'd take Amy Riordan any way he could get her.

Placing the hot chocolates on the table, she sat down across from him. "These are very hot."

Paul scarcely heard. He was too busy feasting on her eyes. Somehow her thick, teal turtleneck sweater made them appear even bluer. He hadn't thought it possible.

"I'm sorry about today," he said, his gaze still locked on hers. "About Maura and Bridget disrupting our plans, I mean."

"I was disappointed, too. But now I know it was for a good cause." Her eyes twinkled like starry sapphires.

"Good cause? I thought those two were cooking up some secret scheme."

"A secret scheme for a good cause," she explained. "Except now it stops being secret. That's where you come in."

"Me? You were the one they were hot to get out to the house." Paul lifted the cup to his lips, keeping an eye on her over the rim.

"They wanted me to help," she said, cupping her hands around the mug. "You see, George's attack of flu has caused a real problem. Bridget thought I might be able to persuade you to help."

"Since when do I need persuading to help my own relatives?" he asked, baffled. This just didn't sound right. "I'd help them any way possible. Anytime!"

"Don't speak too soon, Paul. This is kind of an unusual request," Amy warned, clearly trying not to smile. "Although I think you should give it serious consideration."

Somehow he knew he wasn't going to like this. He leaned in resignation. "Okay, give it to me straight."

"They want you to take George's place as Safety Santa."

"As what?"

"Safety Santa. Don't you know about it?"

Her glared at her. "I know it's something that makes George dress up in a dang fool Santa suit every year. That's all I need to know."

"I take it you don't think much of the idea."

"Why can't they get one of George's buddies from the firehouse to do it?"

"Apparently George wasn't the only one from the fire station stricken with flu. Their duty roster is already down to a skeleton crew. They can't spare anybody."

"You're awfully knowledgeable about all this."

"Why do you think the 'house tour' took so long?" she said with a shrug. "Bridget made sure I knew everything. She's convinced that if she or Maura asked you to do this, you'd refuse."

"Bridget is right."

"Didn't I just hear you say you'd do anything for your relatives?"

Paul tapped restless fingers on the table as he contemplated Amy. It dawned on him that she actually thought he should do it.

"If it involves their health, well-being, livelihood, children or ultimate happiness, I'm theirs," he told her. "But expecting me to parade around in an overstuffed red suit goes over the line. Way over the line."

"Come on, Paul, where's—"

He put up a hand to stop her. "Please don't ask me where my Christmas spirit is."

"Sorry." She stared down at her hot chocolate.

"Look, sweetheart, it's not in my nature to go around town ho-hoing my head off," he tried to explain, her wounded look hitting a bull's-eye on his conscience. "I'm not that kind of man."

"If it makes you that uncomfortable, of course you shouldn't do it."

Thank goodness she saw the light.

"I'd really make a terrible Santa Claus. The kids would be disappointed."

Amy sighed. "They may be disappointed anyway. George will never be well enough by Friday night to do it. And from what I gather, Bridget's already exhausted all other possibilities.''

"You mean I was the last resort?''

She nodded, but told him not to worry.

It then dawned on Paul that Amy hadn't given up. "So you're saying if I don't do it, there will be no Safety Santa.''

"It's a shame. Bridget has told me how much the program means to George. He'll feel terrible about letting kids down. Then again, there's always next year.''

"Am I really the absolute last resort?''

"'Fraid so.''

It sounded like an apology, as if she thought his resistance was weakening. Which it was, Paul realized with some ire. He couldn't believe he was even considering such a thing! Now he knew how Amy had built a successful business—she was one shrewd cookie. Yet what a great way she had about her, he mused with admiration.

He refused to be a complete pushover, however. If he was going to actually submit to the indignities of bushy, white brows and a jelly belly, Paul figured he should get at least one perk.

"Okay, Amy, you win. I'll be Safety Santa.''

"I knew you wouldn't let the children down.'' Beaming, she reached across the table to clasp his hands.

"I have one condition, though,'' he informed her, feeling uncommonly lighthearted. "You have to come with me.''

"You want me to go with you to all those houses?''

"Hey, even Santa has helpers. And it *is* for a good cause.''

Amy stared back at him, clearly realizing she'd been cornered. Her lips quivered with the beginnings of an unstoppable grin and then her shoulders vibrated with laughter. The low, drawling peal of her laugh tantalized him with its bewitching resonance. Paul loved the sound of it.

He loved the effect she had on him even more.

Finally, she breathed in deeply. "You have yourself a deal, sir."

Her beguiling smile sparked another rush of warmth through his veins. His entire body quickened with excitement.

"In that case," he began, his voice growing more husky as the heat inside him intensified, "I suggest we go out to the veranda and seal it with a kiss."

Chapter Ten

Amy gazed out from her room's front window, watching for Paul's red truck. The cold, overcast day was quickly dissolving into dusk; off-and-on snow flurries dusted the inn's grounds. A big snowstorm had been predicted to hit by tomorrow afternoon. She studied the darkening sky, wondering if the storm would actually hold off till then.

She hoped so. Her car was packed with wrapped Christmas toys and a Santa costume was down at the front desk, pressed and ready. Tonight was Safety Santa night.

All she needed now was Mr. Claus.

But Paul had been called to Richmond three days ago on urgent business, his return continuously delayed by "problems" he hadn't even tried to explain. And Amy didn't ask. If he wanted her to know, he'd tell her.

She couldn't wait to see him again, though. His latest run to Richmond had come at the worst time, when so many things—said and unsaid—were up in the air between them. And the clock was ticking on her time here in Tremont. Although Paul had called her from his hotel every night, these phone conversations lacked the immediacy needed by two people starting out on the tricky tightrope of mutual discovery. Amy couldn't help feeling disappointed. She had believed Paul when he said he'd be there for her.

She pushed this niggling kernel of doubt from her mind. Paul hadn't actually done anything to undercut her trust, Amy reminded herself. Business demands popped up even at the most inopportune times—as she knew all too well.

Finally, the red pickup rolled into sight. "Hallelujah," Amy sang out, her heart leaping with excitement. She flew out of her room, making it down the two flights before Paul reached the inn's front steps.

"Safety Santa comes through. I was afraid you were having second thoughts," she teased in an attempt to put a lid on her eagerness. A thirty-one-year-old woman shouldn't act like a giddy teenager, no matter how much she felt like one inside.

"O ye of so little faith." He slid an arm around her waist.

Paul's eyes devoured her as he lowered his mouth to hers. The frigid air still clung to his hair, his skin, his overcoat, making her shiver in his embrace. But his lips tasted warm when he kissed her, and her internal body heat shot up like a rocket.

They finally broke apart when they heard Bernadette enter the hall, pointedly clearing her throat.

"I just caught the latest weather report on the radio. Looks like that storm front has picked up speed," Bernadette said. "You two should have something to eat and then get a move on. Maybe you can get to all the houses before the storm hits."

Amy agreed. One thing she really hated was driving in bad weather. Also, she didn't want a single Tremont child to miss his Safety Santa visit. After helping at the firehouse with the preparations for the big night, Amy had gotten into the spirit of the safety program.

She was in high holiday spirits, as well, following days of lending a hand with decorating the Blue Sky for the holidays. Christmas music filled the common rooms, while eggnog and mulled cider flowed and Martin kept cooking up delectable cookies and candies. The good cheer among the inn's guests and the townspeople was contagious. Amy hadn't felt such excitement about the Christmas holidays since she was a little girl.

Bernadette had their dinner served in the dining room right away, and they ate quickly. As they finished up their coffee, Paul called Bernadette over to the table. "Did a special delivery package come here for me?"

"Something came yesterday, as a matter of fact. It's in my office," she told him. "What is it?"

"Just a little surprise for my friend here." He winked at Amy.

"What kind of surprise?" Amy asked, the gleam in Paul's eyes a little too sly for comfort.

"Guess we'd better hurry and see." He stood up and held out his hand to her. "Shall we?"

As they swept past the front desk, Amy grabbed the box containing the Santa costume. Inside Bernadette's office, Paul found the large, padded packet on a side worktable. "Here you go." He held out the package. "Open it."

She held out the box. "Don't you think you should be changing into this?"

"No, you go first." Taking the box from her, Paul handed her the package.

Mystified, she tore it open. "What on earth?" she gasped as she pulled out a one-piece Lycra pantsuit in leaf green. Fluffy, white fake fur trimmed the collar and edged the sleeve and pant hems. Next came a green stocking cap with a thick, white pom-pom at the tip. Paul had to be joking.

He looked immensely pleased with himself. "I had it rushed from a costume house in New York. I'm pretty sure I guessed the right size," he added, his admiring eyes traveling the length of her body. "Don't you love it?"

"Very funny, Paul. But you certainly don't expect me to wear this thing, do you? I'm not supposed to be in costume."

"You agreed to be my helper didn't you?" he said, his arms opened wide. "Who ever heard of a Santa's helper dressed in blue jeans and a parka?"

"I never agreed to—you never said that—ah, come on Paul, an *elf* costume?"

"Why should I be the only one stuck with a pom-pom dangling from my head? Besides, you'll look fantastic. Promise."

Muttering, Amy led a gleeful Paul upstairs to her room so they could transform themselves into their holiday personas. At least no one from Washington would ever know about the elf suit. She took comfort in that.

Since the Santa costume was more intricate, she offered to help Paul first. She spread the cherry red Santa pieces out on the bed while Paul stripped down to his jeans. Wrapping the special padding around his middle, she couldn't keep her eyes off his sinewy shoulders and taut, muscular back. It seemed such a shame to bury his hard body beneath cushy mounds of fake flesh.

Leaving Paul to deal with the rest of his costume, she took the elf suit into the bathroom. As she pulled the snug knit fabric over her body, she realized how warm it would keep her on this very cold night. In her mind, that was the only good thing about the silly outfit.

"Don't say a word," Amy warned when she emerged from the bathroom.

Paul, practically entombed in his roly-poly costume, greeted her with a wolfish whistle, instead.

Ignoring him, she pulled a pair of warm boots from the closet and then plunked herself down on the edge of the bed. "I feel like Batwoman decked out for St. Patrick's Day," she complained, yanking the first boot over her foot.

"Well, you look fantastic." Paul waddled to her side, giving the unitard's body-clinging fit his undivided attention. "Downright sexy, really."

His hand skimmed slowly over her hip and thigh, causing a distracting spurt of fluttering in her lower body. She closed her eyes for a pleasurable moment. She couldn't, however, close her mind to the jarring image of beardless Santa and his sickly green elf side by side on the bed.

She brushed away Paul's hand. "No fraternizing with the help, Santa."

Amy helped him apply the fluffy white eyebrows. A flowing wig and beard completed his transformation into Safety Santa. After adjusting his fur-trimmed cap, she stepped back, amazed. She would never have recognized

Paul under that suit. "You *are* Santa Claus," she told him.

Bellowing out a deep ho-ho-ho, Paul tossed the costume's huge toy sack over his shoulder. He turned to her with a wink and a grin. "Let's hit the road, sweetheart."

She threw her coat over her costume and followed him out. On their way downstairs, they were stopped several times by passing guests wanting to wish Santa a Merry Christmas. Paul greeted every one with handshakes and a very cheery Merry Christmas. For a man who had initially balked at the job, Paul was throwing himself into the role with surprising gusto.

When they reached the main hall, Bernadette whooped with delight, attracting all sorts of attention from the parties milling about the common rooms. She fussed at Paul's beard and hat. "I never thought I'd see the day!" she exclaimed, giving Paul a big kiss on the cheek. "Now, wait a minute while I get my camera."

By the time the two of them were able to extract themselves from the inn, it was still only flurrying and nothing was sticking.

"Maybe the snow will hold off after all," Paul said as they approached her car.

Two volunteers at the firehouse had helped load dozens of wrapped gifts into the trunk and back seat early this afternoon. To sign up for a visit from Safety Santa, parents had brought nonperishable food or cash donations for the area food bank to the firehouse along with small, prewrapped toys for Santa to give to their kids after the safety check.

"Don't even think about driving," Amy remarked when Paul opened the door on the driver's side. "You'll never fit behind the wheel."

He looked down at his new belly. "Guess you're right."

"A map and a list complete with children's names are in the glove compartment. You can navigate," Amy said as she turned on the ignition. "Did Bridget instruct you on what to do?"

"Went through it with me on the phone, step by step."

Their route began in the heart of Tremont, with five houses in the town center alone. By the third stop, Amy and Paul had their routine down pat. With the appropriate gifts already loaded into Paul's sack, Amy parked her car at a safe distance so as not to be seen. Then she led the way to each front door, shaking a strap of sleigh bells to signal Santa's arrival.

The children's reactions to them ranged from fear to timid wonder to giddy elation. In most instances, Paul won over the frightened ones with an easygoing rendition of Santa cheerfulness and by eliciting their help when he checked the fireplaces and peered up the chimneys. The same technique worked in calming the few kids having trouble controlling their excitement. He had them eating out of his hand. As someone who worked with children every day, Amy was impressed.

Snow was falling lightly when they headed toward the outskirts of town. The houses and farms they had to visit were spread out over the countryside. Miles separated each stop.

The drive on winding, often narrow roads was hampered by poor visibility as the snow intensified. Still, Amy clamped her hands on the steering wheel, breathed in deep and pushed on. After experiencing such fun and joy at each home, she and Paul couldn't stand the thought of disappointing the children still waiting.

By the time they reached the final home on the list, the fast-falling snow was forming a worrisome glaze on the ground. Jack and Mary Frame greeted them with surprise and gratitude.

"We thought for sure you'd given up. The radio is predicting eight to twelve inches," Mary Frame whispered to Amy as Paul ho-hoed his way into the living room. "But now that you're here, maybe the boys will stop fighting about Santa Claus."

Paul stood in the middle of the room, shaking his head. He turned to Amy. "Well, well, my little elf, look what we have here."

Amy followed his gaze from one side of the room to the other. On the floor by a Christmas tree sat a mop-topped little boy in fire-engine red Dr. Denton's, crying his eyes out. He couldn't have been more than three. Across the room sat a seven- or eight-year-old, in pj's and robe, looking very sullen as he stared down at the floor. She could see that Santa and his elf were in trouble now.

Paul tried to comfort the little one, but he wouldn't stop crying. Finally, Paul—with some difficulty—lowered his bulky Santa body down on the floor next to the child. This machination definitely got the boy's attention.

"That's better," Paul noted as the little boy's sobbing gradually ceased. "Tell Santa why you're sad?"

He glared at his older brother. "Joey says you're not the real Santa!"

Joey looked stricken as all eyes turned to him. "And you're nothing but a crybaby tattletale, Andy," he lashed out.

Andy started bawling all over again. Paul stayed beside him, gently patting his small back. "Well, Andy, Joey's right. I'm not the real Santa."

"You're not real?" wailed Andy. Big brother Joey sat up in his chair, taking note.

"Oh, I'm *real* all right. Just touch me." Paul held out his fur-trimmed sleeve. "Feel real, don't I?"

Andy nodded.

"But I'm Safety Santa—sort of a high-ranking helper to the real Santa." He looked up at the older boy, offering him a chance to save face. "You know about Santa's helpers, don't you, Joey?"

Joey nodded solemnly, appearing much less embarrassed than he had minutes earlier. "Like the Santas in the stores are just helpers, too."

"That's right. Because the real Santa is so busy making toys and getting the reindeer ready, he needs all the help he can get," Paul explained. "And I'm helping make sure all the fireplaces and chimneys are safe for him on Christmas Eve. Wouldn't want Santa thrown off his delivery schedule by any mishaps."

"But you look just like Santa," protested Andy.

Paul glanced up at Amy, his eyes pleading for mercy. But she urged him on with a encouraging wave of her hand. He was doing just fine on his own. For a man who, apparently, had little close contact with children, Paul had an innate manner with them that was marvelous. He didn't fawn over them or talk down to them; he was just himself.

"You think I look just like the real Santa, eh?" Paul reiterated in an obvious attempt to collect his thoughts. "That's because I'm his first cousin, and resemblances run strong up in the North Pole. That's why all us Santas look alike."

Amy noticed Joey was sitting forward in the chair, his attention absorbed by Paul's explanation. Clearly he'd bought the story hook, line and sinker—just like his little brother.

"So, what do you say, guys?" Paul said, glancing from one hopeful little face to the other. "Let's have a look at that fireplace."

Both boys cheered and dashed across the room to the fireplace. Their parents headed for the kitchen to get cookies and hot cocoa for everyone. And Amy followed them, offering to help.

"Uh, Miss Elf?" Paul called after her. "Santa needs a hand here."

She turned to find Paul struggling to get up off the floor. All that bulky padding kept throwing him off-balance. "Allow me, Santa," she said, hurrying over to him. She held out her hands and guided him back to his feet. The boys scampered off to the kitchen to check on the cookies.

Soon Paul's hands were around her waist and he nudged her close to his pillowy chest. The look peeping out from beneath his furry brows steamed with un-Santalike intent.

"You've got to be the sexiest elf this side of the North Pole," he murmured. "I've been wanting to do this all night long."

As he lowered his bearded face to hers, her skin felt as if it were being caressed by an airborne cloud. But his lips had an earthier effect, warm and insistent and making her feel ten times more heavenly.

Amy had a vague sense of whispers buzzing behind them, but she was enjoying this kiss too much to investigate. But within seconds, the giggling of two young boys became too boisterous to ignore.

"Mommy! Daddy!" they squealed in unison. "Santa's kissing the elf!"

After a good-humored round of cocoa and cookies, the Frames sent Amy and Paul off with thanks, best wishes and a couple of well-timed winks. They also extended an offer of refuge if the roads proved too dangerous. But Amy was just as eager as Paul to get back to the inn and their civilian clothes.

"Looks like we're in for a fun ride home," she said as they approached her car at the end of the Frames' driveway. The snow was falling at a steady clip. On the ground, the crusty mix of snow and ice crunched beneath their feet.

"I'll drive," Paul said, opening the passenger-side door for her.

She glanced at his oversize middle. "How?"

"By taking this damn belly off." He began unbuttoning the bright red Santa coat.

"You'll freeze doing that."

"Only for a minute until I remove the padding. Then, between this coat and the car heater, I'll be fine. Here." Paul gave her the coat to hold. He was wearing only a cotton T-shirt beneath the padding. "Besides, you're not used to driving in these conditions, and I know these roads."

She could see his point. She also could see the snow falling on his bare arms as he unwrapped the padding from around his chest. The flakes streamed down his muscled arms, forming icy patterns on his skin. To make matters worse, the wind picked up and began whipping through the evergreens along the road. As Paul's entire body shook and his teeth chattered, Amy could practically feel the fierce bite of cold herself. She jumped into the car to start it, turning the heater on full blast.

When he was ready, she helped him with the jacket. Throwing the padding and beard into the back seat, Paul climbed behind the wheel and warmed his hands with the heat blowing from the dashboard.

"I'd say we're about ten miles from town," he said, shifting the car into gear. "Just hang on and we'll get there."

Paul's command of the road reassured Amy, and her car's steel radial tires served them well for the first several miles. Soon it was snowing harder, until visibility was reduced to a white blur. The stretch of repeated hills didn't help as swishing their way up one side became as risky as sliding down the other. Watching Paul's fierce concentration as he steered, Amy bit her lip and gripped the door handle so hard her fingers felt numb.

"Guess my spanking-new radial tires aren't really meant for all weather," she muttered tensely.

"Not the tires' fault. With these kinds of conditions, chains and four-wheel drive are your only hope." Paul tore his eyes from the windshield for a quick glance at her. "Don't worry, we'll be okay."

"I know." If Paul believed this, then she did, too. She respected his word. Somewhere along the line, her faith in him had sprouted and grown to the point where she trusted even her life to him. If anyone else was driving in this storm, she'd be a certified basket case right now.

"You've been an awfully good sport tonight," he said, his eyes now glued to whatever he could see of the road ahead. "About the elf costume and traipsing through all those houses."

"Are you kidding?" Letting go of the door handle, she turned to him. "You definitely get top honors tonight. You didn't want to be Safety Santa in the first place."

"It wasn't so bad after all. Not that I'd want to do it again, you understand."

She chuckled as the car began crawling down yet another hill. "Then I guess I'd better not tell anyone how much you seemed to be enjoy—"

Suddenly the breath was knocked out of her by a violent swerve to the right. The next thing Amy knew the car was skidding downhill. Her body stiffened against the jostling of helter-skelter swerves and shifts. Shouting at her to hold on, Paul worked to control the car, but the skid seemed endless. Her head began spinning faster than the car and her heart was in her throat. After a series of jerks, jolts and bumps, the car finally plowed off the road, stopping with a hard, forceful thud.

"Amy, are you all right?"

She opened her eyes and looked at Paul. The sight of him reassured her instantly. "Yes, I think so. Are you?"

He appeared relieved, but sounded out of breath. "I'm okay. Not so sure about your car, though. I think we've hit a ditch."

They both got out to investigate. It was snowing very hard, making it difficult to see. Yet it was clear that the car had spun off the road and landed in a shallow gully, where it was very stuck. Amy gasped and Paul swore.

"Thank goodness I have the car phone. We can call for help," she told him. "Do you have any idea where we are, though?" Without any houses or buildings around, she felt as if they were in the middle of nowhere.

Paul turned, squinting through the falling wet flakes as he took stock of the surroundings. "Looks like we're in the middle of McArthur's Orchards. See—apples trees on both sides of the road."

Amy just shook her head. She couldn't see past her own nose.

Back in the car, they started calling for assistance. Henry's garage was so busy they said it would be at least three hours before anyone could get out to them—if the roads were even passable by then. The auto club never answered the phone; neither did Dirk Campbell. They even came up empty-handed at the inn. Bernadette wanted to call the state police.

Telling Bernadette to wait until he called back, Paul turned to Amy. "Look, my house is only about three quarters of a mile from here. We could hike it. Otherwise we might be sitting here all night freezing. Who knows when and if the police will get to us."

Amy stared out into the cold dark, more anxious than frightened. The prospect of trudging through this blizzard for almost a mile was daunting. The thought of waiting in this car for help that might never come was plain scary. "You sure you can find the way?"

"It's not far from the orchard's main entrance, which is well marked. Do you keep a flashlight in the car?"

A good sturdy flashlight and extra batteries were stowed in the trunk, along with blankets and other emergency items. After bundling up as much as possible, they covered their heads and shoulders with the blankets and struck out on foot. Paul kept up a good pace. Still, whenever Amy straggled behind, he'd stop and wait for her.

She thanked the stars she had worn her boots tonight, although her toes soon tingled from the cold. As they shuffled through the deepening snow, fighting the wind, Paul patiently urged her on. With the wet snow blowing into her eyes and pelting her face, Amy felt like a frozen, exhausted icicle.

"We're almost there, honey," Paul cried, putting his arm through hers. "There's the McArthur sign."

Thank God, she thought, feeling as if they'd walked ten miles instead of less than one.

Paul gently tugged her along until they reached his curving driveway. "I knew you could do it," he said, giving her a hardy hug. "Just a few more yards."

She was so relieved she didn't know whether to laugh or cry. Instead she squeezed Paul's arm tight as they climbed up the hilly driveway. For a reluctant Santa Claus, he was handling this disaster with admirable restraint. He wouldn't be in this fix right now if it hadn't been for her.

"I'm so sorry for dragging you into this, Paul," she said, breathing hard. "You don't deserve this."

"I insisted you come with me. Even made you wear the elf suit. Then I drove your car into a ditch, causing who knows how much damage. And you're sorry?"

Amy still felt remorseful. "I wasn't one-hundred percent honest when I asked you to be Safety Santa. You weren't the absolute last resort. If all else failed, Bridget was going to try Dirk."

Paul stopped to look down at her. The blanket had slipped from his shoulders when he'd hugged her. His Santa cap, hair, eyebrows and lashes glistened under a coat of snow. "You mean I should have held out? Campbell could have been the fool hiking through this storm instead of me?" He shook his head. "Where's the justice?"

Then he smiled and nudged her onward.

When they got to the house, Paul dug into his deep red pockets for the keys. "Snead's not barking. Dirk must have taken him back to his house while I was away."

Amy didn't know Paul owned a dog. Actually, she knew little about the day-to-day matters in his life. He was still a mystery to her, a question mark in her mind. Yet the connection between them continued to grow despite his private nature and her inherent wariness. And more than just the magnetic pull of physical attraction was at play here.

At least for her.

Unlocking the back door, he led her directly to the mud room off the kitchen, where they stripped off their soaked coats and hats. Amy was shivering so hard Paul sat her on a kitchen stool and pulled off her stiff boots. Then he shooed her off to a guest bedroom to take a hot shower while he phoned people to let them know they were okay.

Amy had no idea how long she stayed in the shower, but it seemed to take forever for her to feel warm again. When she finally emerged from the steamy waters, she discovered Paul had replaced the wet elf unitard she'd left on the bed with a clean, white T-shirt and a hunter green velour robe. The shirt hit a comfortable midthigh length on her petite frame. Paul's robe, on the other hand, draped around her ankles. But it was warm and plush and smelled of his fresh soap.

Wandering through the carpeted hallway in search of Paul, she realized it ran the length of the sprawling one-story house. Midway between the bedrooms and the big, eat-in kitchen, Amy found honey-stained French doors opening out to an enormous great room. She entered the room and was immediately dazzled by a cathedral ceiling of mellow gold wood, thick creamy carpet and lots and lots of windows. On a clear day, the views from the windows had to be fantastic.

"What do you think?"

She turned around to find Paul kneeling in front of the large, stone fireplace. All traces of Santa were gone. He looked decidedly warmer and more handsome in a black turtleneck and blue jeans.

"It's wonderful, Paul. When Maura told me you helped design and build your house, I pictured a small, rustic cabin on top of a hill. Not something as airy or as comfortable as this. You must be very proud."

"It's the home I've always wanted. I plan to be here for a long time." He lit the kindling in the grate and watched the new fire take hold.

His pride showed as he gave her a quick tour of the rest of the house. From the large kitchen with every convenience to the cozy, wood-paneled study, the thought and care he'd given to his home was evident. Yet, as Paul switched on the lights in each of the three sparsely furnished bedrooms, Amy sensed a loneliness in the place. The thought of Paul sitting alone in this beautiful rambling house on long winter nights saddened her.

When he walked her through his bedroom suite, however, Amy began feeling self-conscious. Now that the anxious activity of getting stuck in the snow was over, being alone with this man in the intimate confines of his home had its own set of implications. Was she ready to face them?

For the first time since they'd met, she and Paul were utterly alone with endless hours to spend together. No meddlesome family, no business interruptions. Hadn't she been longing for such an opportunity while Paul was in Richmond? Why was she suddenly riddled with uncertainty?

"I'm sorry I couldn't find anything else for you to wear," he said as he led her back to the sofa in front of the stone fireplace. "Your costume should be dry by morning."

"I'm fine with these. Just fine," she said, trying to shake her nervousness. She wondered if Paul had heard the edge in her voice.

"I've got coffee brewing, but maybe you need something to eat," he suggested. "How about some soup?"

"No, I'm not hungry at all. Just coffee, please."

He looked at her for a long moment. "Are you sure you're all right?"

"I told you I'm fine." Really Amy felt awkward and stiff as she sat on the sofa. She prayed the fire's warmth would relax her. Turning away from Paul, she curled her bare feet under her and gazed directly into the fresh flames. After several seconds of silence, Paul left the room.

She felt terrible about cutting him off like that. But she couldn't help it. Her ingrained self-protective instinct was putting up its guard. Maybe she should heed it for a change. Because every time she'd felt strongly about a man, she'd managed to block out its message. And every time—from her father all the way to Jeff Martin—she'd been, more or less, abandoned.

Paul returned with two mugs of steaming-hot coffee and chocolate-chip cookies on a tray. "I haven't been to the supermarket lately so the refrigerator is pretty empty. But I found an unopened package of cookies in the cupboard." He sat down beside her. "They're not stale. I checked."

The thought of Paul selecting a package of chocolate-chip cookies from a grocery store shelf softened her for a moment. She imagined a good many female heads turned whenever he pushed his cart down the aisles.

Amy took a cookie, even though her stomach was in knots. Then, in her nervousness, she started talking about the house, commenting on everything from the design to the type of wood used for trim. When she finally paused to ask Paul a question, he just stared back at her.

"Amy, I don't want to talk about the house. And I don't think you do, either."

She stiffened. "I don't see how you could know what I want."

"What's going on with you all of a sudden?" He plunked his cup down on the coffee table. "It feels like a wall has gone up between us."

She decided his directness deserved her honesty. "I guess I feel uncomfortable being here like this."

"Uncomfortable being alone with me, you mean?" His eyes winced with hurt. "But I thought—"

"I know what you thought, and what I thought, too." She looked away, unable to think straight with his blue gaze boring into her. "But now I feel I've been put on the spot. We're here alone in your house, basically stranded. Therefore the obvious will have to happen."

"You can't believe I plotted this. That I drove your car into a ditch so I could have my way with you?"

"Of course not. You wouldn't do a thing like that."

"Then what are you afraid of?"

"I'm not afraid."

"No?"

"No. I—I—just don't like having the choice taken away from me."

"Foolish me." Paul slapped his forehead with his hand. "I thought you'd been making choices all along. At least it seemed that way."

This flash of anger made her feel defensive. "I may have gotten ahead of myself. I'm sorry if I—"

"Don't." He reached for her hands, his voice gentler now. "Don't say you're sorry for what's happened between us. And please, please don't treat me like a stranger."

"I'm not—I couldn't. You've been much too good a friend to me."

Her hands felt warm and protected in his grasp, but she fought the sensation. His touch was much too potent for her own good. She had to keep her head clear.

"I don't want to be a friend, Amy." Paul pulled her closer, forcing her to look at him. "I want you."

She lowered her gaze. "I know."

"Having you here in my home like this. Sitting in front of the fire with the snow howling outside. Feeling as if we're the only two people on earth. It's all like a dream come true."

"Dreams aren't real, Paul."

"I'm real. Just touch me." He drew her hand to his heart and pressed it against his chest. She could feel his heart beating hard beneath her fingers. "I want to make love to you."

"Paul, I—"

"Everything that's happened has been driving us to this moment. Maybe fate even had a hand in this snowstorm. Who knows?"

Her confusion was mounting. She had been drawn to him from the very first day, and every step that brought them closer had seemed inevitable. But giving herself to Paul was the ultimate step, a very emotional one. It held more risk than she could afford to take. "Maybe tonight is all wrong for us."

With hope draining from his eyes, Paul sat back in resignation. "No, Amy, everything is right tonight, but if you can't see that . . ."

"Please try to understand," she implored.

"I'm trying. Believe me, I'm trying." He brushed a hand through his thick, gold hair, his frustration obvious. "But perhaps you can help me with the question I'm grappling with right now. 'Cause I'm sure having a hell of a time coming up with an answer.''

"I'll try," she murmured, feeling his wounded anger.

"If not tonight, of all the nights in our lives—'' He paused, gently lifting her chin with his fingers until their eyes were level. "If not tonight, when?''

Amy was captured by his challenging gaze, yet she had no answer. After seemingly endless seconds, Paul released her and got to his feet. There was nothing more to be said. She rose from the sofa. "Should I use the same room I took the shower in?''

Paul nodded and then let her go with a simple goodnight.

As she walked alone down the dimly lit hall, the sense of loss weighed heavy on her heart. Part of her wanted to snatch back the last thirty minutes, rewind the film and replay the scene. This time desire and hope would overcome doubt and fear, and the ending—whichever way it turned out—would be a happy one. But she and Paul were not characters in a movie, and reality ruled. And because endings were never guaranteed, she had to believe her choice was for the best.

Before entering the guest room, she glanced into Paul's room next door. His wide, mahogany sleigh bed stood out, a taunting temptation to her resolve. If her choice was so right, why did she feel so lost?

As she prepared for bed, she heard Paul close up for the night. Inside his room, the muffled sounds of movement filled her with an indescribable loneliness. Amy wondered if Paul was lonely now, too. Or had years of living alone in this big house inured him to the emptiness?

Why was the past such an unrelenting master? she asked herself as she slid under the covers. How well her mother had drummed its lesson into her head after Greg had left. Learn from your mistakes—don't make the same one twice. And never leave yourself open to the wrong man. That was the biggest mistake of all.

Or was not trusting your heart an even greater mistake?

Amy tossed restlessly, unable to sleep. Her muscles ached from the strenuous hike through the snow, but her body ached with longing. She cared so much for Paul— so very, very much. They would never be together like this again. And he would never be as close as he was tonight. All she had to do was reach out...

Paul's question echoed through her mind. *If not tonight, when?*

Unlike before, the hard cold answer struck Amy with its sobering truth, a truth too difficult to bear. *If not tonight... never.*

Amy realized she had to stop being afraid of what might or might not happen in their relationship. Hadn't fear and mistrust kept her from her father all these years? Now she could never be with him. Never.

Bolting out of bed, she pulled on Paul's robe. How things might end was irrelevant, Amy told herself. All that mattered was the beginning.

She stepped into the hushed silence of the hall. It was very dark and still. She didn't need light to find Paul's door, but those few steps seemed to take forever. Reaching down for the knob, she wavered for just a second before twisting it ever so gently. With her heart pounding in her ears, Amy slipped inside Paul's room.

She prayed he still wanted her.

Chapter Eleven

Paul's bedroom was completely dark and still.

Amy hesitated, wondering if he'd already fallen asleep, wondering if she dared wake him. Then she heard the rustling of sheets and the click of a lamp switch.

He sat up in the bed, the blanket and sheets sliding down his taut chest. His fingers combed wheat-colored hair from his eyes as he peered across the room at her.

Amy met his gaze, yet felt rooted to the spot. Her head and heart were spinning with thoughts and feelings she suddenly found impossible to express. She leaned back against the closed door, longing pulsing inside of her.

"You came."

His deep, rich voice tingled through her. "Yes."

"I'm glad." He held out his hand.

It was all the encouragement Amy needed. She crossed the room quickly and slipped her hand in Paul's.

"No regrets?" he asked.

"Only if I hadn't come."

The look in his eyes was a mixture of pleasure and relief. He gently pulled her down to the bed and held her close, covering her mouth with a satisfying full-bodied kiss. She felt him slide the robe off her shoulders, heard it fall on the carpet. Then her mind and body was consumed by the feel of his lips, the taunting of his tongue, the heat of his caressing fingers.

She uttered a soft cry of disappointment when he finally broke the kiss.

"I want you closer," he breathed in her ear. He tossed the bed covers aside and drew her down beside him, pressing her close against his nakedness. Paul's bed was warm; his skin felt hot and she was on fire.

Her arms and hands roamed down his back, her touch delighting in his smooth skin and tight muscles. Amy curved her hands along his arms, their hard strength fueling her need to feel them around her, to experience their power.

"Hold me," she urged, burrowing deep into his embrace. "Hold me, please."

He murmured her name over and over, his arms tightening velvet bands across her back. She could feel his arousal pressed hard against her pelvis. Her passion mounted as she kissed him, slow and long, savoring the taste of his lips, glorying in his urgent response as her tongue sought the moist warmth of his mouth. She had never kissed a man with such hunger; she'd never felt compelled to. Yet with Paul she felt free to enjoy him *and* pleasure him. And it made her feel alive and powerful and so very womanly.

With a growl of unrestrained desire, Paul laid a trail of kisses down her neck and across her shoulders. His hands moved over the T-shirt to cup her breasts. His fingers kneaded their softness and caressed their tips until she gasped with torturous delight.

She stared up into his eyes, deep blue pools reflecting the passion in which she was drowning. "I need you."

He continued to gaze at her, searching her face, her eyes. "We're connected, you and me," he finally said. "I don't know how—I'm not sure why. But we are."

He pulled back, reaching down to the hem of her T-shirt. He glided the soft fabric up the length of her body until Amy helped him lift it over her head. She took the shirt from his hand and dropped it on the floor.

Paul's eyes and hands roamed over her body. "You're so beautiful," he whispered, lowering his mouth to her breast. His tongue curled warmly around her nipple, making it pulse with desire. Her stomach tingled with creamy warmth. Then he showered the same attentions on her other breast, kissing and caressing it until her hips arched with need. She moaned for him to come inside her.

Cradling her to his side, Paul pulled open the night-table drawer. She watched him, moved because—unasked—he'd thought to protect her, wanted to keep her safe. Amy felt cared for, cherished. Even more, she knew she'd been right to trust him.

When he was ready, he reached to turn off the bedside lamp.

"Don't," she said. "I want to see you."

The gleam in his eyes was unmistakable as his body covered hers. "Anything for you, my lady. Anything."

And more than anything she wanted to be filled with his desire. As Paul moved against her, she opened her body up to him, ready to share the untapped passion in her soul. All trepidation and doubt had vanished. In her heart she knew he wanted her for the woman she was, and not for one thing else.

Her eyes widened as he thrust himself inside her. Her body quivered with pure delight as he thrust again and again. These sensations bubbled through her, expanding in her blood, his kisses and whispers thrilling her further. As Amy moved with him, she felt the joy in giving herself freely and the gratification of giving a man physical pleasure.

Excitement rippled through her, hot and fast, until a rush of intensity burst into delicious fulfillment. She clung to him and cried out his name. Paul groaned in response as his body tightened over hers and then shuddered and trembled with his own release.

They held each other for a long time, not moving, not speaking. Weak from the floating warmth of lovemaking, Amy lay beneath him, her thoughts drifting over the weeks and days leading to this moment. Paul had been right; this was inevitable. Fate had decreed them connected—if only for a time. Wrapped in his arms like this, Amy knew giving herself to Paul was something she'd never regret.

Finally, Paul lifted his head and planted a silken kiss on both her eyelids. "I'm so glad you're here with me."

She opened her eyes and found his gaze warm with tenderness. Filled with an overwhelming tenderness of her own, she caressed his rough cheek with her hand. "I wanted to be here—even earlier when I was being so awful to you. I don't know why I—"

He pressed his fingers to her lips to quiet her. "You don't have to explain. We're together now. That's what matters."

* * *

Paul could barely lift his eyelids when the ringing telephone finally roused him. He squinted at the clock radio as he fumbled to answer the phone. Good Lord, it was almost noon. Glancing at the warm, soft woman curled beside him, he couldn't help but smile. She continued sleeping, oblivious to the telephone rings. After Safety Santa and walking a mile through a veritable blizzard, then making love several times during the night, they both had collapsed into a deep sleep.

Keeping his voice low when he answered, Paul listened as Dirk filled him in on road conditions and the situation at work. He was at the office with a skeleton crew and Mr. Snead—whom he'd taken home in anticipation of the storm. As usual, Dirk had everything under control.

Amy began to stir just as Paul hung up the phone. Before she opened her eyes, he prayed there would be no morning-after awkwardness. He'd hate to lose that closeness of spirit they had achieved by the early hours of the morning. He couldn't stand the thought of her being uncomfortable with him after what they'd shared.

She blinked several times until her eyes focused on him. Then she stretched beneath the covers, a lazy, sexy smile zapping his fear to bits. The contented look in her eyes made it clear that her smile was for him and because of him. He was happy to know he'd put it there.

"Was that the phone I heard?" she asked, her voice raspy from sleep.

"It was Dirk. The storm hit Tremont pretty hard," he said, trying not to sound as unreasonably pleased as he felt. "Looks like you and I are snowbound—for today, at least."

Amy's eyes widened when he told her about closed roads and stranded motorists. "Sounds like we'll be lucky if we get plowed out tomorrow," she said as she fluffed up the pillows behind her. Sitting back with the slyest of grins on her face, she added, "What a shame."

Paul wanted to make love to her again right then and there. But both their stomachs were growling audibly, demanding nourishment. He sent her into the shower, while he scrounged through his kitchen for enough food to make a decent breakfast.

His shopping habits had always been spotty, mostly because he didn't care for cooking and eating alone. And today the pickings in his refrigerator were even slimmer than usual because he'd been away for several days. But he had eggs and cheese, and a couple of loaves of bread in the freezer. With his solid supply of gourmet coffees and nonperishable foods in the cupboard, he figured they could eat fairly well for days. Should he be so lucky.

When Amy joined him in the kitchen, scrubbed and glowing in her elf jumpsuit, he gave her a hot cup of coffee and a kiss on the lips. Her freshly washed hair felt soft as it brushed against his chin, and smelled like the crystal-clean snow glistening outside the door.

"Thanks for bringing me the hair dryer. And my clothes, of course," she said between sips of coffee. "I'm kind of getting attached to this silly green thing."

"I'm very attached to it."

"Maybe I should gift-wrap it for you for Christmas."

"Only if you're in it," he replied as he served the eggs and toast.

Clearly famished, she ate with relish, declaring it the best breakfast she'd ever had.

Paul was skeptical. "You just haven't eaten in over twelve hours. Anything would taste good."

"You're too modest, Paul. I can't poach an egg to save my life." She leaned over to kiss his cheek, adding sheepishly, "I'm still hungry. Can I have more?"

As he prepared another helping, she leaned against the counter, marveling over the professional quality of his pots and pans.

"They're Bernadette's doing," he explained. "After this kitchen was completed, I was too busy at work to furnish it. But she kept after me about it. I guess the thought of empty drawers and cabinets was driving her nuts. Finally I handed her my credit card and she went wild with the restaurant-supply catalog." He couldn't help chuckling. "I don't even know what some of these utensils are for."

"You're just lucky Bernadette takes such good care of you," Amy said, her eyes full of mirth, yet her voice tinged with affection. He had sensed Bernadette was growing on her.

Paul showered and dressed quickly after their late breakfast. Then they bundled up and headed outside to shovel the doorways and steps. Snow was everywhere, and the afternoon sun bounced off it, blinding them with its glare. But once their eyes became accustomed to the glistening splendor surrounding them, precious little shoveling got done. The snow was just too tempting. A teasing snowball fight led to creating a band of snow angels in the pristine drifts—which led to yet another round of snow flinging.

Squealing with laughter, Amy hid from his dead aim behind bushes and trees. She smacked him with the occasional icy ball whenever his back was turned, but was no match for him in face-to-face combat. Yet when Paul had ambushed her into a corner, she snuck past him, whooping with triumph as she ran around to the other side of the house.

He held his fire when he caught up with her. She was standing stock-still, her dark hair moving with the gently blowing wind. He followed Amy's gaze to the panorama of snowy hills and mountains spread out before them and understood the wonder in her face. He felt it every time he looked out his windows.

"Now I know why you want to live way out here," she said as he curved his arm around her. "This has to be as close to peace on earth as a person can get."

He snuggled Amy close to his side and kissed the top of her head. Her observation meant more to him than she could know. After the mess in San Francisco, he'd craved the very peace she'd mentioned. He had found it here. Not everyone understood— Bernadette had questioned why he wanted to live out in the hills all by himself. Bridget and Maura, too. Yet, with a few brief words, Amy Riordan had gotten to the heart of the matter.

Amy moved in his arms. "You know, Paul, this looks like a decent sledding hill." She leaned forward to peer down the winding incline. "Have you tried it?"

"I haven't sledded since I was a kid."

She appeared disappointed. "Guess that means you don't have a sled somewhere in the garage."

"Sorry." As he shook his head, however, a boyhood memory came to mind. "I have something else that will do the trick. Wait right here."

His mission didn't take long, and he was shuffling back through the knee-high snow within minutes. Amy zoomed in on the two silvery objects he carried in his hands.

"Cookie sheets?"

"Bernadette told me these would come in handy someday."

She was still staring at the oblong trays. "You want to slide on these?"

"Sure. We used to do it all the time when we were kids." From the surprise on her face, it was clear Amy had never had that particular opportunity. "It'll be great, trust me."

She didn't seem convinced as he instructed her on the art of cookie-sheet sledding. "Hope Santa leaves a real sled under the tree for you this year," she grumbled as he helped position her bottom just so on the cold, flat pan.

"Hold on tight now. I'll be down right after you." A good firm push sent her shooting down the hill, yowling as she picked up speed.

At the bottom, a jubilant Amy jumped up from the tray and began waving at him with excitement. "You're right—it's wonderful," she called up the hill. "Come on down."

They rode down the hill and trudged back up it many times, until their clothes were soaked and their muscles trembled from exertion. "How about one more run before we go in?" Amy suggested.

He looked at her ruddy, wind-chapped cheeks and snow-matted hair. "You're crazy."

"Oh, come on. We'll make it a race. The loser gets kitchen duty tonight."

The shining challenge in her sapphire eyes was impossible to resist. "What does the winner get?" he asked.

"The winner gets whatever she—or he—wants tonight."

The seductive tinge in her voice got his blood pumping double time. The numbing sensation of wet clothes on cold skin melted away. "You're on."

They started at the top side by side and kept an even pace until midway down the hill. Then, with a stroke of luck and a smooth, clear path, Paul pulled ahead when Amy was slowed by a patch choppy with footprints and fallen icicles.

"See you later, sweetheart," he taunted as he slid away.

In a matter of seconds, he heard Amy cry in distress and call his name. Panic surged through him and he struggled to stop. Finally on his feet, he turned to see her rolling over and over in the snow until she rolled into the thick trunk of an old willow oak.

"Amy!" he cried.

She was flat on her back, not responding, not moving. Terrified, Paul ran to her as fast as he could in the deep snow. Reaching her motionless body, he got down on his knees. "My God, Amy. Can you hear me?" He yanked of his gloves to touch her. "Talk to me, Amy," he pleaded.

She was breathing, yet so silent and still. He felt her skin, but his hands were too cold to detect anything. Leaning over her, he slid his fingers beneath her jaw to take her pulse. With his heart pounding in his ears, he began to count. Suddenly, Amy's gloved hand clamped down on his fingers and her eyes flew open.

"My hero," she said with a sigh, breaking into a devilish grin.

His stunned relief evaporated into indignation. "You—you faker. You scared the hell out of me."

"You were wonderful," she said, eyes shining as her hands cupped his shoulders. Then she tugged him down on top of her, capturing his mouth with a hard, impassioned kiss.

Amy held him tight against her as he opened his mouth to her warm tongue, which tasted and prodded, until hot shivers ran from his neck to his loins. They might as well have been stretched out on a bed of hot ice instead of layers of snow. He groaned with pleasure, thrilled by the way she wanted him. She finally let him come up for air, but her contented smile aroused him even more.

"Am I forgiven?" she murmured.

Her kiss had driven the prank from his mind. This reminder scarcely nicked the sensual haze encompassing him. "Just remember—I won the race," he growled in her ear. "The night is mine."

Back at the house, after discarding their wet coats, boots and gloves, Paul opened up his closet to her. She found a deep blue flannel shirt that skirted her shapely thighs and somehow made her dark eyes even bluer. They both knew his long-legged jeans and slacks would do her no good.

"I'm comfortable enough," she said, rolling the shirt's long sleeves up to her elbow. "If my feet and legs get cold, I'll borrow some socks."

He followed Amy into the kitchen, where she put water on for tea and studied the contents of his cupboards. "I'm not the best cook in the world, but I've been told I have a knack with store-bought spaghetti sauce." She pulled a jar of sauce from the pantry. "Just wait, you'll think it's homemade."

Paul knew he'd love anything Amy made for him—almost as much as he loved watching her move about in his big kitchen. When he caught her eye, she gave him a shy smile. Then she shooed him off to the living room. "I'll bring your tea in when it's ready."

He lit a fresh fire, put a soft jazz CD on the stereo and stretched back on the sofa. Gazing into the rising flames, Paul realized this was one of the best days of his life. Perhaps it was the fantasy quality of being snowbound with a soft, beautiful woman: making love, playing in the snow, having her cook for him. It was a different world up here together on the hill. Perhaps it was the way she brightened the day with laughter and sweetened the night with warmth.

When he'd been building this house, he had often daydreamed about the life he would have in it. Home, love, family. The very things he'd lost when his parents had died. The kind of life he'd failed to hold on to in his marriage. With time, however, the daydream had faded into a hazy abstraction—it didn't seem to be in the cards for him. True, there had been women in his life these past four years—but never for very long, never here and never like this with Amy.

Amy stole a glimpse of Paul through the open kitchen door. Her heart somersaulted at the sight of him gazing at the fire, long legs stretched out in front of him, his golden hair damp and shaggy after their hours outside. He seemed lost in thought. Was he thinking about her?

Leaving the pot of spaghetti sauce to simmer, Amy poured two mugs of tea and tucked the stack of unopened mail she'd found on the counter under her arm. When she joined him, Paul's face lit up as if he hadn't seen her for hours. He made room for her on the couch, pulling her close to his side when she sat.

"I thought you'd want to look at your mail," she said as they twined their legs.

"Dirk brought it in for me while I was in Richmond. It sure adds up after a few days." He began shuffling through the envelopes. "I'm always amazed by the number of Christmas cards I get every year. Especially since I don't send any."

"I always do." She felt a pang of guilt about the cards she hadn't gotten around to sending this year. "Because I love receiving them."

"Yeah, it is nice to hear from people I rarely see anymore. Would you mind?"

Shaking her head, Amy sipped her tea and watched Paul open his Christmas cards. She loved the way his eyes smiled when he read each signature aloud and showed her the card. Old army buddies, neighbors from when he lived out West, former newsroom colleagues—she was surprised by the variety of friends who'd thought of him at this time of year.

The next to last card did not bring a smile. "My ex-wife sends a card every year. I'm not sure why."

When he put it down on the coffee table with the others, a small photograph slipped out. Amy reached over to pick it up off the floor. "This is her family?"

He nodded, barely looking at it.

But she couldn't take her eyes off it as Paul went on to the last envelope. It was a typical family pose, husband and wife side by side, children in front. Paul's ex was blond, petite and pretty, her husband attractive, their two boys sweet. The younger child had a silly toddler's grin on his face, but the older boy...

Amy just stared at him, suddenly shaken to her core. After years of working with children, she could determine a child's age with little more than a glance. And her professional eye screamed that this blond, blue-eyed boy was seven or eight years old.

Paul had been divorced only four years.

Maura's vague impressions and Bernadette's evasive answers reverberated through her stunned mind. What was going on? Clutching the photo with trembling fingers, Amy didn't know what to think. Paul had a child no one knew about? A child he didn't acknowledge? A child he had no contact with?

"Amy, you're as pale as a ghost. What's wrong?"

She searched his startled face, hoping for a sign or clue that would allay her anxiety. There was none. Untangling her legs from his, she sat up straight and gave him back the photograph. "Why would your ex-wife send you a picture of her family?"

"Shelly's extremely sentimental. Even about me." He reached out to reassure her. "It doesn't mean anything."

"It doesn't?" She shrank from his touch. "Then why won't you look at that picture?"

"What is the matter with you?" He still hadn't even glanced at the photo.

"What's the older's boy name?" She didn't know why it even mattered at this point, but she couldn't help pressing.

Paul's eyes narrowed with uncertainty. "Andrew."

He didn't want to tell her, she saw that clearly now. Disappointment made her voice shake. "How old is Andrew?"

His face ashen, he finally looked down at the picture in his hand. Then he lifted his gaze to hers. "He's not mine, Amy."

"Not your son?"

She didn't know if she believed him, and this doubt angered her. And Paul knew it. The steely glint in his eyes as he shot off the sofa made that very clear.

"There was a time I would have given my soul to be that boy's father. His real father." He threw the photo down on the coffee table. "But that man is *the* father— biological, custodial and any other damn way you want to call it."

He crossed over to the stone mantel and gazed down into the fire. Amy stared at his back, her stomach knotted with tension, her head aching with confusion. The Paul she knew was unflappable. Strong, commanding, certainly private, stern and even angry at times. But she had never seen him upset. Not like this.

"Paul, please—" Her voice cracked with emotion. "Please, I don't understand."

"I was a father to Andrew for the first three and a half years of his life. I was in the labor room when he was born—my name was on his birth certificate. I helped him take his first steps—I even taught him to sing 'Jingle Bells.'" Paul turned around to face her. "Then his real father came back, and it was over."

Amy went to his side. "This isn't easy for you to talk about, is it?" she said, drawing him back to the sofa.

"It's been four long years. Maybe it's time I did."

She clasped his hand in hers, encouraging him to take his time, to tell her how little or how much he wanted. He began with how he and Shelly, a general assignment reporter at the TV station, started dating after Bob Wickwire left her for a prestigious overseas assignment. The story poured out of Paul. He seemed compelled to tell her every last bit of it, making Amy realize he had probably never talked about it before.

"We'd been dating steadily for weeks when Shelly found out she was pregnant with Wickwire's baby," Paul revealed. "She came to me in tears, insisting we break up. But Wickwire was long gone, her contract at the station was up for renewal and she was determined to have her baby come hell or high water. The station management was too conservative to permit an unwed pregnant woman to go on the air. I knew they'd never renew her contract."

"You married her to save her job?"

"If it had been as simple as that, we all would have been spared a lot of pain," he said ruefully.

"You were in love with her, then?"

"I was very attracted to her from the start. We came to care a great deal for each other as time passed, and our marriage was a marriage in the fullest sense." He picked up his mug of lukewarm tea and sipped some. "When Shelly came along I was searching for some meaning to my life. I was an anchorman on automatic pilot, earning more money than I knew what to do with, going out every night—yet I had no life. I was ready to settle down. Perhaps it was foolish, but I convinced Shelly that getting married and raising the baby as mine was the right thing to do."

As Paul told her about the wedding, the pregnancy and the baby, her empathy deepened. He had committed himself completely to wife and son, believing he finally had a family of his own for the first time since he was eight years old. It pained her to hear how it had been torn away from him when Bob Wickwire transferred to L.A. over three years later.

"I loved Andrew more than life itself, Amy," he admitted, his voice tight. "It threw our lives upside down when Bob showed up in San Francisco and put two and two together. He wanted his son and he wanted Shelly. He claimed he'd never stopped loving her."

"And Shelly?"

"She turned him away at first, even when Bob first sued for visitation rights. But he kept pressing and pressing, until it was painfully obvious that she was still in love with him." Paul looked at the waning flames of his unfed fire. "Things just got messier after that, especially when the press got wind of it. They hounded us for months."

It sounded like hell. Amy couldn't fathom how Paul had survived. And she couldn't understand how Shelly could tear her son from the only father he'd known, a father who truly loved him. It wasn't right. It wasn't fair.

"But, Paul, surely you had legal rights. How did they get them away from you?"

Paul sat silent for a moment. Then, with a weary sigh, he turned to her, his expression somber. "I didn't *lose* my rights, Amy. I gave them up."

His words buzzed in her head, but she couldn't believe he'd said them. "You gave up your son?"

"Andrew isn't my son."

"I can tell you didn't feel that way."

"Well, Bob Wickwire did. Besides, Shelly and Andrew were moving to Los Angeles with him. Even if Wickwire had been receptive to liberal visitation—which he definitely wasn't—my involvement with Andrew would have been part-time at best."

"A part-time father is better than one who disappears completely. Believe me."

"What happened with you and Greg was different."

She knew her own experience and memories were getting all tangled up in this. It was difficult to separate them in her mind when the differences weren't as clear-cut to her as they seemed to be to Paul. Exasperated by the tug-of-war within herself, she went over to the huge picture window. The misty gray-blue of dusk was falling fast over the snowy hills. The tracks their cookie-sheet sleds had left behind on the snow were barely visible now.

Paul came up behind her. "Try to understand."

She couldn't look at him. "You should have fought for him."

"I started to. Had the lawyers filing court papers left and right. But in the end, I couldn't go through with it. Andrew's life had already been shaken up enough."

"That's why you let him go?"

"His mother and father loved each other and wanted to be together. Bob wanted to be a true father to him. Had I stuck around, I would have only confused Andrew." Paul touched her shoulders, his kneading fingers imploring her to understand. "How could I not let him go? How could I, of all people, deny him a whole family?"

Amy closed her eyes as all the pieces fell into place. Now she understood. Paul had given up everything—the family he'd always wanted, the life he'd made for them, the future he'd planned—to ensure Andrew a proper family. That took a strength few men could muster, a depth of heart few possessed. And yet, what about the poor child who lost his "daddy"? She couldn't help thinking about how awful it must have been for him.

She turned to him, sliding her arms beneath his, pressing against him. He whispered her name as he clung to her, and she held him as close as she could. Life had given this man a lot of heartache, yet he hadn't turned bitter or cold. Revealing the details of his marriage and divorce must have been excruciating. No wonder he had refused to discuss them with Bridget and Maura. But Amy was glad he had told her, despite how difficult some of it had been to accept.

His every word confirmed what her heart had known last night in his bed—she loved him. She loved his passion, his strength, his voice, his laugh. She even loved the pain of his past, because it, too, made Paul Hanley so very special to her.

His arms tightened around her, as if he sensed the deep emotion coming to life within her. "I need you, Amy," he murmured. "I need you so much."

Curving her arms behind his neck, she stretched up on her toes to reach his lips. She kissed him with all the new love in her soul, to prove she was there for him. More than anything, Amy wished she could take away years of hurtful memories. Yesterdays were not in her realm, however. Only the here and now. But she could give him all the longing in her heart and all the warmth of her body.

Amy leaned back in his arms, her eyes locking on Paul's darkened gaze. She took his hand from her waist and silently led to the dusky shadows of his room. Standing by his bed, Amy unfastened his belt buckle and helped him slip out of his sweater and jeans. A familiar flush of yearning made her legs quiver as Paul undid the long row of buttons on her flannel shirt. He let it fall to the floor at her feet.

Without a word, she drew him down on the bed. She covered his hard, strong body with her own. Her desire sizzled as her taut nipples pressed into his chest, but she wouldn't allow it to distract her from the giving. Her tongue tasted and kissed. Her hand taunted and caressed. She whispered and moaned. All for him, all from deep inside of her. And the more she gave, the hotter her own passion burned.

Paul cared about her, Greg Riordan's daughter, not her wealth or connections. That's what made this giving the most intimate act of her life. She had never felt so free with a man, and never so close.

"I want you," Paul rasped, his fingers raking through her hair, "want you now." He rolled her onto her back, pinning her beneath his broad shoulders. For the longest moment he looked into her eyes with a tenderness she wanted to lock away in her heart forever. Clutching his back, she enclosed him in her fire, moving with him until their bodies shuddered and trembled together, and Amy's cry of joyous pleasure echoed his.

Afterward, Paul lifted his head and captured her gaze with a soul-deep intensity that took her breath away. "You're mine now, Amy. No matter where our paths take us, even if we're apart, you'll always be mine."

She knew what Paul was saying. What they had shared today—and tonight—would stay with them for a long, long time.

He held her close long after his breathing had settled, his chin nuzzling her hair. A glowing satisfaction thrummed in her veins. The room grew darker as dusk gave way to night. The aroma of her simmering spaghetti sauce swirled around them and they talked of rescuing it before it cooked away. But neither one of them was eager to leave his bed.

Amy drifted off, snug and secure in Paul's arms, until a humming roar jolted her awake.

"It's all right. You're all right," he soothed, tightening his arms around her. Yet she detected disappointment in his voice.

The roar seemed to be rolling closer, growing louder. "What is that?" she asked.

"The state highway crew. They're clearing and sanding the main road." He planted a kiss on the top of her head.

Her heart sank. The outside world was crashing in too soon.

"Technically, we're no longer snowbound," he told her, sounding as low as she felt. "The local plow will be just a few hours behind these guys. We'll be plowed out by morning."

Chapter Twelve

Amy felt a warm hand on her bare shoulder. Fingers of steam and a toasty aroma roused her awake from a deep, delicious sleep. She lifted her lids to find Paul, fully dressed, sitting on the edge of the bed, holding a mug of hot coffee. He greeted her with a kiss as, groggy-eyed, she slowly sat back against the pillows, tucking the sheet over her breasts.

He put the steaming mug in her hands. "Dirk called. He's on his way up to drive us back to town."

"Already?" She saw he had placed the dry elf unitard at the bottom of the bed.

"The roads are all clear. Tremont is back to normal, and my office needs me," he said with forced cheerfulness. "Your car has already been towed back to the inn—none the worse for having been stuck, apparently."

"Sounds like everything's under control," she said lamely, feeling as though everything were out of *their* control.

Amy had no idea what would happen between them once they left here. She didn't know how they would bridge the gap from the intimate isolation of the past two nights to the busy, crowded worlds awaiting them.

Paul left her to shower and dress. By the time she was ready, Dirk Campbell had arrived with Paul's truck and dog. The golden retriever barked with happiness at seeing his master again, and spent some time checking out Amy with sniffs of curiosity.

Leaving Mr. Snead at the house, Paul drove them back to town. He dropped Dirk off at the Valley News Group first, then headed for the inn. They rode in silence until they reached the steep drive leading to the Blue Sky where Paul pulled the truck over to the side of the road.

Amy's heart fluttered as he turned to her, his thick hair golden beneath the morning sun's brilliance. Yet his angular face, so handsome in her eyes, was shadowed with concern, his gaze serious. Uncertainty tempered her heart.

"I want to see you again tonight."

"Yes, of course." They didn't have many nights left.

"There's something else I want."

"Anything."

Smiling, he reached across the seat for her hand. "Don't be so quick to say that. I probably don't have the right to ask this."

She squeezed his hand in encouragement.

"You still have a decision to make about the inn—and it's one-hundred percent your call. Not Bernadette's. Not Bridget's or Maura's. I know that now."

He looked down at their clasped hands. His thumb gently caressed her fingers. "But a lot has happened to you and me because of the Blue Sky—it's been the link between us. I want you to keep a connection with the inn—with Bernadette and the girls. With me." He lifted his gaze to hers. "Somehow—in a way that makes sense to you, in a way that you can live with."

"Paul, I—"

"Don't say anything now. Just think about it before you decide—that's all I want." He started the truck's engine and drove the rest of the way up the hill.

Amy gazed out the window at the inn's snow-covered grounds, quietly moved by his request, his consideration. In truth, she'd already been contemplating her options regarding the Blue Sky. She'd thought about little else since the scary, yet wonderful realization that she was falling in love with Paul Hanley.

After Paul had dropped her off at the front steps, she stood gazing at the inn for a long time. Trimmed and aglow for the holidays, the Blue Sky looked picture perfect in the fresh white snow. Amy remembered her bittersweet feelings when she had first laid eyes on the place, how she felt like an outsider in her father's world. Today she was filled with a sense of coming home.

As soon as she entered the main hall, Bernadette rushed from the office to greet her with open arms. Her solicitous warmth touched Amy. It was the kind of uncritical welcome she'd be unlikely to receive from her own mother—especially after being snowbound with a man for two days.

"Come have some breakfast," Bernadette urged, taking her by the hand into the dining room. "I hope Paul took decent care of you up there."

Amy felt herself redden at the unabashed twinkle in the older woman's eye. But there was sincere affection behind the knowing look, as well, convincing Amy there was no reason for her not to twinkle right back. "He did just fine."

Bernadette lips broke into a not-so-cryptic grin as she found Amy a table and fetched the coffeepot. "I've got good news. George is much better, so he and Bridget and the kids, and hopefully Maura, are coming to the cottage tonight to decorate the family tree. I want you to join us, Amy. And of course, I'm sure Paul will come."

"It sounds like fun."

"It will be, won't it?" Bernadette poured herself a cup of coffee and sat down with Amy. "This is our first Christmas without Greg, and I haven't had much holiday spirit. I thought I didn't want a tree at the cottage this year," she admitted. "But Willy and Jenny are just up to their eyeballs with excitement. And your being here is a special blessing. So I just know your father would want me to keep up the family tradition."

Blinking back a tear, Amy touched Bernadette's hand. "Thank you for including me in it."

"Don't you know?" she said, her own eyes wet. "To me, Amy Riordan, you *are* family."

After a light breakfast, Amy went up to her room, thankful to be taking off the elf costume for the last time. She was exhausted, her muscles and limbs deliciously sore from all the hiking and sledding in the snow. And from making love. But before crawling into bed, she made quick calls to Julie at the office, to her mother and to a favorite sporting goods store in D.C. Then, with Paul and her memories crooning in her head like a lullaby, she drifted off to sleep.

* * *

Amy came downstairs late in the afternoon just as the common rooms began buzzing with predinner activity. Finding Bernadette on a stepladder rehanging a fallen rope of evergreen over the dining room entrance, she offered assistance.

"I'm practically done here. But I've finally got a small tree up in the Pub Room. Could you start decorating it?" the older woman asked. "The balls and tinsel are in the boxes on the bar. I'll send in the others to help when they arrive."

As the bar hadn't opened yet, the Pub Room was deserted. Amy collected the red and gold glass balls and started hooking them on the fir's prickly branches. When she had just about covered the top half of the tree, Bud arrived for work whistling a chipper rendition of "Let It Snow."

"Well, well, I see my favorite helper is back," Bud greeted, hanging his coat and scarf on a wall hook behind the bar. "Glad you've finally been dug out."

She looked at him, startled. "You know about that?"

"Honey, the whole town knows about it. Loose-lipped Harry towed your car in, didn't he?"

With an exasperated groan, Amy returned to her decorating. As Bud prepped the bar, he described with great detail the great blizzard of '79 when the entire town had been snowed under for a week. "When you're young that kind of thing is lots of fun," Bud concluded. "But for an elderly person, being snowed in can be terrifying."

"I hope this storm didn't pose problems for your mother-in-law."

"My mother-in-law? Didn't bother her at all," he said with a shrug.

"She must be coming along fine, then." She stepped back from the tree to view her progress.

"Coming along?"

"From last week—when you didn't come to work."

"Are you talking about last Saturday night?" Bud looked at her, puzzled. "Bernadette told me to take the night off with pay. I'm not sure why—it wasn't necessary."

This sounded odd. Had she somehow misunderstood Bernadette's explanation? "Didn't you have a family emergency that night?"

Before Bud could reply, however, Willy and Jenny came bounding into the room, calling to Amy with delight. Bridget and George followed right behind, greeting her with hugs and thank-yous for her help with Safety Santa. Bud called the kids to the bar for a soda and poured their father a beer, while Bridget helped Amy finish the tree.

"Maura is already up at the cottage, getting the food ready, and Mom's giving final instructions to the staff. They're on their own tonight," Bridget explained as she tossed silver tinsel onto the branches. "And Mom says to tell you Paul is on his way."

"No, Mommy. Paul's there!" Willy squealed, pointing to the door while spinning on the bar stool.

Amy's gaze flew to the Pub Room's entrance. Paul's eyes met hers, responding with a knowing gleam meant for her alone. Giddy excitement shivered down her spine. She marveled at what the mere sight of this man did to her, although he did look exceptionally handsome tonight in a tweedy gray sport jacket. His thick, dark blond hair was a warming, rich gold contrast to the sleek black of his turtleneck and slacks.

There was no time for them to speak before Bernadatte appeared with coats folded over her arm, announcing it was time to leave for the cottage. Paul took Amy's coat as the family filed out.

"You look wonderful tonight," he murmured, slipping the coat over her long-waisted soft jersey dress. His hands cupped her shoulders as he nuzzled the back of her hair. "You're as ravishing in red as you are in elf green."

Amy winced. Stifling a chuckle, she turned to Paul with a teasing leer. "I'm not sure I can ever wear green again. And I'm gonna burn that suit."

"Don't you dare." He hugged her to him, squeezing her warmly in his arms.

Arriving at the cottage arm in arm, Amy and Paul were just as surprised as the rest of the family to find Dirk Campbell helping Maura set up the dinner buffet. The comments, the glances, the jokes caused Maura to throw up her arms in despair. "Okay, the Christmas spirit got the better of me. I admit it. But when he stopped by the shop for last minute gifts to send to his family in Florida, it struck me that even Dirk Campbell deserves some holiday cheer. Especially for *finally* shopping in my store. So, I brought him with me."

"The more the merrier," George chipped in, hugging Bridget to his side.

"And for the sake of peace on earth, goodwill toward men," Dirk continued amid the good-natured ribbing, "we have made a pact to be civil to each other—"

Maura pushed her way in front of him. "Until January 2."

Bernadette laughed the loudest, her eyes sparkling with hope as she looked at Maura and Dirk. "The saints be praised and let's eat."

This camaraderie continued through dinner and the tree trimming. There were so many hands helping that decorating didn't take long, regardless of all the laughing and reminiscing. Finally, George lifted Willy onto his shoulders to place the star on top of the tree. Amy scanned the group circling the tree, faces smiling and all eyes uplifted to the glittery star clasped in tiny hands. She realized how very dear these people had become to her. Despite the initial suspicions and resentment—on both sides—the Ryans had embraced her as part of their family. A sense of belonging glowed within Amy, as warm as the Christmas star shining in their eyes, and as real as the tall, vital man beside her, arm wrapped around her waist. On this night of family and belonging, Amy couldn't help thinking of all Paul had lost. She'd do everything she could to make it up to him this Christmas.

After the gathering disbanded late in the evening, Amy walked Paul to his truck in the inn parking lot. "A group activity wasn't actually what I had mind when I said I wanted to see you tonight," Paul said, drawing her against him.

"No?" Her fingers danced lightly on his chest as her eyes flirted with his. "What did you have in mind?"

"Having you all to myself. All night long."

A surge of pleasure curled through her. "Maybe, if you make it worth my while, I'll reconsider."

"Okay." Smiling, he kissed the tip of her nose. "How about a fully restocked refrigerator and a meal to knock your socks off?"

"Better than my spaghetti?" she asked, purposely reminding him of how they had feasted after making love last night.

"Darlin', nothing will ever be as good as that spaghetti." Paul leaned close to plant kisses along the curve of her neck.

"I'll come anyway," she rasped, her spine tingling with delight.

As Paul had to stop at the supermarket before preparing this sock-knocking meal, they agreed to meet at his place late the following afternoon. Once she assured him she could indeed find her way back to his house, he gave her the back door key and a long, breath-robbing goodnight kiss.

Paul tossed items into the grocery cart with hurried abandon. He was running late and Amy was waiting at home for him. Waiting for him. That sounded so good, and the image in his mind was even better.

God, it was amazing how much everything could change in a few weeks. His life had been thrown upside down and inside out by a pretty dark-haired lady he hadn't even expected to like. Now he was crazy about her. Somehow Amy had worked her Riordan magic, making him feel alive in a way he'd never known, filling him with the kind of hope that had been sapped from his soul by too many years alone.

Outside the store, Paul threw a wad of bills into the bell-ringing Santa's pot in the spirit of comradeship with a fellow St. Nick. He hummed along with the carols blaring over the shopping center's public-address system, very much in a holiday mood for the first time in years. December 25 was still a couple of days away. But for him, Christmas had already arrived in the person of Amy Riordan.

The road leading home was clear and dry, and Paul took advantage of it. He couldn't wait to get to Amy. Her sweet eyes and sexy smile, her warm, giving body—just knowing these were minutes away from his sight and touch made his blood hum.

Rolling up his long driveway, Paul spotted Amy's silver sedan parked close to the house. When he pulled in behind it, he noticed another car was parked in the yard, as well—one he didn't recognize—a blue station wagon with D.C. plates. Mystified, he grabbed the two sacks of groceries and went in through the back door. The kitchen was empty, but he heard voices coming from the living room. Leaving the groceries on the counter, he quietly walked into the living room.

Amy, sitting on the sofa with another woman, saw him right away. She greeted him with an awkward smile. "You have a visitor, Paul."

The blonde next to her stood up. "Hello, Paul. It's been a long time."

Feeling like the wind had been knocked out of him, he just stared as she crossed the room to him. She clutched his hand between hers and kissed his cheek.

He managed to find his voice. "Shelly, how did you get here?" he asked, truly rattled by his ex-wife's unexpected appearance at his house. He hadn't seen her since their last day in court over four years ago. She hadn't changed much at all.

"I went to the inn, figuring Bernadette would know where to find you," she explained. "It was nice to actually meet her after all this time. She's just as you described her."

"Bernadette knows you're here?"

"Yes, I met her and Amy, too." Shelly glanced back at the sofa. "When I heard she was coming to see you, I asked if I could follow her."

Paul looked at Amy, who sat there, uncomfortable, unsure. He wanted to go to her, but Shelly still clung to his hand, blocking his path.

"Why didn't you answer my letter?" she asked. "Or call me back? I left several messages on your answering machine."

"I thought my silence *was* an answer."

Shelly stepped back. "I wouldn't have come out here like this if it wasn't important. We have to talk, Paul. It's about Andrew."

"What about Andrew? Is he ill?"

"No, nothing like that," Shelly quickly reassured. "He's a happy, well-adjusted seven-year-old who's asking a lot of questions. About you."

Amy started to rise from the couch. "Maybe I should leave you two alone to talk."

He went to her, pressing her back down. "I want you to stay. Please."

"Are you sure?"

Nodding, he sat beside her and looked up at Shelly. "Amy knows all about what happened."

Shelly offered no objections as she sat on the over-stuffed club chair next to the sofa. "On our family therapist's advice, we've tried to be open about you with Andrew from the beginning," she began to explain. "It wouldn't have been healthy to deny your existence when you were such an important person in his life."

"Your husband must have loved that."

"Please remember Bob felt threatened by you. He's eased up considerably now that his relationship with Andrew is secure. Besides, he only wants what's best for his son."

"Where is this leading, Shelly?"

"Andrew wants to see you again."

"He doesn't remember who the hell I am," he snapped, impatient, yet not sure why. Amy put a hand on his arm to calm him.

"He certainly does," Shelly insisted. "He knows you were his stand-in dad, who took care of him until his real daddy could be with us. I saved some pictures of the two of you together, and he still likes to look at them."

"I see. He's remembering the pictures of me."

Shelly leaned forward in the chair. "Andrew is very precocious, very sensitive. He has two or three really intense memories of you from that last year together. Like the day you two found starfish on the beach in Oregon. I don't have pictures of that. I wasn't even there."

Paul closed his eyes. Lord, he'd forgotten about that himself. Andrew had been afraid to go near the starfish at first, but once he'd touched them, he'd gotten so excited that all he wanted to do was hunt starfish for the rest of their vacation.

"When we first moved to L.A., he'd ask about you all the time," Shelly admitted. "I'd tell him he couldn't see Daddy Paul because you had moved to Virginia. Now that's come back to haunt me. Bright second grader that he is, Andrew knows Washington, D.C., is near Virginia. He made me promise to contact you."

He couldn't believe this was happening. He'd never expected to see Shelly or Andrew again. Why now, after all the years of struggling to put that part of his life behind him? Why now, when he'd just found Amy? How could he possibly take a step backward like that?

Paul got to his feet. "Tell him you can't find me."

"I could do that," Shelly said, obviously disappointed. "But seeing you will help him bring that part of his life full circle. I think he needs that. Why else would the questions continue?"

"If he's as happy and as well adjusted as you say, he'll get over it. Andrew's got a mother, a father and a brother. He doesn't need me."

"I can't believe you're refusing him. I thought for sure once you heard the whole story—"

Resentment churned through his gut. "Refuse him? In case you've forgotten, I gave up everything for that boy."

"I haven't forgotten."

"Then how could you come barging into my home— into my life?"

"Paul!" Amy came to his side.

"It's all right, Amy," Shelly said, reaching for her coat and purse. She rose from the chair and turned to him. "Mothers will try anything for the sake of their children. I'm only doing what I think best for Andrew. Still, you're right. I could be making too much of this. He may be fine without your help." She hooked the purse strap over her arm. "But please know, Paul, I've always felt terrible about how things turned out."

He shook his head. "It wasn't anybody's fault."

"Maybe not. But it hurt you terribly. I guess I had the notion that helping Andrew this way might help you. Must be leftover guilt."

"You don't need to feel guilty. And I don't need help."

Shelly took a long look at Amy standing behind his shoulder. "No. I can see you don't."

When Paul returned from walking Shelly to her car, he found Amy lost in thought, gazing out one of the living room windows. The tension Shelly had created still hung in the air. Damn! His ex-wife's visit made him feel bad enough as it was, but it riled him to realize the evening he and Amy had planned was now in jeopardy.

He was determined to save it.

Quietly he came up behind Amy, circling his arms around her slender waist, holding her tense spine tight against his chest. He lowered his mouth to the back of her neck, kissing the silky nape. Her body melted into his, giving Paul hope.

"I'm sorry Shelly came here like that," he murmured, his cheek caressed by her lustrous, dark hair. "I don't want it to wreck our night."

"Neither do I." She turned in his arms, looking up at him beseechingly. "But, Paul, won't you please reconsider about seeing Andrew? It's a terrible mistake to leave him wonder—"

"Amy, I realize all this must be hard on you. But don't confuse it with you and Greg. It's not the—"

"Don't tell me it's not the same." She pushed away from him. "Andrew is as much a child of divorce as I am. No matter how young he was, no matter if you're not his natural father—he loved you like a son."

"Well, he can't love me like a son anymore. Didn't you hear? I'm 'Daddy Paul'."

"You have every reason to feel resentful. Still, it's not right to act like he no longer exists."

Paul struggled with his temper. Amy couldn't know how Andrew haunted his every thought. "I resent wasting time arguing about this when you and I should be holding each other, making the most of tonight."

She stood silent for a moment, her gaze clearly pained. Then, murmuring apologies, she walked back into his arms. "Maybe I am confusing the issues. I just don't want you to deny Andrew—and yourself—the resolution my father and I never had."

Paul tightened his arms around her, but he couldn't hold her close enough. He kissed her hair, her forehead, her lips. "I want us to look ahead to what *we* have together—not at what we've both lost in the past."

"That's what I want, too," she said, breathless, her heart pounding hard against his chest. "That's all I want."

"You're the best thing to ever happen to me," Paul said, his head reeling with the white smoke of desire as Amy clung to him. He trailed impassioned kisses along her neck and over her ear, until her body shivered in his arms. "Let me love you," he whispered. "Let me love you."

Chapter Thirteen

Dawn broke just as Amy pulled into the Blue Sky's parking lot. The inn looked shuttered and dark, which is exactly what she had hoped. She didn't care how Paul laughed or teased, she just couldn't waltz into the inn during the busy breakfast hour after spending the entire night at his house—under nonsnowbound conditions. Maybe some of his penchant for privacy was rubbing off on her.

Difficult as it had been to drag herself away from Paul's warm bed, she had plans she was anxious to get on with. She had people to call, arrangements to make and lots of Christmas shopping to do before she went back to Washington for the holiday.

Now, however, the pressure and dread associated with her return home no longer existed. During the long, lovely night in Paul's arms, Amy had decided to give herself the gift of time for Christmas. Time to absorb the new relationships and lessons of the past weeks. Time to contemplate what she wanted to do and where she wanted to be. Time to know Paul.

She felt relieved and excited. And she loved this new morning. The town was blanketed with snow, the sky was as deep and as bright as the inn's name, and the air so crisp. Amy wanted to drink it all in and make it part of her. It was perfect. Today everything was perfect... almost.

Alone now, she could admit she was troubled by Paul's reaction to his ex-wife's request. Yes, she understood his misgivings. Yet she couldn't get it out of her mind that he had actually walked away from Andrew four years ago, and denied him contact even now. No matter how noble his reasons for giving up his rights to the boy, he had, in effect, abandoned his son. Maybe she was taking it all too personally. Perhaps the situation *did* hit too close to home. Still, in her heart, she felt Paul's refusal to see Andrew was wrong.

Amy prayed she could make Paul understand this.

She hit the mall in Winchester at eleven and was out by two in the afternoon. Amy was happy with the toys she chose for Willy and Jenny, and the mohair sweaters, leather gloves and silk scarves she bought for George, Bridget and Maura. Her best find was the pair of hand-crafted silver earrings she knew Bernadette would love. Who would have believed she'd be buying Christmas gifts for her father's other "family"? Or how very happy it would make her to do so?

Although her trip to the mall had been successful, she drove to Maura's shop for the few remaining gifts she needed for her Washington friends. New Worlds bustled with last minute Christmas shoppers, so Amy browsed through the sizable selections of New Age music CDs while Maura helped her customers.

"Thank goodness Christmas is the day after tomorrow. I love all the extra business, but I could use a break," Maura declared when the two women finally had a moment together. As usual, she was full of chatter about everything in her universe, and it didn't take long for her to get around to Amy and Paul.

"You two were very chummy the other night at Mom's. Is there something going on I should know about?"

"Depends on what you think you *should* know," Amy answered with a wry smile before returning her attention to the CDs.

"You and Paul have clicked—that much is obvious." She shook her head and chuckled. "That mother of mine is one smart cookie—I never give her enough credit."

"What do you mean?"

"Don't mind me," Maura said, dismissing herself with a wave of a hand. "Are you looking for music for anyone in particular?"

"For my business partner's husband. Julie and I always get together to exchange gifts on Christmas morning. But heaven help me if I show up without something for Max," explained Amy. "He takes gifts very seriously."

Maura's mouth dropped open. "You mean you're not going to be here on Christmas Day?"

"I told you—I promised my mother I'd come home."

"Yes, but I'd hoped you'd change your mind. I mean, once you go back, will we really ever get to see you again?" Maura fretted. "What about Paul? And the inn? Have you made up your mind what to do about it?"

"Relax, Maura, I'll be visiting Tremont on a regular basis."

"Really? Does that mean what I think it means?"

Amy nodded. "I haven't said a word to anyone else, but I'm going to keep my half interest in the inn."

Amy realized she had probably decided the morning Paul brought her back to the inn after the storm. But the past two days had solidified the choice in her heart and mind. She didn't want to break her tie to her father's memory and the Blue Sky, or to the Ryans. And she especially didn't want to lose her link to Paul—not if he was the love she'd been hoping for all her life, not if he was the one man she could trust with her love.

Now she would have time to find out.

Maura practically screamed with delight. "I can't believe it!" She ran around the checkout counter to hug Amy. "This is the best news ever. But why haven't you told anyone?"

"Haven't had the chance. I just called my lawyers this morning to get the ball rolling. They're looking into how much I'll need to invest to keep the Blue Sky afloat and to pay off some of its debts."

"You're willing to do all that?" Maura hugged her again. "You don't know how much this will mean to my mother."

Amy smiled. "Oh, I have some idea."

"How she prayed for this." Maura's eyes widened suddenly. "Paul, too! He'll be so relieved. Now Mama can pay him back all that money he loaned her. And not a moment too soon, either."

"Paul lent Bernadette some money?"

"Not *some* money. *A lot* of money. Right after Greg died," Maura revealed. "Mama would have lost it all if he hadn't."

"It's lucky he could afford to help her."

"Yeah, but now the Valley News Group has hit a real tough patch, and Paul needs that cash—badly."

Amy felt uneasiness creeping up on her. "How badly?"

"We're talking job layoffs, which will kill Paul to do. And it could really damage his reputation in this town. A lot of people didn't like the way he came back and bought out the Tullys."

Amy nodded, remembering various remarks she'd heard over the weeks. Why hadn't she paid more attention to them?

"And you know what Dirk told me the other night?" Maura lowered her voice, although there was no one else in the store to hear. "Paul had to take a second mortgage on his house to raise some fast money for the business. Trouble is there's a huge balloon payment due early on. Dirk is real worried about that."

"Oh, God, you mean Paul could lose the house."

"Well, he *could have*. Except you're saving the day," Maura reminded. "But please don't say anything to Mama about Paul's second mortgage. She's not supposed to know about it—none of us are."

Amy stiffened. "You're right. Paul wouldn't want any of us to know."

"That's my cousin," Maura said with affection. "He'd do just about anything for Mama."

Of course Amy knew that. She'd known that since her first night in Tremont. Yet somehow she'd lost sight of the fact over the past several days.

Her mind was in a daze as Maura suggested CDs for Max Bauman. Amy bought two and quickly left the store. She was dumbfounded, stunned. Paul had never said a word to her about his financial stake in the Blue Sky.

She told herself to stay calm, to think through what Maura had said, before jumping to conclusions. But as she drove out of Winchester, she couldn't help wracking her brain over the past weeks. Amy had no illusions about Bernadette's motivation for getting her down to Tremont in the first place and drawing her into the family. It was all to save the inn. She'd known that from the beginning.

Until now, however, she hadn't recognized that Bernadette had contrived situations to throw her and Paul together. Like the night Amy had volunteered to tend bar in the Pub Room because of Bud's family emergency. Bernadette couldn't get Paul over there fast enough to help her. But, as Amy had discovered later, Bud had had no family emergency—Bernadette had made it up.

Had Bernadette detected a spark of attraction in her eyes and decided to put it to use? Was Paul added insurance, in case the inn and memories of Greg Riordan weren't enough to hold her? Amy had to hand it to her— Bernadette *was* one smart cookie.

Exasperating as she found Bernadette's manipulations, Amy wasn't shocked or even that angered by them. The older woman's agenda wasn't exactly hidden—Amy knew what Bernadette wanted from her.

But Paul? Did he have an agenda of his own? It was almost too painful to contemplate. She ran everything he'd said or done through her head with the calculating scrutiny years of necessity had sharpened to a fine point.

For a man described as being private, Paul had revealed some extremely personal things about himself to her—from the death of his parents to the loss of his wife and son. She had believed—or wanted to believe—an in-

trinsic bond existed between them, a bond that had led
Paul to share himself with her. Had that been a silly romantic notion on her part, and a clever manipulation on
his? After all, Paul knew her vulnerable spots, especially
where losing her father was concerned. All he had needed
to win her heart was a few suitable and well-timed conversations.

Amy gripped the steering wheel so tight her knuckles
turned white. She hated thinking this way about Paul.
The soul in his eyes, the tenderness in his voice, the passion in his touch—they had to have been genuine. They
couldn't have been all lies. Paul was not grasping and
selfish like Jeff Martin. He was not irresponsible and
unreliable like her father. Although he'd never actually
said the words, Paul cared for her as no other man had
before.

She wanted so much for that to be true, yet she
couldn't trust herself to believe it. She'd engaged in such
magical thinking before. A familiar black frustration
shrouded her heart as she had to face the inevitable
question. Did Paul want and need her for herself? Or was
he after her for the power and money she possessed to
save not only his beloved aunt's inn but his business and
home, as well?

Amy didn't know the answer. But the fact that the
question had to be asked was tearing her apart. She
thought she had, finally, found a man who didn't want a
blessed thing from her except her love. She had thought
Paul was a man she could trust.

Apparently she was wrong.

Arriving at the inn, Amy grabbed the shopping bag
containing the Ryan gifts and went in search of Bernadette. She found her in the office.

"I see your expedition to the mall was a success," Bernadette said, her sparkly gray eyes roaming over the store-wrapped packages.

Amy felt a twinge of sadness as she asked Bernadette to put the presents for the family under the cottage tree.

"If you'd like," Bernadette agreed. "But you can bring them tomorrow night and do the honors yourself."

"I'm afraid I won't be spending Christmas Eve with your family after all. I've decided to return to Washington today—as soon as I pack my things."

The color drained from Bernadette's face. "I don't understand."

"It's just time for me to go home," she said, hanging on to her composure with all her strength. She didn't want to upset Bernadette with anger or tears. "You should know I've decided to maintain half ownership of the inn as a silent partner. All outstanding debts will be covered, and you'll remain completely in charge. My lawyers will be contacting you after the holidays."

"Your lawyers? But when are you coming back?"

Amy looked away. "I don't know."

"What about Paul?" She sounded stunned.

"Tell him—" To keep her voice from breaking, she took a deep breath. "Tell him I'll have funds transferred to you as soon as possible."

"He doesn't know you're leaving?"

Amy didn't answer. She walked out of the office and ran up the stairs to her room.

Fighting tears, she grabbed her suitcase and emptied out the drawers and closet as quickly as she could. Only the green elf suit remained hanging in the closet. The memories it aroused paralyzed her for countless moments until she finally yanked it off the hanger and dropped it into the wastebasket.

After clearing her toiletries from the bathroom, Amy called Julie Bauman and told her she'd be in the office the next morning. The call was interrupted by a hard rapping on her room door. Her heart clutched when Paul called her name.

She steeled herself against the sad dread threatening her composure. Amy took a deep breath and calmly opened the door. "Bernadette didn't waste any time," she noted as Paul whisked past her.

He stood in the middle of the room, his gaze roaming from her to the packed suitcases on the bed to the elf suit drooping over the sides of the wicker wastebasket. Casting a cool glance her way, he seized the green costume from the basket. "What the hell are you doing?"

"I'm going home for Christmas, just as I'd always planned."

"But we'd planned to spend Christmas Eve together," he said, twisting the green unitard in his hands. "And Bernadette has the notion that you're not coming back."

"She's right. I'm not." She went over to the bed to close the suitcases. "I've found the answers I came for, and I've made the necessary decisions. Now it's high time I get back to my life."

Grasping her arm, Paul swung her around to face him. "What about us?"

The burning bewilderment in his eyes floored her. She didn't know which she wanted to do more, slap his face or hold him close. She swallowed hard, instead, and fought to keep her emotions in check.

"Paul, you don't have to play the game anymore—Bernadette's getting exactly what she wanted. And your money troubles are over."

"Money troubles?" His grip on her wrist tightened. "What are you talking about?"

She twisted away from him and turned back to her luggage. She couldn't bear looking at his fake confusion. "I know all about your loan to Bernadette, and your cash flow problems at the papers and the risky second mortgage on your house. It's a shame such a generous act backfired on you. But everything will smooth itself out now."

"Where did you hear this?"

"Does it matter? I mean everybody in town seems to know one thing or another about your financial situation. Only I've been too dense to pay attention." Amy snapped the locks on her suitcases and pulled them onto the floor. "You should have just told me what you and Bernadette needed. Certainly you shouldn't have let my tales of woe about being used scare you off. Being honest would have saved you a lot of emotional effort and me a heck of a lot of time."

"You can't believe that I . . ." Paul threw the costume on the bed. His gaze darkened with disbelief as his expression hardened. "You really think I'd make love to you for the sake of the inn? Or that I'd tell you about the most painful time in my life in hope of solvency? My God, Amy."

"I think you'd do anything in your power to protect Bernadette's happiness." She stared him straight in the eye. "And the same applies to keeping your business from going down the drain."

"You don't mean that. You can't." He grabbed her shoulders, pulling her taut against his chest. "Don't you know I love you?"

"Paul, don't—"

He shook her gently. "I love you."

She wished he hadn't said it. It was the one thing she didn't need to hear from him. "What good are the words if I can't trust them? You told me you loved Andrew more than anything. Still, you've turned your back on him. How can I believe in your love?"

"Because it's real—all of it. Every second, every day," he insisted. "After the beautiful nights together, the way we've held each other—how can you doubt me?"

Pulling away from him, Amy squinted back tears of regret. No matter how much she wanted to believe Paul, it was too late. The seed of doubt had already been planted, the mistrust expressed. Nothing would be the same between them. She felt such loss, such sadness. But falling apart now would mean certain disaster. She wouldn't be able to resist his comforting arms.

"I've been fooled before, Paul," she said, sounding as callous as she could and meaning every word. "You're no different from the others."

His pained expression made her heart sink. But the fury in his voice ripped right through her. "I thought *you* were different, Amy. I'd convinced myself you were the one woman who could love me for the man I am. Right or wrong, good times or bad, you'd be there for me, just as I would be for you. The trouble is, you don't trust me. Never did, never will."

"I tried. I really tried."

"Possibly." He gave her a skeptical look, although his anger remained clear. "But in the end your mistrust won out. I never stood a chance."

She lowered her gaze to the floor, unable to take his intense, blue stare any longer, unwilling to deal with his accusation. "I'm sorry things turned out this way," she murmured, knowing she'd never see him again.

"Not half as sorry as I am."

Without so much as a goodbye, Paul walked out on her.

Chapter Fourteen

"I hate to leave you alone this afternoon, Amy," Thomas Windom said, wrapping a black, wool scarf around his neck. "Sure you won't change your mind about coming to Angier's open house?"

Amy gave her stepfather a peck on the cheek. "I'd rather stay and help Mrs. Jenkins get Christmas dinner ready. Besides, Angier's never forgiven me for accidentally breaking his crèche angel all those years ago."

"Darling, you were only ten. He doesn't even remember it."

"Oh, no? Then why does he cringe every year when he sees me walk in?"

Thomas acknowledged this with a smile. "He's nothing but an old fussbudget anyway. Maybe your mother and I should just skip it, too."

"And disappoint all your old buddies? Not on my account, Dad," Amy insisted. "Besides, I could use an hour or two to myself to regroup."

"If that's what you need. You seem very distracted today," Thomas commented, his tone hinting—again—that he wanted her to reveal more about her stay in Tremont. "Are you sure you're all right?"

"For the tenth time, yes." She straightened his coat collar and nudged him toward the library door. "I just need time to get back in the swing of things around here. The pace is a lot slower in Tremont."

"I hope you'll tell me about Greg's inn. You must have been impressed with it to retain your half interest. I was certain you would give it up."

"We'll talk in a few days, Dad, I promise."

Right now, her emotions were too raw to speak of the beautiful, old mansion on the hill and the family that had swept her up into their lives. Although she was glad to finally be back in Washington, where she belonged, Amy thought about the Ryans constantly—and Dirk Campbell, Janie Lee Pratt, Bud and all the others in that gentle little Virginia town.

Nor could Amy tell her stepfather about the man who had stolen her love. She couldn't bear to even think about Paul Hanley. Because when she did, she found herself either raging against his denied subterfuge or missing him terribly.

Her solution was to keep busy, to ride the holidays out on a wave of work, family and friends. And to refuse Paul's phone calls.

Yesterday she had gone into the office to catch up on a month's worth of lost time. Only, she had felt out of sync with the agency's flow, as if she didn't belong there anymore. The few kids dropping by the office had grown tremendously and had acted shy around her. Yet this didn't bother her as much as it should have. It didn't seem to matter.

This morning, as the three of them exchanged gifts, Julie and Max had assured Amy that her enthusiasm for the agency would return with the new year.

She hoped they were right.

Thomas went to round up her mother, leaving Amy in the library with the family Christmas tree. As always, Joan Windom's tree was the perfect height, shape and density. The expensive silver bells and crystal balls were distributed evenly among the branches. Amy held one of the delicate balls in her hand. It probably cost more than all the Ryans' homemade ornaments and old family treasures combined. Still, all these exquisite decorations couldn't match the magical beauty of Bernadette's cottage tree. Perhaps the magic had been in the hands and hearts of the people who had decorated it that night.

Amy sat on the floor at the foot of the tree, disheartened to think that wonderful night had happened only last week. It seemed like a lifetime ago now.

"Amy! Why on earth are you sitting on the floor like that?"

Looking over her shoulder at her mother, Amy shrugged her reply. "Didn't you go with Dad?"

"I decided that if you didn't have to go to the open house, neither did I." Joan sat on the leather wing chair directly behind Amy. "Angier is such a bore."

This remark startled Amy—almost as much as her mother's decision to sit out a traditional holiday social gathering. That was not like her at all.

"You still haven't told me why you're here staring at the tree."

Amy shrugged again. "Just thinking."

"Just thinking," repeated Joan. "You *have* been in quite the mood today. Really, your visit to that dreary little town has had an abysmal effect on your disposition."

Irked by her mother's snappish tone, Amy scooted around on her bottom to face her. "Something on your mind, Mother?"

She looked taken aback. "If you must know, it's that—I—I just can't understand it."

"Can't understand what?"

"The whole thing! Staying down there so long with that woman—giving her all that money—deciding to keep that tie with Gregory Riordan. Honestly, Amy, I was beginning to wonder if you were ever coming back."

Joan averted her gaze and nervously smoothed an imaginary wrinkle in her champagne-colored knit skirt. But Amy had caught the flicker of fear in her mother's eyes. All of a sudden, she realized what that fear meant. Joan was afraid of losing her—to the inn, to "that woman" and, ultimately, to Greg.

Now she knew why her mother had skipped Angier's open house. It was an opportunity to be alone with her daughter, her first opportunity to find out what had happened in Tremont. Amy could see that Joan wanted to know. She was just too proud to say so. Feeling an unaccustomed sympathy for her mother, Amy reached for her hand and explained why it was important to her to keep Greg's dream alive.

"I don't know why you care." Joan removed her hand from Amy's. "He let you down—his very own daughter. He let us both down."

Her mother's bitterness was nothing new, but the tinge of sadness was. For Amy, it was like a crack in an impenetrable wall of restraint—all she had to do was wedge her way in. Paul had advised her to find out the reason behind her mother's unceasing acrimony toward her father. Perhaps now was her chance to learn the truth.

Joan brushed off her initial attempt, insisting it was pointless to wallow in the past. But Amy pressed gently until her mother told her things she'd never heard before.

"To this day I've never met a man as handsome as Greg," Joan revealed, staring past the tree into the invisible movie screen of her memory. "You look so much like him, you know."

"You never told me." Still sitting on the floor, Amy gazed up at her mother. Joan's expression had softened.

"I thought it a million times while you were growing up, but the words just burned in my throat. There were such hard feelings between him and me after the divorce. Later, when he disappeared on you, I was furious," her mother admitted. "It was one thing to disappoint me. But his own daughter?"

"How did he disappoint you, Mother?"

Joan leaned back in the wing chair. "I married Greg over my parents' objections. He had no family, no money, no profession. But I was enthralled by him, and he'd vowed to give me the best life possible. And I believed him. Yet when my father offered him a management position at his bank, Greg refused. After that, my parents never let me forget I married beneath myself."

Amy remembered her late grandparents well. Although they had indulged her materially, they had not been the least bit demonstrative. They'd been outspoken yet distant, and more than capable of making her parents' lives difficult.

"Why wouldn't Greg take the job?"

Joan gave a haughty laugh. "Greg Riordan marched to a different drummer. No starched-shirt life of routine for him. Which is why I fell in love with him, I suppose. He wasn't like the young men I'd grown up with here in Washington."

"The two of you were happy for a while. Right?"

"In the beginning it was all very romantic. We moved out to the country, where Greg found all sorts of jobs. Unfortunately they usually didn't last very long." She sighed and clutched the chair's arms. "Living from hand to mouth all the time grew unbearable—especially after you were born. I stood it for as long as I could, because you adored him and so did I. When my father offered him yet another job and a house here in town, I begged Greg to accept. If he really loved me, he had to take it."

Amy had never heard her mother's voice tremble so. "But he still refused?"

Joan nodded. "Even though he knew our marriage was on the line. I don't know, maybe I shouldn't have backed him into a corner, but I was young and very scared. So I packed you up and moved back home. Deep down, I had hoped my leaving would shake him up enough to do right by us. But Greg was too stubborn and proud for that."

Amy's heart went out to Joan. Before now, she hadn't known how much her mother had loved Greg, or the depth of her pain and disappointment. Before now, Amy doubted she could have understood the devastation of being let down by the man you loved heart and soul. Until now—until Paul—she had never loved that deeply.

She clasped her mother's hands between hers, wishing she had known her mother's side of the story a long time ago. Maybe she and Joan could have been closer. "I'm sorry he hurt you, Mother."

Joan looked down at her, eyes glistening with unshed tears. "Thomas means the world to me—you know that. But I had pinned my hopes and dreams on Greg. He was the love of my life." A solitary tear drifted down her powdered cheek. "Perhaps that's why I could never forgive him."

Forgiveness might have relieved Joan of her bitterness, but Amy doubted it would have spared her the lingering pain of losing the man she'd loved. She found it all terribly sad.

Passion and hope, expectations and disappointments, dreams and despair—they all were a part of love. They all made it a dangerous endeavor. True, love brought great joy, but it could rob one's soul of it, as well. Her mother was a prime example. The years of sadness reflected in Joan's eyes told Amy all she needed to know about the cost of love's loss.

Bernadette opened the cottage door before Paul had a chance to knock. "I'm glad you've come. I've been worrying about you all day."

"I don't know why. Every time you or one of the girls called, I said I was fine."

Bernadette helped him with his jacket. "We hated the thought of you staying away on Christmas Day," she insisted. "Especially since you didn't come by last night, either."

"I told you I needed time alone. I thought you understood."

He tried to keep his impatience from showing. Bernadette was beside herself with concern for him and distress over Amy's abrupt departure; she meant well. He just wished she'd accept his need to come to grips with

Amy's leaving in private. Since that seemed unlikely, he'd broken down and come over.

"God will bless you for indulging a worried old lady," she said, hooking her arm through his. "The others have all gone home. It's just you and me now."

Paul supposed he should be grateful for that. As much as he loved Bridget and Maura, he didn't need an audience to witness his anger and hurt. And he was hurting—more than he ever had before.

Bernadette led him into the study. "Express Delivery left a gift here for you yesterday afternoon. I put it under the tree just as Amy asked me to."

"What?"

"Several days ago, Amy said she was having a present for you sent here and would I mind putting it under my tree. I'm sure she's forgotten about it with all the fuss. But there it is." Bernadette pointed below the tree.

Paul couldn't believe his eyes. Beneath a huge, fluffy, red satin bow was a spanking new adult-size sled with shiny red handles and runners. Amy had said something about Santa putting a sled beneath the Christmas tree for him. Then she'd gone ahead and arranged it all herself. To surprise him. To make him smile.

He sure as hell wasn't smiling, and his surprise quickly evaporated into dejection. He'd spent the past two days attempting to erase all reminders of Amy Riordan from his house and heart. Struggling like crazy to blot out the lush delight of making love to her and the sweet warmth of talking with her long into the night, Paul had convinced himself he would indeed survive this blow. But the damn sled had unraveled any hope of that. Now he had to face the truth.

Amy was the best thing to ever happen to him. How in the name of heaven did he think he'd get over her?

Paul stooped down to read the gift tag attached to the bow.

"This sled is big enough for two on purpose! Meet you at the hill. All my love, Amy."

He stared at the card until the anger that was part and parcel of his despair emerged from deep within him. All her love?

Amy's love had been a sublime gift. Except it hadn't lasted very long and was devoid of all trust. For Paul, Amy's love was like the sled—a painful reminder of what might have been, sad evidence of what was lost. His soul ached with emptiness.

He felt a hand on his shoulder. "You've got to find Amy and set things right, Paul."

"Bernadette, don't start. Please." He pushed the sled back beneath the tree and stood up. "If you must know, I've tried to call her several times. She didn't answer her phone at all last night. Today the housekeeper at her mother's told me 'Miss Riordan is not available.' Amy doesn't want to talk to me."

"Oh, that's nothing but her father's stubbornness and pride coming through. I'll call her. She'll take my call."

"I wouldn't be so sure about that."

Bernadette's shoulders sank and she looked as if she was about to cry. "I didn't mean to hurt her—or you. I was trying to help."

"Come on, let's sit down." Curving an arm behind her back, Paul walked her to the sofa. "What happened isn't your fault. Okay?"

"But I did try to throw you two together. After I had Bridget find out who that Jeff Martin person was, I arranged certain things," Bernadette confessed. "Because I didn't want you to be alone anymore, Paul. And I knew

Amy was the girl for you. I knew it the moment I saw her.''

"You knew?" He peered at her with a skeptical eye, knowing she possessed a keen Irish sentimentality. Especially when it came to Greg Riordan.

"All right, I admit I fancied the idea of Greg's daughter settling down in Tremont with you and someday running the inn on her own. What's wrong with that?"

Paul squeezed her hand gently. "You can't push your dreams on people."

"Push, you say?" Bernadette rolled her eyes to the ceiling. "I barely had to tap the two of you together. Face it, Paul, you love Amy and she loves you."

"She doesn't even trust me. She thinks I'm after her money." The mere thought of Amy's accusation made him burn with resentment. Did she really believe he could be that low?

"She must be confused. Or afraid of her feelings," insisted Bernadette. "Coming here the way she did couldn't have been easy. Amy is still carrying some emotional baggage to work out where her father is concerned."

"I know that. Don't you think I wanted to help her?"

"Then why, for heaven's sake, are you here instead of in Washington?"

The challenge in his aunt's brown eyes provoked his ire. "Because I'm absolutely furious with her. Hell, she accepts calls from her ex-fiancé—a jerk who was really out to use her—but she refuses me."

"There, you see? She really is in love with you."

He glared at his aunt. "And that's how she shows it?"

"You matter so much to her it hurts. And remember," she added, "Amy refused Greg, too."

Paul ran a weary hand through his hair. He'd forgotten what had happened with Greg.

"Please, don't repeat Greg's mistake. Don't give up on Amy the way he did all those years ago." Bernadette placed a hand on his arm. "Please don't *you* give up this time."

He met her pleading gaze. She didn't have to say anything else. He knew she was referring to how he'd given up Andrew.

Paul made no promises when he left Bernadette. But as he drove home, her logic was hard to dispute. He, too, believed Amy loved him, a fact that had fed his resentment. Yet it was easier to be indignant than to confront her head-on. It was simpler just to let her go.

Although she'd never come out and said it, Amy faulted him for not fighting for Andrew—for his son. She thought he should have. Paul still believed he'd done the best thing for everyone concerned at the time. He wasn't about to second-guess his decision four years after the fact. He glanced over at the passenger seat, where he'd left the Christmas card Shelly had sent. Andrew's smiling face looked up at him. It was too late to change the past. But the future?

Tightening his grip on the steering wheel, Paul committed himself to fight this time. To fight for all the passion and light this special woman brought to his life. A fight for Amy.

Now all he needed was a way to get through to her....

Two days after Christmas, the agency was in a deep holiday lull. Amy was glad to have the chance to wade through routine paperwork. Busywork kept her mind off Paul and how he'd stopped calling. But not always. Disappointment often harassed her peace of mind. Still, what did she expect from him? That he'd keep trying to call her indefinitely? She had served her purpose, enabling him to continue his business free of financial concern. Paul probably had decided to get on with life—just as she had. And that was for the best.

So why couldn't her heart get the message and accept it was over?

With a sigh, Amy sifted through a backlog of nonpriority mail as Julie rattled on about the Jamaican resort she and husband Max were jetting off to on New Year's Day. Their secretary, Melissa, listened, fascinated. The phones rarely rang.

After regaling them about her vacation, Julie turned to her. "Did you get to look at Shawna's audition tapes? Is she going to sell a lot of toothpaste or what?"

She nodded. "They were great—Shawna was great. I can't believe how much she's progressed in one month. No wonder she got the Mighty Whites bleach job. You've done a great job with her, Jules."

"It took a few days for her to warm up to me. But then we became great pals and she relaxed—a lot."

It showed in Shawna's tapes. She was confident, cute, sweet and looked very much at home in front of the camera. Gone was the shy little girl who would stop, mid-dialogue, to peer behind the camera for Amy's reassurance. She'd known Shawna would pull it all together eventually. Amy was taken aback, however, that it had happened this quickly and without her help.

The telephone jangled to life. "Thomas Windom for you, Amy," Melissa announced.

A phone call from Thomas in the middle of the workday was unusual. She picked up the line. "Is something wrong, Dad?"

"Wrong? Of course not," he said, sounding amused. "I was just sitting here thinking how nice it would be to have lunch together. Can you join me?"

"Today?" she asked, startled. Her stepfather was not given to impulse.

"Aren't you free?"

She assured him she was. "Where shall I meet you?"

"Just come up to my office. Say, in about an hour?"

After hanging up, Amy thought it odd he had suggested meeting at his office instead of a restaurant. There were many excellent places to dine between her office and his. Something had to be up, and she had a good idea of what it was. Thomas wanted to discuss her decision about the Blue Sky.

She *had* promised him she would. She saw no point in putting it off. Explaining about the inn, Tremont, the Ryans and Greg Riordan would never be easy—emotionally speaking. Maybe Thomas could help her put it all in some sort of perspective. He'd always been good at that. Besides, she had questions for him regarding a certain photo album. Before leaving the office, she grabbed the album from her briefcase and tucked it under her arm.

Amy was surprised to find Thomas outside his office, sitting at the secretary's desk. "Dad?"

"Hello, dear." He spotted the bulky album under her arm. "What have you got there?"

She had planned to show it to during lunch, but decided there was no time like the present. She placed it on the desk. "Go ahead. Take a look."

Opening to the first page of photographs, Thomas grew very still. He stared at the first set of pictures for a long time before finally lifting his eyes to Amy. "You know where he got these?"

"Bernadette told me."

"I see."

"I need you to tell me why."

"That would mean explaining many, many complicated feelings and issues." He glanced at his closed office door. "But, basically, I couldn't stop thinking about how I'd feel in Riordan's shoes, how I'd feel if I lost all contact with you."

Tears stinging her eyes, Amy leaned over to kiss the top of her stepfather's head. "Thank you for remembering him, Dad," she whispered. "I'll always be grateful."

He patted her hand. "I felt terrible keeping it secret from your mother. You understand why I couldn't tell her, don't you?"

"She'd see it as a betrayal."

"Unfortunately," Thomas said, closing the album. "In her defense, I think you should know how very distressed she was by Greg's death. She wept the night Mrs. Ryan called with the news."

"If you had told me that a week ago, I would have been shocked. Now I believe it." Amy wiped an errant tear with the back of hand. Taking a deep breath before she really lost her composure, she cracked a wry smile. "Tell me, why *are* you sitting out here?"

"You'd better sit down. It's quite a story."

Baffled, she pulled a chair closer to the desk. "What's going on?"

"Your mother and I had an unexpected visitor early this morning. *Very* early. Young man practically dragged us out of bed."

"Young man?"

"A most impressive young man," Thomas said, leaning back in the secretary's swivel chair. "A man who cares very deeply for you."

"Paul," she gasped, her body feeling as if it were in free-fall.

"Yes, Paul. He had quite a lot to say to us."

"I bet he did."

"In any case, I'll make a long story short." Standing up, Thomas pushed the chair neatly beneath his secretary's desk. "This man is sitting in my office, wanting very much to talk to you."

"I—I—don't know." She stared blankly at her silver-haired stepfather. Her mind was torn by fear and hope.

"What you do is totally up to you. Still, I suggest—with all the love in my heart—that you not repeat your parents' mistake. If you *are* in love with this man, go to him and work out a life for yourself."

"How can I be sure, Dad? I've made so many stupid mistakes."

"And each mistake has led you right here, because you've learned from them. I can see it," he reassured.

"You can?"

He nodded. "Trust yourself, Amy. It's time." Stepping up to his office door, he curved his hand around the knob. "Shall I?"

Her knees trembling, she rose from the chair and nodded. Thomas pushed the door open. "Good luck, dear."

When she walked in, Paul was gazing at the expansive view from the floor-to-ceiling window behind Thomas's desk. He wore his customary brown, leather jacket and denim jeans, and his thick, gold hair appeared a bit disheveled. Amy felt her heart slam against her chest. He looked exactly as he had the first time she'd laid eyes on him.

When she clicked the door shut behind her, Paul turned around. His sky blue eyes drank her in. A smile of hope brightened his face. "You came."

His deep, honeyed voice filled the gnawing hole in her heart. God help her, how she loved him. No matter what happened now or in the years down the road, Amy knew she would always love Paul Hanley.

"You went to a lot of trouble." She leaned against the edge of her stepfather's desk. "I guess I can listen to what you have to say."

Paul lifted a hand to touch her, but stopped. Instead he rested his hands on the high back of Thomas's leather desk chair. "You and I have been hiding behind the shadows of the past for way too long."

She gave him a sidelong glance. "Hiding from what?"

"From the opportunity to love, to find some happiness. Until you, I didn't think such things were possible for me," he admitted, "because the past tends to overshadow the possibilities. But I refuse to hide from the truth any longer, and I'm not going to let you do it, either."

The determination in his voice unnerved her. Amy moved over to the window, needing to focus on the familiar, like the stretch of mall between the monuments and the curving grace of the Potomac River in the distance. She needed to hold on to who she was and where she belonged. Yet, looking in every direction possible, she felt nothing.

"You and I belong together, Amy. I believe that deep in my soul."

Paul came up behind her, close enough that she could smell the trace of wood smoke in his jacket. It reminded her of his handsome stone fireplace and how they had held each other in front of the dancing flames.

"I'm sorry your father left you," he continued. "And I'm sorry for the men who have used you. God knows I've made mistakes, but I really love you. I love you for your warmth, your eyes, your laugh, the way you hold me after we make love.''

Finally, he cupped her shoulders between his hands, his embrace firm as he murmured in her ear, ''I'm a man who wants to love you, not hurt you. Believe it, Amy. Take a leap of faith and believe in me.''

She turned around to face him, her heart in her throat. Searching his eyes, she touched his cheek. Then, with a fierce surge of emotion, she flung herself into his arms. ''I love you,'' she whispered over and over between kisses, pressing close against him.

Paul held her so tight she could scarcely breathe. And she didn't care. She never wanted him to let her go. ''Tell me you believe in me, Amy,'' he said, his fingers entwined in her hair. ''I need to hear it.''

Her heart was so full, she wanted to tell him so much. She wanted to make him sure. Leaning her head back, she sought his gaze. ''It takes some kind of man to track Thomas Windom down at the crack of dawn—how could I not believe in you? How could I not love you?''

''Enough to take your chances?''

She nodded. ''My mother and father were once madly in love, yet they weren't capable of taking that leap of faith. And they suffered for it. Loving demands a lot, so does sharing a life. Except the alternative is bitter regret—my parents taught me that. But, as of this moment, I'm breaking that chain.''

Paul lowered his head, kissing her with deep emotion. She felt its passionate heat suffuse her heart and body with his love.

''Marry me, Amy,'' he breathed against her lips, and then kissed her once more. ''Marry me soon and share your life with me.''

"I will. You know I will," she answered, breathless. "But there are certain conditions."

"Anything." The look in his eyes told her he meant it.

"I want to live with you in Tremont, in your beautiful house."

"*Our* beautiful house."

She smiled. "I'm going to become Bernadette's assistant at the inn, and you know how hectic that line of work can be. You're going to have to share me with the Blue Sky."

"I'll do that gladly." Paul hugged her to him. "But what about the agency? Your town house? Washington? I'm not expecting you to give that all up."

"I've been feeling like a fish out of water ever since I came back," she revealed. It was a relief to finally be able to admit it. "My heart isn't in the agency—I just keep thinking about the inn. I don't care about Washington anymore. I just want to be with you, in Tremont."

"Are you sure? You've been back only a few days."

Amy stepped out of Paul's arms and led him closer to the window. "When I look out there I see a great, exciting city, but it doesn't feel like home any more," she explained, caressing his cheek with her hand. "Do you know why I finally gave in to Bernadette's demands to visit the inn? Because I found out what my father named it. Touch the Blue Sky. Do you know where Greg got the name?"

Paul shook his head. "I don't think I ever heard it discussed."

"Bernadette doesn't know, nor anyone else as far as I can tell. Except for me."

Amy told Paul about the swing game Greg had made up for her. "It's one of the few memories I have of him. When I realized he named the inn after it, I had to go there. Now I know it was some of sort of sign. Because I found you, and the rest—Bernadette, Bridget and Maura, the town. All the pieces began falling into place for me. I belong there.''

"With me," Paul said, giving her hands a loving squeeze, "and Mr. Snead and the house—"

"And our kids?"

"As many as you want." His eyes sparkled with love, making her heart thrum with contentment. She couldn't wait to get him back home to Tremont.

"Who shall we tell first?" she asked, unbearable happiness welling up inside. "I wonder if Thomas is still sitting outside here."

"I can't wait to see Bernadette's face when we tell her," Paul added.

"And Bridget and Maura? What a kick."

Paul laughed. "You might want to reconsider marrying into this family."

"Too late, I already belong."

Amy put her hand in Paul's, and together they started the journey back to the rolling hills and welcoming arms of the prettiest town on earth, back to plan a life they had never imagined possible. They were going home.

Epilogue

Paul stood in the gazebo, gazing out at the inn's emerald green grounds. Looking down at the tiny village at the foot of the hill, he saw Tremont in its full spring glory. He couldn't remember a May afternoon as glorious as this one, the mountain panorama crystal clear, the sky the most incredible blue. It was a perfect day for marrying the perfect woman for him.

Dirk Campbell, all decked out in formal best-man attire, skipped up the gazebo steps. His eyes flashed with surprise at the flowers, ribbons and greenery that had transformed the gazebo into a wedding altar. "Wow, look at this place."

"Maura decorated the whole thing," Paul informed him.

"You've got to be kidding. From her I'd expect wind chimes and strawberry incense." Dirk shook his head. "Your cousin is a constant amazement to me."

Paul spotted Bernadette scurrying between the rows of folding chairs, squinting up at the gazebo. She called to Dirk. "George wants you to go over the ring and pillow bit with Willy one more time. And, Paul Hanley, come down here," she added. "I want to get a good look at you."

He met her at the bottom of the steps. "Do I pass muster?"

She fidgeted with his collar and tie before stepping back. "You look so handsome. And happier than I've ever seen you. It's all so wonderful—I can't believe it's happening."

"Come here." He put his arms around his aunt, embracing her warmly. "Thank you for taking care of me when no one else would. And for always being there for me. I don't know if I'd be marrying a great woman like Amy if you hadn't been in my life."

"Don't get me going. I promised myself I wouldn't start bawling at least until the ceremony." She dabbed at her eyes with a scrunched-up tissue. "I also came to tell you that Shelly and Andrew have arrived. I knew you'd like to say hello before the ceremony."

"Thanks, love." He planted a kiss on her forehead. "I'll go find them."

Paul was glad his ex and her son had made it down for the wedding. In the past few months, he and Andrew had developed a nice, easy-going relationship. And, with Amy's encouragement, he and Shelly had finally come to terms with what had happened between them.

"Paul! Over here!" Andrew called out as Paul wove his way through the growing crowd of guests.

Paul shook his head with disbelief. Andrew looked so grown-up in his blue suit and striped necktie. The cuddly toddler he used to carry on his shoulders was all boy.

But even now he wasn't too big to be lifted up for a warm hug. "I'm so happy you're here today. It means a lot to me."

"I've never been to a wedding before. Have I, Mom?"

Standing behind her son, Shelly smiled and shook her head. "This is a first for him."

"I'm honored." Paul straightened Andrew's jacket and tie. "And I'll tell Bernadette to make sure you get an extra big piece of wedding cake."

"I brought you a wedding present," Andrew announced, handing him a loosely wrapped object. "I made it in Cub Scouts."

After tearing off the wrapping paper, Paul gazed at the roughly carved wooden candle holder for a long time. To him, it was almost as precious as the clay model of Sneed Andrew had made on his first day of nursery school. He got down on his knees to embrace the boy again. "It's beautiful, son, just beautiful. I know Amy will love it."

He glanced up at Shelly and she met his gaze with glistening eyes.

"I'm so happy for you, Paul. No one deserves happiness more," she murmured. "And I'm glad Andrew and I can be part of your special day."

Holding Andrew close to him, he reached for Shelly's hand. "So am I, Shell. So am I."

He meant it with all his heart. Laying rest to the past had not been without its thorns, but the rewards were abundant. Today was the happiest day of his life. Now he and his beautiful bride were free to embrace the future together.

From a window of an upstairs suite, Amy smiled as she watched Paul with Andrew and Shelly. Her heart was near to bursting with pride and happiness. She couldn't believe she had finally found a man she could trust and love for the rest of her days.

"Amy, turn around, dear. Let me check the front of your veil."

She turned to her mother, allowing Joan to primp at her to her heart's content. She was just so grateful to have her mother with her—really with her.

Joan surveyed Amy from head to toe. "You look beautiful, darling. Absolutely perfect."

She smiled at her mother's unqualified praise, quietly reflecting on how far the two of them had come since Christmas. Amy reached for Joan's hand. "Thank you for honoring my wish to have the wedding here at the Blue Sky. Coming here can't have been easy for you."

"I needed to do this for both of us," Joan said, holding tight to Amy's hand. "When Paul showed up at the house that day after Christmas, I saw right away how much you meant to him. I didn't want you to lose that. And I made a promise, to Thomas and myself, that I wasn't going to do to you what my parents did to me."

Amy felt teary, but took several deep breaths to keep her composure.

"Now, Amy, I've been talking to the girls, and I know you have something borrowed, blue and new. I told them I was providing the something old." Joan pulled a delicate lace-trim handkerchief from her purse. Amy had never seen it before. "I carried this on the day I married Greg. It was his mother's."

Her eyes wide, she accepted the handkerchief from her mother. "I can't believe you kept it. And for all these years?"

"On that day, I loved your father more than anything," Joan whispered, tears threatening her voice.

"Oh, Mother, thank you." Amy hugged her close.

"Now, we really must stop this," Joan said, finally breaking away when Julie Bauman entered the room, "or we'll both ruin our makeup."

Julie carried in two bouquets of spring flowers. "It's time to start," she announced, handing Amy the larger bouquet.

Joan gathered up her belongings. "Let me go round up Thomas."

"Bridget and Maura are all dressed and set downstairs. I thought it best if they kept an eye on our little flower girl and ring bearer."

"You're the most efficient matron of honor a woman could have," Amy teased.

"Hey, I'm just so happy to get you married off I'm making sure everything goes off without a hitch," countered Julie. "Although I'm gonna kind of miss your smiling face around the office. So I'll be making a lot of long-distance consultation calls."

"Any time I can help."

Bernadette poked her head in the door. "Thomas is ready, but can I sneak a peek at you first?"

"Peek away," Julie said with a parting wave to Amy. "I'll see you downstairs."

When they were alone, Bernadette hugged Amy. "Your groom is walking on air out there. He's not the least bit nervous," she informed her. "Promise me you'll always be good to my boy. No one deserves some happiness more than he does."

"I know. And I do promise." She patted Bernadette's hand. Then, remembering the handkerchief, Amy showed it to her.

"I'm happy your mother saved it for you." She ran her fingers over the fine, old linen. "You know, I feel Greg is in this room with us right now. And surely he's the happiest one here. Do I sound like a dotty old fool?"

Amy felt her lips curve into a tender smile, and she gently touched Bernadette's faded red hair. "I feel his presence whenever I'm with you."

Bernadette dabbed at her eyes and then threw up her hands. "I'm not going to cry until the ceremony!"

Thomas was waiting for her at the top of the stairs. "This is the proudest day of my life," he told her as she clutched his arm tightly.

They walked down the elegant staircase and out to the veranda, where the rest of the bridal party awaited. Bridget and Maura, the sisters she'd always wanted and now had, looked lovely in their satin gowns. They offered her encouragement as they lined up behind Willy and Jenny for the walk down the aisle.

The string quartet started up the wedding march, but before she and Thomas began down the aisle, Amy took a long, loving look at those gathered to witness this much-wanted union. Among the many faces, she saw Martin and Bud taking a moment from their catering duties; Jake and Janie Lee Pratt beaming in their best Sunday outfits; several of her kids from the agency; Shelly and Andrew and her mother and Bernadette sitting proudly in the front row.

Then she looked ahead to the steps of the gazebo, where Paul stood waiting, tall, handsome and beaming with happiness. Amy closed her eyes, wanting to lock the memory of him at this moment in her heart forever. When she looked again, Paul caught her eye and winked.

"Are you ready?" Thomas whispered.

"Ready."

Her heart filled with deep love for the man at the end of the aisle and with affection for the family and friends surrounding them, Amy was ready to take the first step toward her future.

* * * * *

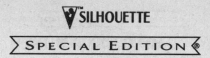

SILHOUETTE

◆SPECIAL EDITION◆

An invitation to three

Sweet Hope Weddings

from AMY FRAZIER

Marriages are made in Sweet Hope, Georgia—where the brides and grooms-to-be are the last to find out!

♥ ♥ ♥ ♥ ♥

NEW BRIDE IN TOWN
October 1996

WAITING AT THE ALTAR
November 1996

A GOOD GROOM IS HARD TO FIND
December 1996

♥ ♥ ♥ ♥ ♥

SILHOUETTE

> SPECIAL EDITION ®

COMING NEXT MONTH

EXPECTANT FATHER Leanne Banks

In one shocking night, Glory Danson and Caleb Masters made a baby!
Caleb was a brilliant scientist bent on saving the world—certainly not
father material. Could a tiny infant turn this confirmed bachelor into a
family man?

SUMMERS PAST Laurey Bright

When Seth Keegan returned home after years in prison, he expected his
mother's scorn and the neighbours' glares. But he was shocked to find
Ghislaine Pargiter, the woman he'd once loved, living high in his
family house, her young daughter mysteriously the heir to the Keegan
fortune...

NEW BRIDE IN TOWN Amy Frazier

Sweet Hope Weddings

Belle Sherman decided to live life to the full and moved to Sweet Hope
to do just that. This recently jilted bride had almost given up hope of
finding—and keeping—Mr Right. But when she met sexy Boone
O'Malley, Belle knew this was one eligible bachelor she couldn't let
pass her by!

MARRY ME, NOW! Allison Hayes

Nick Reynolds was Dacy Fallon's first love, the man she could never
forget. They'd been just seventeen when life had taken them on
different paths. Now fate had brought Dacy back to town—and she was
determined to reclaim her man...

MOLLY DARLING Laurie Paige

That's My Baby!

When scandal threatened Sam Frazier's custody of his child, a marriage
of convenience to Molly Clelland made her an instant, loving mum.
But would sexy Sam ever make the strait-laced schoolteacher his
blushing, breathless bride?

RAINSINGER Ruth Wind

Winona Snow came to New Mexico expecting to claim her inheritance
and establish a new life for herself and her troubled young sister. Love
was the last thing she wanted. But she hadn't bargained on Daniel
Lynch, the new resident in her abandoned house...

GET 4 BOOKS
AND A SILVER PLATED
PHOTO FRAME

Return this coupon and we'll send you 4 Silhouette Special Edition® novels and a silver plated photo frame absolutely FREE! We'll even pay the postage and packing for you.

We're making you this offer to introduce you to the benefits of Reader Service: FREE home delivery of brand-new Silhouette® romances, at least a month before they are available in the shops, FREE gifts and a monthly Newsletter packed with information.

Accepting these FREE books and gift places you under no obligation to buy, you may cancel at any time, even after receiving just your free shipment. Simply complete the coupon below and send it to:

SILHOUETTE READER SERVICE, FREEPOST, CROYDON, SURREY, CR9 3WZ.

No stamp needed

Yes, please send me 4 free Silhouette Special Edition novels and a silver plated photo frame. I understand that unless you hear from me, I will receive 6 superb new titles every month for just £2.30* each postage and packing free. I am under no obligation to purchase any books and I may cancel or suspend my subscription at any time, but the free books and gifts will be mine to keep in any case. (I am over 18 years of age)

E6IE

Ms/Mrs/Miss/Mr _____

Address _____

_____

_____ Postcode _____

COMING NEXT MONTH FROM

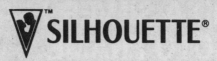 **SILHOUETTE**®

Intrigue
Danger, deception and desire

BEAUTY VS. THE BEAST M.J. Rodgers
LUCKY DEVIL Patricia Rosemoor
TRIPLECROSS Linda Stevens
TANGLED VOWS Rebecca York

Desire
Provocative, sensual love stories for the woman of today

BABY DREAMS Raye Morgan
THE UNWILLING BRIDE Jennifer Greene
APACHE DREAM BRIDE Joan Elliott Pickart
CONNAL Diana Palmer
INSTANT HUSBAND Judith McWilliams
BABY BONUS Amanda Kramer

Sensation
A thrilling mix of passion, adventure and drama

GUARDING RAINE Kylie Brant
KEEPER Patricia Gardner Evans
HOMECOMING Sally Tyler Hayes
PERFECT DOUBLE Merline Lovelace